COURT ME KILL ME

David Bradwell

COURT ME KILL ME

What if the only person you can trust is secretly plotting to kill you?

Fashion photographer Anna Burgin faces a career in ruins after her studio is destroyed, but when armed police burst into her home, she realises it's the least of her worries.

Murders in Seattle, Frankfurt, Venice and London all point to one common killer - and the chief suspect has just been in her house. The evidence is compelling, the body count is rising, but as news emerges of a corrupt business network that reaches into the heart of the police, nothing can be taken for granted - especially the promises of the person who offers to protect her.

Packed with twists, intrigue and dark humour, Court Me Kill Me is book 5 in the bestselling Anna Burgin series.

ABOUT THE AUTHOR

David Bradwell grew up in the north east of England but now lives in Hitchin in Hertfordshire. He has written for publications as diverse as Smash Hits and the Sunday Times and is a former winner of the PPA British Magazine Writer of the Year Award. Aside from writing, he runs a hosiery company with web sites at www.stockingshq.com and www.tightsandmore.com.

Get in touch at:
www.davidbradwell.com

COURT ME KILL ME

A Gripping British Mystery Thriller - Anna Burgin Book 5

Court Me Kill Me was first published in 2019 by Pure Fiction
Copyright © David Bradwell, 2019
www.davidbradwell.com

ISBN: 978-1-9993394-3-2

DEDICATION

Sometimes the hardest part of writing a book is to decide on the dedication. This time it was supposed to be easy.

But who knows the workings of the human mind? Who understands the euphoria when you feel that you've found someone truly special? When you've dared to believe that the mental and physical connection is real, and flows in both directions? And who can describe the pain when things end, unexpectedly, just when you thought you were both in such a happy place? It hurts like nothing on earth.

But we're strong. And when the tears dry, and the awful, empty hollowness begins to abate, we brush ourselves down and face the world again. Wiser and braver, knowing that we'd welcome them back in a heartbeat, with no questions asked, because despite the agony, the world seems so much less daunting when we're holding their hand. But we no longer dare to dream, because ultimately, unless the other person wants the same thing, no amount of thinking of them will ever bring them back.

And so, that means a late change of plan. And instead of naming that one truly special person, this book is instead dedicated to someone different. It is for all those who have ever suffered a broken heart.

Anna, 2019

Chapter 1

Monday December 18th, 1995

OUTSIDE, the heavy rain and leaden skies over north east London set a fitting tone for a funeral. Even for one that was little more than a sham.

Detective Sergeant Amy Cranston arrived early and took a seat towards the back of the chapel. It was the perfect place to observe without attracting attention. Mourners filed in, guided by the tall, greying Detective Superintendent Joe Leyland, acting as usher for the day. Colleagues, criminals, those she decided were members of the family, and others that she didn't recognise at all. But she'd identify them soon, if everything went according to plan.

Joe Leyland was showing a woman to the front row. Amy's attention intensified. She'd imagined Rafaela March to be a plain Spanish woman in her fifties, but in the flesh, she looked far younger, possibly not even forty. She was wearing the customary black, but carrying the look with effortless style, as though she was the star of the show, rather than her husband. Once seated, she stayed silent, head bowed. Nobody came to sit alongside her until the DSI returned, just before the service was due to start.

· · ·

Detective Chief Superintendent Paul Curtis looked briefly at his notes, cleared his throat and then began the eulogy, aware that all those assembled would recognise the insincerity in his words. Detective Chief Inspector Graham March would be greatly missed. Amy laughed to herself. He certainly would. The world would be a much better place.

There was no mention of the cause of death. That he'd been shot by a group of police marksmen while holding a hostage and firing his own gun twice at an innocent civilian. Now wasn't the time. Everyone already knew. Equally, there was no mention of his corruption, his previous suspension, or the allegations of evidence removal, trafficking, loan-sharking and frequent visits to prostitutes. Amy knew the score. Better to die a hero at the expense of a widow's pension than to be a posthumous embarrassment to the Met.

The surprise was just how many of the mourners looked genuinely upset. The local lowlife she could understand. They'd been onto a good thing. An astute backhander to the late Mr March always let them continue unhindered. But the others? There were real tears. A genuine sense of loss. She hadn't been expecting that.

The service ended and the mourners filed out. Amy waited until she was alone with DSI Joe Leyland.

"Well?" she said.

"Interesting," he replied.

"Good turnout."

"At least in number."

They left the chapel together. Across the street, a Nissan Primera taxicab was parked. Close enough to watch. Not close enough to attract attention. Amy nodded discreetly to the driver.

. . .

From behind the steering wheel, Clare Woodbrook saw the nod and knew that for now her job was done. She put the camera down on the passenger seat and turned the ignition. The traffic was heavy, but her mind was elsewhere. She pulled out slowly, trying to comprehend what she'd seen.

Chapter 2

Three months later: Thursday, March 14th 1996

I HAD every reason in the world to feel happy. Things were on the up. Work was good, the flat was tidy, I'd even conquered the mountain of ironing that had been plaguing me for weeks. Yes, there were still the tiny irritations that we all have to deal with on a day-to-day basis, but nothing that uplifting thoughts and a nice cup of tea couldn't fix.

A solid, and untypical nine hours of sleep had left me rejuvenated, my skin feeling fresh, and although my hair was rather unruly, that in itself was nothing new. It had been such a busy few weeks, culminating in a hectic couple of days in Venice. It was my first photoshoot for a hat company, but the pictures looked amazing. And I'd been allowed to keep one of the hats, which was temporarily fixing the hair issue. Happy days.

Most exciting of all, though, Danny was coming home. Two more days and then we'd be reunited. The last three months had reminded me of the joys and freedoms of living alone, but I couldn't wait to have my best friend back - even if he'd be insufferable within a day, making inappropriate suggestions about nurses' uniforms, and generally expecting me to look after him in ways that he'd be entirely capable of doing for himself. But I wouldn't care, and I wouldn't get annoyed, because it had been a long road to recovery. Gunshot wounds have a habit of taking time to clear, and I'd so nearly lost him forever.

Nothing could possibly go wrong.

Not a thing.

Unless, of course, it did.

I edged my dark blue Mercedes SLK out of its parking place just outside our flat in Camden's Rochester Square, still enraptured by the new car aroma and the novelty of having central locking that worked. The Honda Prelude had served me well, but this was a significant upgrade, and a justifiable reward to myself, for all of the long hours and relentless hard work I'd put in building my business. Of course, I'd never actually lower the roof, but it was good to know I could if I wanted to.

Just one quick, late-afternoon trip to my studio, to make a start on a backlog of important paperwork, and then I'd be free to devote all my energies to the most triumphant of homecomings.

Danny had been my closest friend and confidant since we'd met as students, seven years before. He was a national newspaper journalist, carving out a reputation as a fearless investigator, although his last exposé had ended in near disaster. He'd had impeccable training from his former boss and mentor, Clare Woodbrook, until she took an unexpected career change and he was left to run his department on his own.

Clare was now firmly ensconced as my second best friend. Admittedly, that hadn't always been the case. She'd proved an unlikely ally in some ways, not least due to her rather complex approach to life, but in recent times we'd developed an understanding and - I hoped - a mutual appreciation.

There were things about her that made me nervous, but she'd

only ever pointed a gun at me once, and even then she hadn't actually fired it. But that was ancient history, and since then she'd saved my life on numerous occasions. To most people she was a darkly dangerous fugitive, the investigative journalist who went rogue. But I'd seen a different side: the vulnerable woman who was dealing with her demons, albeit in unconventional ways.

I had her number on speed dial on the private phone she'd given me, so I always had a way of getting in touch. I pressed the button to connect a call.

"Anna," she said, and I thought I detected a smile in her soft voice, tinged with the faintest of accents from her native Wearside. "Long time no speak. How are things?"

"I know. It's been, what? Five days." I couldn't hide my enthusiasm. "Genuinely never better."

"That's good. Are you over the hangover?"

I smiled at the recollection. She'd visited me in Venice, the day before the shoot, taken me to lunch, and after almost three bottles of wine, had agreed to answer any questions, hoping I'd be too drunk to remember her answers.

"I'm fine. Just thinking of some of the things you told me."

"What's the expression? What's said in Venice stays in Venice?"

"Not sure that was Venice, but my lips are sealed."

"Good. But just remind me never to go drinking with you again. As cathartic as it was. What are you up to?"

"I'm on my way to the studio. It's the first time I've had a chance since getting back. Things are good. I've just about finished shooting autumn-winter so I'll be casting the net again soon. And I've got to start looking for a new assistant."

"What happened to Diana?"

"Better job, I assume." I floored the accelerator to catch a green light, just as it changed to amber.

"Better than working for you?"

"I know. Hard to believe, but there you have it. Maybe I'm just a shit boss and she hated me."

"Haha. I'll come and work for you."

That made me laugh.

"Do you know how weird that sounds?"

"We'd be good. You could take pictures and I'd scare everyone into paying early."

"Don't take this the wrong way but I value my clients. I appreciate the offer, but I suspect you're overqualified."

"Shame."

It was only a short drive. I could have walked but I loved my new car, and the novelty had yet to wear off.

"Where are you?" I asked. "Hiding in some underground lair in the middle of Switzerland?"

"You have such an impression of me." To be fair it was an impression based on significant evidence. "No, I can't get a phone signal down there. I'm in Cologne but I'm coming to London first thing on Saturday. I was hoping you'd let me come round to welcome Danny home."

"That would be fantastic. I'm sure he'd love to see you."

"Really?"

"Of course."

"You don't think he'd be traumatised?"

"No." I thought back to the night that it happened. Danny walking forward, putting his life on the line in an attempt to save me. "It was Graham March who pulled the trigger. I think he'd be delighted. How long are you here for?"

"It's not always possible to say."

"No, of course not. Have you got somewhere to stay?"

"Yes."

I knew better than to follow up with the obvious supplementary.

"I'm glad of a few days of calm," she continued. "It's already been a busy year."

"I can imagine. You must be exhausted. It sounds like it's been non-stop travel."

"Did I tell you about that?"

"You told me about everything."

"I can't believe I let you take advantage of me."

If there was one thing I'd learned about Clare, nobody ever took advantage of her. I still wasn't sure quite why she'd decided to open up to me, but I knew that it was on her own terms. Had it been as simple as loneliness? It must be hard, living in a twilight world, wanted for murder, continually changing appearance and identity to avoid arrest. And yet she seemed to have come to some sort of understanding with the police, in London at least. They hadn't arrested her when they'd had the chance. Maybe she was more useful to them on the outside, using her extensive knowledge of international crime to bring down the really bad guys.

"What are you doing when you get to London?" I asked.

"I've got to tie up a few loose ends, a few obligations, but once I've done those I can have a few days off. What time are you picking up Danny?"

"On Saturday? I'm not. He says he's getting a lift. Apparently he doesn't need me. Not that I'm hurt."

"Oh, Anna. He definitely needs you."

"He'll need me to run round after him. He's due early afternoon. One-ish."

"Perfect."

I turned the car into the entrance to the small row of units. My studio was at the end. Nobody had taken my parking space. I was truly blessed. I switched off the engine, and picked up my bag, with the phone wedged on my shoulder. I pressed the button on the fob to lock the doors. Magic.

"I'll pop round early if you like," Clare continued. "I can help blow up balloons."

I'm not sure what she said next. I wasn't really listening. I had my key ready to unlock the studio door, but the lock was broken. And when I pushed open the door, everything else paled into insignificance. The shock was total. It was a shell of a building. Everything had gone. All of my equipment. All of my furniture. As my legs gave way, it struck me that the only thing left was the stench of a fire that hadn't completely taken hold. As mercies go, it was a very small one indeed.

Chapter 3

DS Amy Cranston replaced the phone handset and paused for a moment, unsure whether to swear or scream. She sat back and closed her eyes, and ran her hands through her short brown hair, thankful that her colleagues were oblivious, so far, to the latest potential disaster. They'd find out soon enough. This couldn't be happening, not after all this time.

But it was.

When she reopened her eyes, everything looked different. The walls appeared closer, the fluorescent strip lights colder and harsher. The furniture even shabbier. Her colleagues more distant. The phone sat silently blinking, taunting her, as though it could burst into life again, and make things even worse than it had already.

With a deep breath, she stood up and made her way to the lift. It was time to visit the fourth floor. But then she bypassed the lift, opting instead, for the concrete staircase. It would give her more time to think. She paused outside for a moment in the busy corridor, to gather her thoughts and get her breath back. His door was slightly open.

"Boss, you got a minute?"

Detective Superintendent Joe Leyland looked up over the top of his reading glasses and signalled for her to enter.

"What is it?" he asked, his voice reassuringly calm and authoritative. "You look like a ghost."

She avoided the question, for now.

"Good holiday?" she asked, although this wasn't a social visit.

"Hardly a holiday. But I don't suppose you came here to check if I had a suntan."

"Did you go anywhere?"

"Just working on the house. But I don't expect you're checking my DIY skills either."

"No." She edged forward, tentatively, knowing everything was about to change.

"So what is it?" he asked.

"It's bad. Concerning Clare Woodbrook."

"Oh, Christ." He put down his pen. "I hardly dare ask. Come in, shut the door and take a seat."

Amy did as commanded, then immediately regretted it. Some things were better said while standing.

"So?"

She took another breath.

"Nothing's confirmed but I've just taken a call from the Polizia di Stato in Venice." She consulted her pad. "A Sergeant Simona Ricci, working with an Inspector Crescentini."

"Paolo?"

"Yes. Do you know him?"

"Not really, but I've heard the name."

Amy put her pad on the coffee table in front of her. This wasn't going to be easy.

"You're not going to like this. But according to Sergeant Ricci, they've found a woman's body in a hotel room on the Lido."

His mouth fell open.

"Tell me not Clare? When?"

"No, not Clare. But somebody else we know. Marzia Neri. And Friday last week."

That caught his attention. She could see him processing the information, forming the links.

"That's the third of them," he said.

"Exactly."

"It's getting beyond a coincidence."

"Way beyond. But it's worse than that. The hotel staff said Neri was in the bar that evening. With a woman. They left together. And there's no sign of forced entry. Which means…"

The DSI gave a low whistle.

"They think the woman in the bar went back to the room? And let me guess. Sergeant Ricci says the description matches with our Ms Woodbrook?"

"They think so. She's sending through a photograph. But you know as well as I do that Clare's appearance varies."

He nodded, then stood up and walked to the window, buying time. He cut an imposing figure, dominating the room. Amy didn't rush him. After the murders in Seattle and Frankfurt, they'd discussed wild theories, but that's all they were ever supposed to be. Fantasy hypotheses over glasses of whiskey, away from the ears of the rest of the Station, and between two colleagues who had developed a friendship based on the mutual desire to eradicate corruption. Now things were looking ominous.

"But it could have been anyone," he said. "And even if it was Clare in the bar, it's not a crime to go for a drink. Even to go upstairs with someone." He turned back to face the room, and then walked round his desk to take the chair opposite Amy. She was no more convinced than he appeared to be.

She shook her head.

"I'd love to believe that. But then Sergeant Ricci mentioned the time of death. It's currently estimated to within an hour of them leaving the bar. Could be less."

"And do we know what time the friend left the room?"

"They don't have a witness for that."

"And presumably there was nobody else in the vicinity?"

"I asked. According to Sergeant Ricci it's a busy hotel, but no, just the two women. The victim and the one they think is Clare. They're trying to trace her."

"Good luck there." He shook his head. "So why are they calling us, exactly? Because they want to confirm a photograph?"

"No, it's beyond that. They want us to run a check on our DNA database. They found the stub of an English cigarette. In the room."

"Of course they have. And if it matches?"

"Then we have to face the facts," said Amy. "There's no point pretending otherwise any longer, no matter how that makes us feel. She's linked, evidentially, to all three. Which means..."

"She's reverted to type. And she needs to be stopped." The DSI sighed deeply and looked to the ceiling.

"We always knew it was a risk," Amy continued. "Leopards, spots, and all of that."

"But seriously? Now? I'm this close to the end." He pinched together the thumb and forefinger of his right hand. Amy waited, giving him a moment to collect his thoughts.

"Okay," he said eventually. "We're going to have to follow this up. Set up an incident room. Make it official. And whatever else happens, we're going to have to find her. It's time to stop this madness, whatever she's up to."

"Agreed."

"Do you have any idea where she's holed up?"

Amy shook her head, feeling the weight of responsibility and a sense of foreboding.

"Not at the moment. I take it she's stopped calling you?"

"I expect she will now." He stood up and returned to his desk, picking up his phone. "Have you met DCI Court?"

"The new guy from Vice? Rogan? Only in passing."

"Let me call him up here. He'd be useful on this."

He dialled an internal number. When the call was finished, he leaned forward and lowered his voice.

"Before he gets here, I just want to say be careful. I know you will. There are lots of things we don't know. You know how difficult this is going to be?"

"Of course."

"Nothing has changed. DCI Court will run things, but you still come and talk to me. Keep me updated, personally."

After a few minutes, there was a knock at the door. DCI Rogan Court entered, wearing a navy suit that accentuated his athletic frame, the same as his close-cropped beard accentuated his jawline. DSI Leyland made the introductions.

"How can I help," asked the new arrival, once he'd taken a seat.

"I'll cut to the chase," Joe began. Amy was impressed by his switch from friend to DSI. "You've heard of Clare Woodbrook?"

"I don't think there's anyone who hasn't."

"Good. In essence, we need to find her. I need you to work with DS Cranston, penetrate Woodbrook's network, find out where she's hiding, and bring her in."

"Okay. But can I ask why? I mean, I can guess why, but why now?"

"Because she's killed three people in the last two weeks, and it's time to put a stop to it," Joe said, with grim determination.

Slumped against the bare wall of my studio, I was still holding the phone, but my head was full of white noise. I looked across to where my desk should have been. My lights. My cameras. And all I could see was charcoal-blackened paintwork and a vast empty space that represented a career in utter devastation. I felt a rush of nausea, and then retched as I staggered back outside.

"Anna!"

Suddenly I became aware of a voice. I looked at the phone. Was that where it was coming from? All my usual points of reference had evaporated. The voice was still coming. I put the phone to my ear.

"Hello?"

"There you are. What on earth is going on?"

"Clare?"

"Of course it's me. Who else did you think it'd be?"

"I'm going to have to call you back."

"Don't you dare hang up on me. What's going on? Talk to me."

But I could hardly bring myself to say it. To do so would be to make it real. I apologised, said goodbye and ended the call. And then sat back against my car, looking at my studio door as though I was looking at the jaws of death itself.

After a few minutes, and lots of deep breathing, my senses began to return. And with them a strong sense of outrage, anger and injustice. Who the fuck had done this to me?

Life was continuing as normal in the rest of the block. I could hear voices and music from the other units. Nobody seemed aware of my trauma. Maybe I'd imagined it.

I walked back to the studio and reopened the door. It was like falling back asleep, only to find you're still within the same nightmare. I walked through to my darkroom. Or at least where my darkroom used to be. Again it was empty. Even the kitchen was bereft of any sign I'd ever been there. Every cup, plate, and piece of cutlery had gone. It must have taken ages. I felt the sharp sting of tears in my eyes. I still didn't understand. It still couldn't be happening - but standing, feeling sorry for myself, wasn't going to catch the bastards who'd done this.

I called 999 and asked for the police, then waited for them to arrive. The person I really wanted to call was Danny. He was my soulmate, but at that moment he was lying in a hospital bed. So instead, I pressed the speed dial to reconnect with Clare. She'd know what to do. She answered on the first ring.

"Anna, what on earth is going on?"

I explained as best as I could, but it still didn't make sense. When had it even happened? While I was away in Venice or since I'd returned home? I felt physically sick at the thought of somebody doing this to me, at the thought of going about my daily life, oblivious to the carnage.

"This doesn't make sense, Anna," she said.

"Nothing makes sense any more."

"I'll be there as soon as I can, but... Shit."

"What's up?"

"I'm not even in the country. This is so typical."

"Don't worry."

"But I do worry. Of course I worry. If I can get an earlier flight I will."

"The police are coming."

"That's good, but God knows how long they'll take. Anna, look, whatever happens, whatever they say, keep me informed, okay? We *will* sort this out."

Flashing blue lights meant it was time to end the call. I said I'd keep Clare abreast of developments then she disappeared back into her own mysterious ether. Two uniformed officers emerged from the car. I led them inside, but as they started to take details, asking me about my movements and anybody who may have held a grudge, I just wanted to collapse to the floor and cry.

Chapter 4

DSI Joe Leyland continued his briefing. About the CCTV evidence from Seattle that clearly showed Clare Woodbrook entering the private suite of hotelier Olof Lindberg, in one of his own hotels, shortly before his body was discovered. About a hair, recovered from the scene, that matched her DNA. About the discovery of the body of energy company boss Axel Meier in Germany, dressed in stockings and lingerie in the back room of a brothel in Frankfurt. About how Clare Woodbrook was believed to be the last person to have seen him alive. And now the discovery of financier Marzia Neri in Venice, and yet more photographic and potential DNA evidence that placed Clare Woodbrook at the scene, precisely at the time that the Italian had been killed.

"I'm going to level with the pair of you," he concluded. "I've got two months left and then I'm retiring. Much as I've put my neck on the line with Clare in the past, I really do not want the end of my career to be tarnished by this. It's an absolute disaster, because we trusted her. So if it is Clare, I want her brought in and charged, okay? No excuses. No delays. And you can do absolutely whatever it takes. Understood?"

"Is there anything to link the victims?" asked Rogan. "It's three murders in three countries across two continents. Are they random or are you seeing connections?"

Amy looked at her superior for permission to speak. It was granted.

"You were involved in the clean-up after we broke the Euston trafficking ring?" she asked.

"Yes, it came to Vice. I was part of it."

"So you've also heard of DCI Graham March, then?"

"The one who was killed on the rooftop? Of course."

"Just be grateful you never had to work with him." Amy had a flashback, and shuddered inside.

"That was his redemption, though, wasn't it?" asked Rogan. "Back from suspension, clearing his name?"

"If you believe his side of the story, but let's put you right there. He wasn't just a DCI. He was a bent bastard, and when he was killed it was because he was pointing a gun, having taken a civilian hostage." Her memories of the night were still vivid.

"I'd heard about that as well," said Rogan.

"Good. So let's just be clear from the outset, he was not one of the good guys. But then, at his funeral, he was given quite the send-off."

"In what way?"

"He was a serving officer at the time, so he still qualified for a full police funeral, despite the fact it was clear that he was far from a shining example to the rest of the service. But as well as family members, colleagues and assorted lowlife, there was a group of other mourners who we've been trying to identify."

"Such as?"

Joe took over.

"Nils Bengtsson, until recently the partner of Olof Lindberg," he said. "Lover, not business. And then Axel Meier, himself, who'd come all the way from Germany, and Marzia Neri who'd made a similar trip from Italy."

"So the three that have since been killed?"

"Two and a partner."

"And these were all at March's funeral? Why?"

The DSI shrugged.

"That's what we've been trying to work out. There were others too, but we're still trying to identify them. The key thing is that yes, all three of those - if you include Olof Lindberg by proxy - have now been murdered and Clare is, let's just say, a person of considerable interest."

Rogan switched his glance between Joe and Amy. There was more to come.

"The issue we have," Amy continued, "or at least one of the issues, is that we don't yet have a motive. Is she just killing Graham's friends out of spite, for the hell of it? Is there something more to it? Some link we've yet to discover? And if she is, are the other mourners also at risk?"

"How well do you know her?" asked Rogan. "Is that the sort of thing she'd do?"

"Reasonably well. And yeah, if you want the honest answer, I really don't know. I wouldn't have thought so. You'd have to be a psychopath or plain insane, but Clare is a special case. She's highly intelligent but ruthless and unpredictable. She's certainly capable of doing it. I doubt she'd lose much sleep if she thought she had justification."

"Was there any justification?"

Amy shook her head.

"Not so far as we've discovered."

Rogan looked thoughtful.

"You mentioned DNA evidence," he said.

"In Seattle and Venice, yes," said Amy.

"But not Frankfurt?"

"No."

"So maybe that could be a coincidence? Is there anything else pointing to her?"

"Meier was a known associate," said Joe, taking over. "But we also know they had history over business deals that went south. He was found in particularly humiliating circumstances, dressed in lingerie in the laundry room of a brothel."

"Maybe that was his thing?"

"He was dressed post-mortem. The body was left in such a way as to cause maximum embarrassment."

"Which backs up the spite theory," added Amy, as Joe started to gather some papers on his desk. "It's the sort of thing that would amuse her."

"I've got to go to a briefing," said the DSI, standing up and reaching for his jacket. "The press are going to be onto this. The whole thing is going to explode. Rogan, I need you to run the team, with Amy. Get Lisa Miller involved. She knows Clare. Amy can introduce you. Come back to me with a plan and then keep me updated at absolutely every stage, okay? We're going to start getting serious pressure from above on this, so we need to be quick and decisive."

"Finding Clare is easier said than done," added Amy, looking at Rogan. "So that's all the more reason to act quickly. Catch her in the hope she's off her guard."

"Exactly," added Joe. "Amy, bring Rogan up to speed and we'll meet tomorrow at ten. Anything you need from me in the meantime, you have my mobile."

Amy and Rogan stood as the meeting concluded. Joe shook them both by the hand, which she thought was strangely formal, but nothing about the search for Clare was likely to follow convention.

"Welcome to Holborn," said Amy to Rogan as they made their way down the stairs. "You're in at the deep end."

"Thank you." They paused to let someone past, carrying armfuls of box files. "Is this Clare really that notorious?"

"You must have heard the stories," said Amy as they resumed their descent.

"I know the basics. Investigative journalist, went rogue. Something about an art fraud?"

"That's not even the start of it."

"Maybe you can tell me over dinner?"

Amy stopped and sighed, irritation immediate. Both barrels or softly-softly? She chose the latter, for now.

"Listen, word to the wise, okay? This isn't Vice. We do things properly. I don't care where you've come from and I don't care how big an opinion you've got of yourself, but you need to learn the way things happen here. And if you ever suggest anything other than a professional relationship, you'll be out of here faster than you can say 'sexual harassment', okay?"

"Hey, I didn't mean to cause offence. I'm just the new boy. Sorry. I should have said drinks."

"You'll also find we've got a very low tolerance for bullshit. Which is ten times worse."

"I'm sorry. Cup of tea, then?"

"That's better. Let's go to the canteen."

Rogan paid for two styrofoam cups of tea. As he carried them across the tired linoleum floor to the table, Amy ended a call and pocketed her phone.

"Sorry - we've got off on the wrong track," he said. "Yes, I was trying it on and I apologise. Lesson firmly learned. But there was a genuine professional reason too. I want to get up to speed on what happens here, and I know there's a lot to take in."

"Apology accepted," said Amy, taking one of the cups.

"I promise you I won't do it again. So please, forgive me. But I would appreciate a ten-minute summary. Who's who. Who's good, who I need to watch my back with. I've heard lots of rumours about this place."

"You mean about Graham March."

"Essentially."

"Bad news travels."

"Was he really as bad as all that?"

"Probably worse. But he's history." Amy recalled her former boss. He was a larger-than-life figure in many ways, but deeply corrupt, and equally obnoxious. "Let's just say there weren't too many tears at the news. Shock, yes, because it's always terrible to hear about things like that, but he's no loss to the Force."

"You didn't get on then?"

"Can we change the subject?"

"Okay." Rogan offered sugar, but Amy declined. "Who's Lisa Miller?"

"She's an angel. Young, but good. You've probably seen her. Late twenties, red hair?"

"I think so."

"I'll introduce you. She was working with March just before he died, but you don't have to worry about that. I can vouch for her. I'll get her to track down all of Clare's known acquaintances in London."

They paused while someone asked if one of their chairs was free. Amy nodded and it was moved to another table.

"Are there many acquaintances?" asked Rogan, once they were ready to resume.

"Who knows?" said Amy. "Clare moves in mysterious ways."

The next table was empty, but Amy still felt the need to lower her voice.

"We'll start with the two we know for definite," she continued. "There's a photographer called Anna Burgin, and then Anna's flatmate, Danny Churchill. He used to work with Clare at the Echo."

"Those names ring a bell."

"Danny was shot by March. He's been in hospital ever since. He's a good guy. Lisa knows him, well. Anna's got a heart of gold."

"So they're not accomplices then?"

"No, but I'd imagine if anyone knows where Clare is, it's probably Anna." She paused. "That doesn't mean she'll tell us, though, and Clare has a habit of being elusive."

"But we can apply pressure?"

Amy looked up, surprised at his tone.

"I think we'll find they respond better if we treat them like responsible adults." She struggled to keep the irritation out of her voice. But Rogan was only getting started.

"Listen, *sergeant*, when I want lessons in interviewing suspects I'll let you know," he said, with a thin smile. "But until then, we'd both do well to remember our ranks. Okay?"

"Yes, sir." Where had that come from? Was it his reaction to being spurned for dinner?

"Good," he continued, but then his voice softened. "So who else do I need to be careful about?"

Amy suddenly felt less like being helpful.

"At Holborn? You just do your job, and you don't need to be careful of anyone," she said. "It's a good group now, but there are a lot of people here. You'll end up working with all of them, probably. Just remember we take things like March personally. It was a stain on the reputation of the Met and Holborn specifically. We've moved on but there's still damage to repair. Rest assured we're doing everything we can to prove that we're not defined by a blip. A bygone."

Rogan nodded, then took a sip of his tea. Amy watched him, cautiously, trying not to jump to early conclusions, but with doubts playing on her mind.

"Okay, so tell me more about Clare Woodbrook," he asked after a moment.

"What have you heard so far?" Amy reached for her own cup

and took a sip. It was still too hot to be fully drinkable, but the taste was enough to make her wince.

"Aside from what we were just discussing, only what I've read," Rogan continued. "Investigative journalist. High-flyer. Then seemingly went mad and started killing people."

Amy smiled, despite herself.

"I suppose that's a fair assessment. It's a bit more complicated, though."

"Go on."

"Okay, so she was involved in some sort of art fraud, tried to impersonate a police officer by pretending she was DC Lisa Miller..."

"Our one?"

Amy nodded.

"Then she ended up killing her partners and disappeared, after faking her own death in a helicopter crash."

"Wow. Okay. And since then?"

"She crops up occasionally. She's a bit of an enigma."

"And she's managed to escape arrest?"

"Kind of." Amy thought for a moment. There was so much to tell, but it was best to drip-feed slowly, especially given her rapidly forming opinion of her companion. "Let's just say, she was assessed as being more use to us on the outside. She's got contacts. Knows things, knows people. And the value of that was deemed more significant than the value of bringing her in."

Rogan frowned.

"She sounds intriguing."

"She is, and the arrangement served her well for a while. She was pivotal in bringing March down. And the Euston trafficking ring. But now it looks like she's back to killing people, which goes against the terms of the deal. So as of now, she's back on the wanted list. Is that enough?"

"It's a start."

Amy checked her watch, mindful that she still had the DNA database request to process.

"We're going to have to be careful," she said. "We might get lucky. She may be in London. She could be anywhere. But if you don't mind taking advice from a mere sergeant, sir, I'd suggest we don't underestimate the scale of this. If she gets wind of the fact that we're looking for her, she'll vanish. She's a master of the disappearing act."

Rogan looked at his colleague.

"I appreciate the advice," he said. "But I don't appreciate the tone. We need to work as a team so we have to understand the meaning of respect, okay?"

"Of course," said Amy. She didn't add that respect always had to be earned.

Chapter 5

Friday, March 15th 1996

I DIDN'T sleep well. After the shock of the devastation at my studio, I thought the very least I deserved was a nice bottle of wine. Opening the second, however, was an error, even if I hadn't finished it before passing out.

After a shower that failed to do much more than steam up the bathroom and make a puddle on the floor, I got dressed in my comfort clothes of jeans and big knitted jumper, and downed a couple of ibuprofen. I flinched at the bright light coming in through the kitchen window, despite the drizzle. Toast, I decided, would be about the most I could muster - both in terms of cookery and keeping something down. I made a mug of Yorkshire tea, while looking longingly at the rest of the ibuprofen, wondering how long, exactly, it would take the first two to kick in. Then I had a couple of paracetamol for good measure.

All of my paperwork had been kept at the studio, so with the first stirrings of a filthy, hangover-augmented temper, I took the tea through to my desk in the living room and called directory enquiries for the number of my insurance company, just grateful that I could at least remember their name. The thought of starting again was daunting, and the interruption to my business would have lasting effects, but I tried to console myself with the thought that at least I'd have shiny new equipment. And then protect it with even better locks. But I was far from happy at the thought of the injustice. I loved my cameras. They'd been with me on the entire journey, and shiny newness was no real substitute for hard-earned trust.

Just after nine, I called the insurance company, and after the obligatory duel with the automated answering service, I finally got through to the claims department. After I'd given my address, date of birth, and mother's maiden name (don't even start me on my mother), they located my policy.

"So, what do you need?" I asked. "I have a crime reference number. I can supply a list of equipment, although all the receipts have gone, obviously. I'm not sure how this works."

"Miss Burgin - can I call you Anna?" said the insurance lady.

"Of course."

"I just need to check something with my manager. Are you okay to hold?"

"Yes," I said. And then she disappeared, leaving me with nothing but jangly guitar pop when I'd have preferred something with a synthesiser, or even better, nothing at all. Eventually she returned.

"Okay, I've double-checked the policy," she said. "And I'm afraid there's a bit of a problem."

Had I been less hungover, I'd have spotted the warning signs.

"I'm afraid your policy has lapsed."

It took a moment for that to sink in.

"What?" I said eventually.

"We've processed your cancellation request, I'm afraid, which means the cover has ended."

"What cancellation request?"

"We have your letter here, from two weeks ago. We posted a cheque on Tuesday for the refund."

My blood pressure rose to that of a forty-a-day smoker.

"What refund? What letter? I've never sent a letter."

"I'm afraid you did."

"I'm afraid I absolutely didn't."

"I'm sorry, Anna..."

"I think we should go back to Miss Burgin."

"Miss Burgin, you cancelled the policy."

"What the fuck... Sorry, excuse my language. What on earth are you talking about?"

"I'm sorry."

"Are you saying I've got no insurance?"

"Exactly that. Not since you sent the letter."

"What fucking letter?"

"If you're going to take that tone, I'm going to end the call."

"I'm not taking a tone." I paused, trying to calm myself, but it wasn't successful. "I've been paying you bastards for the last three years, so don't now tell me that the time I've actually got a claim to make, that I've sent some fucking letter which I absolutely have not, just so you can get out of paying what you owe me."

"Miss Burgin..."

"Seriously, you're pissing me off."

"Miss Burgin..."

"Will you fuck off with the Miss Burgin?"

"I'm going to end the call now. You cancelled the insurance so no, you're not covered. And I don't need to listen to that kind of language."

"I apologise for my language, but do not tell me I've sent a letter when I haven't and that I've cancelled my policy when I really, really need you."

"But you did cancel the policy."

"I didn't!"

"I'm afraid we have the letter here. You said..."

"Oh fuck. Off."

And with that she ended the call. I threw the phone down with a combination of disbelief, fear, and rising resentment. I wasn't having it. She was clearly confusing me with some other policyholder. I called back and got put through to someone else, who told me the same. And after apologising for lapsing into further Mancunian brusqueness, I got cut off again.

By the time it began to really sink in, I wanted to punch something. There was nothing to punch, and I'm not really a violent person, so I resorted to shouting instead. And then kicking my wastepaper basket so hard, it flew across the room, depositing sheets of A4 paper, tissues, crisp wrappers and pencil shavings all over my carpet, which pissed me off even more.

I collapsed on my sofa, head pounding, incredibly close to tears. I absolutely had never sent a letter.

I called Clare.

"I'm fucked," I said when she answered.

"What do you mean you're fucked?"

"I've got no insurance."

"What do you mean you've got no insurance?"

"Will you stop repeating whatever I say to you?"

"I'm technically not repeating anything, just asking you to clarify what you mean."

God, she was annoying at times.

"What I mean is that the insurance company is refusing to pay out because they claim they've got some bastard letter I allegedly sent them two weeks ago, cancelling the policy," I said.

"Oh."

Now it was my turn.

"What do you mean, 'oh'?"

"I mean that's not good."

"Jesus. I ring you because I'm hoping you'll know what to do, and now I discover you're a master of the bleeding obvious."

"Anna, please calm down."

"Calm down? *Calm down?* Clare, my studio has been cleared out. Everything I've worked for, for years - *years* - has been destroyed. And the one redeeming feature of the whole fiasco is that the insurance company will put things right, except now I find I'm not even covered."

"There's obviously some mistake."

"Which is exactly what I said to them and they put the phone down."

"They put the phone down?"

"I may have sworn."

"Heaven's sake, Anna."

"Oooh."

I punched the cushion.

"So what do I do now?" I asked.

"You try to stay calm."

"That's easy for you to say."

"We've all had setbacks."

"*Setbacks?*" My head was pounding even worse now.

"Yes. Listen, I'll be with you tomorrow. We'll sort it out, okay?"

"How are we going to do that?"

"I'll think of something. But in the meantime, try not to worry about it."

"How can I not worry about it?" That probably came out snappier than I'd intended.

"Because you've come to me and I'm your friend and I'll help put things right."

"You're not a magician."

"Oh, Anna."

"They said they'd sent me a refund." I thought of the pile of post that had been accumulating in my studio, and which had only been growing since my assistant left. If I'd had time to open it all, I might have found the cheque and called them and sorted everything out before it became critical. But now the cheque had been stolen along with everything else. Talk about taking the piss.

"I'm going to find out who has done this and I'll sort it out," said Clare.

"But how?"

"I don't know yet. But I will."

"But seriously, how?"

"I don't know, yet. I don't know what's happened. All I know is that it shouldn't have done. You don't deserve it."

I took a deep breath. My chest hurt along with my head.

"But Clare," I said, "I'm not being funny. I know you're good but I'm completely up shit creek here."

"So you keep saying. And you're not. Trust me. I'll fix this, okay?"

"Okay." My blood pressure wasn't conveying the same message.

"I'll see you tomorrow for Danny's homecoming. I'll talk to you then."

I started to laugh. Despite everything.

"What's funny?" asked Clare.

"Nothing's funny."

"But you were laughing."

"I'm getting hysterical."

"Well, don't."

"But it's like you say you'll pop round tomorrow, and it's like you're a normal person, popping round to see friends."

"And the problem with that?"

"You're a wanted international fugitive."

Clare laughed.

"I think things are okay on that score."

"Christ, I won't ask."

"Better not to. But Danny will be home, we'll have a big party, and everything will be okay. All you need to do is trust me. What time are you collecting him?"

"I'm not. I told you. The hospital are giving him a lift."

"Ah yes, I remember."

Clare ended the call, but not before reiterating that I should remain calm, followed up by the instruction to be very, very careful. If she thought she was being reassuring, she was being anything but.

———

Danny Churchill sat up in the hospital bed, and smiled when his visitor entered the room. She leaned forward, and kissed him.

"How are you feeling?" asked DC Lisa Miller.

"Going crazy," said Danny.

"You should be celebrating. It's your last day."

He reached out his hand. She took it and he pulled her closer. They kissed again. Longer this time.

"I just can't wait to get out," said Danny. "To get home, and back in my own bed. I'm struggling to even remember what the curtains look like."

"Nobody can ever remember what curtains look like," said Lisa, smiling. "Although I'm deeply hurt that you mentioned your own bed rather than mine."

Now it was Danny's turn to smile.

"Well, that as well, obviously."

"What if we find we're completely incompatible?" Lisa continued, teasing him. "You might be into weird stuff. I'll have to hide the handcuffs."

Danny squeezed her hand slightly harder.

"You do know it still hurts to laugh?"

"Maybe I just like the thought of inflicting pain."

She sat down on the edge of the bed and they lapsed into an easy, comfortable silence.

"Are you nervous?" she asked eventually, her voice dropping to not much more than a whisper.

"About what? Going home? Or your new-found sadistic side?"

"Going home."

"Only one part of it."

She took a deep breath. She knew what he meant. It had been discussed countless times, but now the moment was getting closer, there was added urgency in his voice.

"Do you think she'll be okay about us?"

Danny looked up, directly into Lisa's pale green eyes. They were so pure, so kind, despite the terrible things she must have seen at work. They didn't judge him. She had a look of genuine caring, almost an innocence, but with a sexy, mischievous glint when the mood struck. He loved her eyes. They were one of the first things he'd noticed about her, the first time they'd met in daylight. He'd felt an instant, almost overwhelming attraction, but could never have foreseen that she'd have even been single, much less given him a second glance. That she'd visit him so often in the hospital. And that the police duty of care would evolve into something altogether more intimate.

"The thing about Anna is that she's my best friend," he said. "Kind of a soulmate. It's going to take time to adjust."

"But she clearly loves you."

"As a friend. We've always been close, but we've never risked that by taking it further. Anyway, she's relationship-averse."

"But she's not going to be happy."

Danny lay back on the pillows, assessing the scale of that particular understatement.

"Look, she doesn't have great history in this kind of thing. She was fixated on Clare for a while, when she thought I had a crush on her..."

"You had a crush on Clare?"

"No. But that's not the point."

"Am I not dangerous enough for you? Am I not enough of an enigma? Is that what you're saying?"

"I don't have a crush on Clare!"

"Oh, it's all coming out now."

"Stop it." He laughed, then winced. "Look, Anna will be fine. She may be a bit frosty, that's all. But she's going to have to get used to it."

"I hope so."

Lisa's pager bleeped. She read the message and frowned.

"I'm going to have to go. Briefing with Amy, Will you be all right till the morning?"

"I'll manage. Just don't be late."

"I'll clean the car specially."

She kissed him again, and then headed back to work.

Chapter 6

DS Amy Cranston turned up the collar of her coat against the morning drizzle, and quickened her pace. She hated being late, hated looking anything other than the perfect professional. And especially today, because today was the first big briefing in the hunt for Clare Woodbrook, and she was determined to be at the centre of the investigation. Especially with a new boss to impress. Even if he seemed like a dick.

By the time she arrived at her desk, the office was already alive with activity. The pile of paperwork had grown, and there were three new Post-It notes stuck to her screen.

She picked up the phone.

"Lisa, where are you?"

"I'm on my way. Should be there in ten. Sorry, I was at the hospital."

"Are you going anywhere near a coffee shop?"

"I can do."

"Perfect. Small cappuccino would be lovely."

"Leave it with me."

Lisa was more than just a colleague. Amy felt a duty to

nurture and protect her. Lisa was a good detective, balancing the demands of her young child with the dedication required to make a meaningful contribution. The culture of the Force had changed in recent years, but it still wasn't easy for either of them. Talking of which...

DCI Rogan Court was approaching from the other side of the room.

"Can I have a word?" he said, when he was within speaking range.

Amy looked at her watch. The briefing was in fifteen minutes but it would be good to be prepared. She followed him to an empty meeting room.

"You were late," he said, once the door was closed.

"Sorry, sir. The Tube was suspended at Caledonian Road so I had to get the bus."

"Do I look like I care? I was expecting you forty-five minutes ago."

"Word to the wise then, sir. Nobody will work harder to find Clare, so don't for one minute question my attitude or commitment."

That only inflamed him.

"And the second thing, Sergeant, is to not tell me what I can or can't question. Where's DC Miller?"

"She's on her way. She'll be here by ten."

"God, what is this place? Some sort of holiday camp?"

"I don't know how things worked at Vice," said Amy, struggling to keep the irritation out of her voice, "but here there's a culture of respect and self-discipline. We don't clock-watch because we don't knock off at home time. But we absolutely get the job done."

"Yeah? Well, we'll see how well that continues to work. Any word on the DNA match from Venice?"

She sighed.

"You know what? I just got in. As you already pointed out.

There are messages galore for me, but I didn't have time to check them before you dragged me in here to give me a bollocking for something completely spurious." Immediately she regretted saying it out loud. "I will find out, and be fully up to speed by the time we meet DSI Leyland."

"This is not a bollocking, Sergeant," said Rogan, with a hard edge to his voice. "This is a friendly chat. Believe me, if you deserve a bollocking you'll very much know about it when one arrives."

"Yes, sir. Duly noted."

"Now get to work." He held open the door, and Amy returned to her desk, quietly seething. Her phone was already ringing but there was no time to answer if she was going to get the DNA result before the briefing. It was going to be one of those days.

She scanned the Post-Its. All three were marked urgent. Ignoring them, she picked up the phone to make a call of her own. But DCI Court was back at her desk.

"While you're here, and on my watch, you answer the phone. Understood?" he said. "That was your DNA match from Venice. And yes, it's Woodbrook."

"Thanks, sir," she said. And then swore silently as he left.

Briefings were normally punctual, but by 10.15 there was still no sign of DSI Joe Leyland. Amy had nearly finished her cappuccino when Detective Chief Superintendent Paul Curtis strode into the room and called all those working on the Clare Woodbrook case to a meeting room. A dozen officers assembled around the table. Some seated, some standing, with Curtis at the head. There was still no sign of Joe.

"Gentleman, and ladies," he began, with a nod to Amy and Lisa, "I'm afraid I have some bad news. DSI Leyland will not be with us today as his wife has been involved in a road traffic accident. I'm sure you're all concerned so I will update you on her condition as soon as we receive news."

"Is she all right?" asked DCI Court, immediately looking concerned. Amy watched with a cynical eye. She doubted he cared about anything other than making a good impression with the management.

"We don't know yet, just that her car came off the road near their retirement home in the Lake District," said DCS Curtis, taking a seat. "I will, of course, convey your best wishes and send flowers, etcetera, etcetera. In the meantime I will be covering his caseload, which rather pisses me off, as I was supposed to be on two weeks' leave, but that does mean you lucky people have the pleasure of working with me on the apprehension of the elusive Clare Woodbrook." He surveyed the assembled team. "And when I say pleasure, it is on the assumption that you will be successful in extremely short order. Do I make myself clear? DCI Court, an update please."

Rogan gave a synopsis, covering the links between the murders in Frankfurt, Seattle and Venice, and, glancing at Amy, the DNA evidence from a cigarette from the Venetian hotel that was now confirmed to be a match. He called up CCTV images from the hotel in Seattle and mentioned the further DNA evidence from a hair found at the scene. All pointed in one direction.

"And is that it?" asked the DCS. "No leads, no idea of her whereabouts? If you value your careers, people, we need her under lock and key by nightfall."

It was Amy's turn to speak.

"Sir, we've had lots of experience of Clare. She could be anywhere in the world at the moment, so we will be checking ports and speaking to Interpol. But if she's in London, I am confident we will apprehend her extremely quickly."

"And you are?"

"DS Amy Cranston, sir."

"Okay, DS Cranston. Tell me this. What conclusive proof do we have that she's done this? We can't go to the CPS with a grainy picture, a human hair and a fag butt. Any defence lawyer would laugh at us. Of course she stays at hotels. She could have been an innocent visitor. Wrong place, wrong time. I need actual evidence. Preferably a confession. There's no DNA or CCTV from Frankfurt?"

"Not that we've recovered, so far. I've put in a call to the police there to forward a copy of the case notes. But at the moment yes, at best it's circumstantial."

"You're not filling me with confidence, Sergeant."

Amy was aware everyone was looking at her.

"There are links between all the victims, and we're working to establish exactly the extent of that," she said. "But we do know Clare has previous history with all of them. They fit her MO. And we know she's had dealings with a gang in Germany that thinks nothing of wiping out rivals. We'll find the evidence, but first we're concentrating on finding Clare before anyone else is killed."

DCS Curtis paused, looking at her. Not blinking.

"You think this is the beginning of the spree?" he asked.

"That's certainly one of our current theories."

"All right." He looked around the room, at the expectant faces. "What were her last movements?"

"She was here in December," said Lisa. "The night Graham March died."

"And you are?"

"DC Lisa Miller, sir."

"I like that. A DC willing to speak up. And since then?"

"No confirmed sightings."

Amy didn't want to mention asking for Clare's assistance at the funeral. Nobody apart from DSI Joe Leyland was aware of that.

"So she could be anywhere?"

"Literally anywhere."

"Not good enough." He slapped his hand on the desk, with surprising ferocity. "Who are her contacts? Where does she stay? Business dealings? Boyfriends? I want every bit of information on my desk by this afternoon. Everyone she knows. Everyone she talks to. Speak to all of them. Someone must know something. She can't just vanish. She's got two friends here, yes? The photographer and the journalist. Are they implicated?"

Lisa looked across to Amy. It was an awkward moment. Amy nodded, then took over.

"We know them both well," she said.

"Who are they?"

"Anna Burgin, fashion photographer, and her flatmate Danny Churchill. They share a house in Camden. Danny worked with Clare as her researcher on the Echo. He stayed on and took her old job when she left."

"Could they be hiding her?"

There was a momentary silence, until Lisa took over, face slightly reddening.

"I can best answer that, sir," she began.

"Go on, no time like the present."

"Okay. Well, Anna and Danny were both on the rooftop the night DCI March died. March was holding Anna as a hostage. Danny tried to rescue her and took a bullet in the process. He's been in hospital ever since."

"Okay, so that's his alibi. But the other one. Burgin?"

"We've been in touch with her regularly over the last three months," Lisa continued, "and if she was hiding Clare we'd know about it. But Clare's independent. She's capable of hiding on her own. She doesn't need protection."

"Sounds plausible."

"There's one other thing," said Lisa, face reddening even more. "For the sake of full disclosure I've become very close to Danny Churchill recently, on a personal level. I understand if that means you want me off the case."

"Oh Christ." The DCS looked on the verge of losing his temper. "How close? Don't tell me you're shagging a main suspect?"

"Danny isn't a suspect."

"You don't decide if he's a suspect. Everyone's a fucking suspect."

"With respect, he's been in hospital since December. I've been visiting him regularly. So I can guarantee he's not hiding Clare. He's due out tomorrow, though, so I can keep an eye on things, in case she makes contact."

"Yes, do that."

"But if you'd rather..."

"What?" She felt the full force of his glare. "Christ no. Stay close and get closer. We've got to use everything we can. Anyone shagging the photographer while we're mid-confessional?"

"I know Anna, and to the best of my knowledge she's not shagging anyone," said Amy. There were a few laughs in the room. "She works hard. But she's straight. Again, there's nothing to suggest she's been in touch with Clare since that night but I'll speak to her. You should know that she's also just suffered a burglary at her studio."

"Christ, that's all we need. What sort of burglary?"

"It was completely cleaned out, sir. She phoned it through yesterday."

"I'm seeing them both tomorrow," added Lisa. "I'm due to take Danny home from the hospital so I'll be with the pair of them. Unless you want to speak to Anna first?"

"No," said Curtis. "We don't want to spook them. Keep them onside. If they don't know we're looking for Woodbrook, they're more likely to drop it into conversation if they've spoken to her. What time are you seeing them?"

"Danny's getting discharged around lunchtime if all goes to plan," said Lisa. "Should be early afternoon."

"For the sake of a day, stick to that then. In the meantime, make a list of anyone else Woodbrook knows. And the first sign of her, we pounce. Okay? Whatever it takes, whatever force. She's a dangerous woman. But one last thing before I let you people get back out into the real world. We do not discuss this with anyone, okay? Actually, that implied I was looking for your agreement. You don't get that option. We've got strict orders to keep this under wraps. Nail Woodbrook. Keep your mouth shut. Loose talk costs jobs. Do I make myself very clear?"

There was a general murmur of assent. DCS Paul Curtis stood and called the meeting to a close.

"Can I have a quick word?" Amy asked Lisa, as everyone else filed out.

"Of course."

"Shut the door."

Lisa waited for the last of her colleagues to leave the room, then did as directed.

"I'm glad you're working with me on this," said Amy. "But just a word to the wise, okay?"

"Of course."

"Graham March wasn't working alone. Someone in this building was protecting him. Someone wants this resolved and they'll be watching their back."

"Curtis?"

"I don't know. Maybe. Just go careful, Lisa. The thing that worries me is that Clare is killing people for a reason. We don't yet know the reason. But we need to make sure we're not caught in the crossfire."

Amy left her desk and took the lift to the ground floor. She passed through reception, and once out in the street, made a phone call. It was answered on the fifth ring.

"Boss, I've just heard the news, I'm so sorry. How is she?" she said.

The DSI sounded in a bad way.

"It's not good. She lost control and, well - you know what the roads are like round here. I had the call last night. I came straight up."

"But is she okay?"

"I don't know, Amy. It's so hard to see her like that. She's in intensive care. The next few hours will be..." His voice trailed off, full of emotion.

"I'm so sorry. Is there anything I can do?"

"You can keep me updated on the case."

"Boss! You shouldn't be worrying about that."

"Amy, can you please just call me Joe? I'm off duty now."

"Okay, Joe, but seriously. You shouldn't worry about work. There are much more important things."

She heard him sniff, as though fighting back tears.

"You know the heartbreaking thing? She was up here getting things for the dream home we're looking to spend the rest of our lives in. And if she doesn't make it..." His voice faded again.

"What happened?"

"They don't know. It could have been mechanical. The car seems to have missed a corner and it plummeted... I'm just amazed she survived at all, looking at the wreckage."

"God. It sounds awful." Amy tried to picture the scene, but it was too traumatic to contemplate. Then a dark thought crossed her mind. Was it too early to ask such a thing? Tactless? It had to be done.

"I hate to say this," she said, hoping she was doing the right thing, "but you don't think the car could have been tampered with?"

"Oh, Amy." He paused for a moment. "Let's just say the thought crossed my mind. But who? Clare? Why?"

"There are strange things going on, Boss. Joe. Maybe I'm

being ridiculous. Surely even Clare wouldn't do that."

"I can't even think about that."

"You shouldn't. Concentrate on your wife. She needs you more than the Met does. But keep me updated, okay? I'll be thinking of you."

She could hear a siren. She pictured Joe, standing outside the hospital, scared, not knowing, just hoping. His entire future dependent on a fragile heartbeat.

"Listen, I'm going to be hard to get hold of for the next few days," said Joe. "The signal isn't great and I can't have the phone on if I'm in the hospital, but keep me updated if you can. Who's running the case?"

"DCS Paul Curtis."

There was a moment of silence.

"Joe, are you still there?"

"Curtis?"

"Yeah. What's up?"

"I just... don't know what to make of that."

"I've never worked with him directly."

"You've heard of him, though?"

"Of course."

"Look Amy, watch your back. Okay? The way I look at this, we've got two problems. Clare's back to her tricks, but she wasn't March's sponsor in the Force. We know that. So whoever was behind that and giving him licence to get away with being a bent bastard is still active."

"Exactly what I've been thinking. You don't think it was Curtis?"

"I'll tell you this as a friend, not your superior. And frankly I'm out of there soon, anyway. But there's something about him. Find Clare for me. For all of us. But mainly be careful, okay?"

"Yes, Joe."

She ended the call and pocketed the phone, with a strong sense that there were dangerous times ahead.

Chapter 7

Saturday March 16th, 1996

I ENJOY a hug at the best of times, the worst of times, and pretty much any time in between. So when Clare knocked on the door, just before noon, and then stood on the step with her arms held open, I kind of fell into them.

She held me tight, towering over me in significantly high shoes, and for a moment things felt better. Just for a moment, though. Because the empty, sick feeling of panic was never far away.

Eventually she released her grip and I led her into the front room. I'd hung streamers and started to blow up balloons. I'd even attempted to make a cake, which hadn't been altogether successful, but I'd decorated it in red and white icing in tribute to Danny's favourite football team.

"It looks lovely," said Clare, trying her best to cheer me up. Luckily I was wise to it, and ignored the compliment. "Do you need a hand with the balloons?"

"Yes please. I hate blowing up balloons. I'll make the tea."

A few minutes later I returned with two mugs of Yorkshire's

finest, and discovered Clare had made significant progress. How she had the lung capacity, given her prodigious smoking, was anyone's guess.

"So," she said. "Are you looking forward to having him home?"

"You know what? I've had such a shit two days, it's the only thing that's kept me going."

"Have you got the nurse's outfit ready?"

"What is it with everyone and the nurse's outfit? He can take me as I am and be done with it. Although obviously for a special occasion, I'd be willing to compromise." I winked, almost fooling myself into thinking the situation could ever arise.

"Do I detect a softening in your resolve? Are you going to finally make your move?"

"What move?"

"With Danny?"

I may have blushed. May not have. I couldn't see the mirror, but it certainly felt like it.

"Let's just say I'll be very happy to have him home. I've missed him."

"Oooh, I think you have. There'll be a wedding by the end of the year." She was enjoying this.

"We're just very good friends."

"You were never just very good friends. You were just too scared of commitment." She may have had a point there.

"Yeah, well."

"Life doesn't wait for any of us, Anna. You're perfect for each other. I've never known two people get on so well, live in the same house, and occasionally share a bed...

"That's your fault."

"... and never actually, you know, do what comes naturally."

I was definitely blushing now.

"Drink your tea," I said, "and change the subject."

"Oh, you *are* going to make your move. I'm so happy for you."

"Will you please just shut up?"

"I'm so, so happy. I love a romance."

"Clare. Stop. Seriously. I'll put it another way for you. I nearly lost Danny. He nearly died. And yes, if that had happened, then my world would have ended. So it's put things in perspective - how much he means to me, and how much I love him and how I never want to lose him again."

"You said the L-word."

"But whatever you think," I continued, ignoring her, "it's irrelevant. Because even if I had finally decided that it was worth risking the friendship by moving it onto another level, there's no guarantee that he feels the same. So put your hypothetical wedding on hold and drink your tea."

"Danny adores you," she said, ignoring me too. "For as long as I've known you, you'd have only ever needed to click your fingers and he'd have been with you in a heartbeat."

"Well, we'll soon see, won't we?"

She reached across and squeezed my hand.

"Can I be a bridesmaid?"

"Oh, will you sod off?"

"I'll help you with the dress. You're going to look gorgeous."

"Right, I'm going to go now, and lock myself in a room, and come out when you've gone." But she'd hit a nerve.

I had, in moments of wild fantasy, pictured what I'd look like at the altar, with Danny standing beside me, whispering "I do" and then kissing me in a way that wasn't just a platonic peck on the cheek. And yes, I'd thought long and hard about how he'd react if I ever suggested a change to our basic best friend status, and almost made myself feel sick with the combination of excitement, and then the hollow despair I'd feel if he said he liked things just the way they were.

But I'd reached a point in life when I'd started to really know what - and who - were the closest and most important to me, even if it wasn't something I wanted to discuss just now. At least not until I'd spoken to Danny, and offered him my heart in a way that I hoped he would find hard to resist.

So yes, I was excited to have him home. But more than that, I'd come to the realisation that this was the day I'd been building up to since we'd first met as students, seven years before. No nerves then.

"Can we talk about my studio now?" I said to Clare, desperate to avoid feeling like I was going to throw up. Although the thought of my career being over actually made things worse.

"Of course," said Clare, after drinking some of her tea. "Have the police had any leads?"

"Not a sniff. They took statements. Said they'd be in touch with any news, then nothing."

"That doesn't surprise me."

"I forget you're not the biggest fan of the police."

Her expression was unfathomable.

"It's not that. It was just too professional a job by the sound of things," she said. "For someone to go to that much effort, and preface it by cancelling your insurance - they're not going to leave clues."

That wasn't what I wanted to hear, but she had a point.

"So what do I do?"

"You do what you do best."

"Drink wine?"

She laughed.

"That'll help in the short term. But no, I think just be you. Stay lovely. Be funny. Look after Danny. And let me look into it for you. Can you take me up there later?"

"Of course, if you want to see, but there's nothing much there."

"It would help me get a perspective."

Then I caught a glimpse of the clock, and it was time for a full-blown panic.

Danny was due any minute. I moved to the window, expecting to see an ambulance moving along the row of terraced houses in Rochester Square, or possibly executing a three-point turn at the end. But instead there was just a grey Ford Mondeo reversing into a space. I quickly dashed to the kitchen to get the bottle of Champagne from the fridge, ready to pop the cork for his triumphant homecoming.

"Do you need a hand with anything?" asked Clare, her voice carrying from the front room.

"No, I think we're fine." And then I saw a shape moving towards the glass of the front door, and my heart did a somersault. He was home. I'd dreamed of this moment for three long months.

I put down the bottle and ran to the door, and opened it, and there he was. But weirdly, DC Lisa Miller was standing next to him, and they were holding hands.

"Danny! Welcome home. I'm so pleased to see you," I said, sensing Clare appear at my shoulder.

"Uh-oh," she said.

Danny stood there, looking slightly less buoyant than I'd hoped.

"Are you going to let us in?" he asked. But I was becoming increasingly fixated by the hand-holding. And the "us". It didn't look like she was merely keeping him upright. "Anna?" I moved to the side to let them pass. But Danny tried to give me a hug. "It's so good to see you."

"Likewise," I said, not returning the hug, and feeling my world fall apart.

"Come in, the pair of you," said Clare, as I stood transfixed, not moving. Trying my absolute hardest not to cry.

"Clare, this is Lisa," said Danny.

"I know who you are," said Clare, in a reassuringly sombre tone.

"And Lisa, meet Clare. Albeit occasionally she calls herself DC Lisa Miller as well." Danny laughed, looking embarrassed, as well he might. The absolute outrage. Lisa let go of Danny's hand so she could shake with Clare, and he put his bloody arm round her. One of his lovely arms. The bastard.

"Excuse me, I'll be back in a moment," I said, and started to move towards the kitchen.

"We've spoken on the phone but we've never met," said Lisa as I passed.

"Have we?" asked Clare.

I didn't hear the rest of it as I'd slammed the door.

A few moments later there was a gentle knock. I didn't respond. I was standing at the sink, looking out of the window. The door creaked slowly open, but I ignored that too.

"Anna?" said Clare, in a soft voice.

"Don't talk to me," I said.

To her credit, she didn't. But she came towards me and put an arm around my shoulder, pulling me close.

"Is that what I think it was?" I said at last, struggling to form the words.

"I'm afraid so."

"I made the bastard a cake. A bloody cake."

"And it's a beautiful cake."

"Which I now hope they choke on. On the upside, at least it doesn't look like she's going to arrest you." I let myself be supported by Clare. My legs would have given way otherwise. I'd made such an effort with my outfit as well. The absolute two-timing shit.

"Sorry, can I have a word?" I turned to find Danny standing at the door, looking serious.

"I'll pop outside for a cigarette," said Clare, moving to the back door.

"Still smoking then?" I said, ignoring the new arrival. "I thought you were giving up?"

"Why would you think that?"

"Because you said you were."

"Did I?"

But before I'd had the chance to remind her of what she'd told me in Venice, she'd opened the door and was gone.

I stood looking at Danny, feeling my legs become increasingly powerless. I held onto the sink to steady myself.

"Come here," he said.

"No." I wasn't going anywhere.

"I want to talk to you."

"Well, you can do it from there." My voice wavered, and I doubt it sounded as commanding as I hoped.

"I know it must be a shock."

"A shock?"

"Yes, me coming back with Lisa."

"Your very own police escort. You're obviously very special." I admit there was an edge of bitterness. "How long?"

"How long what?"

"You know exactly how long what. How long has this been going on for? While I've sat here every night worrying about you."

"Just a few weeks."

"A few weeks! You were in a fucking coma a few weeks ago."

"Since then. She came to see me, to take statements once I came round, and we found we got on, and then we got close, and well, things just happened."

"I don't want to hear about the things that have happened." I could feel the tears forming but I was determined not to let them ruin my make-up.

"I don't mean like that," said Danny. "But this doesn't change anything. I'm still here. We're still best friends."

"Are we?"

"Of course we are. I've just got a relationship. But it doesn't change anything between us."

"You reckon?"

"Of course not. I'd love your blessing. I thought you'd be happy for me."

I turned back to the window. There was no sign of Clare. She'd done well to get out of my line of sight.

A moment later Danny put his arm around me.

"Please don't touch me," I said.

"Oh come on, Anna, don't be like that." He let go.

I took a step away from him, but still faced in the other direction. We stood in silence. It seemed like minutes.

"She's a lovely person," he said eventually. "She works hard, she's got a daughter called Jessica, she's been a fantastic support for me."

"In a way that I haven't?"

"Of course you have too. But I'm allowed to fall in love, aren't I?"

But I didn't get a chance to answer that little affront. Because right at that moment the front door caved in, and a small platoon of armed police infantry came bursting through the flat.

Chapter 8

I DIDN'T think things could get any worse. How wrong
I was.

"Where is she?" said a man I didn't recognise.

"Who?" I said, feebly.

"Clare Woodbrook."

"No idea. And who are you, and why are you in my flat? It's polite to knock."

"Don't piss me about. I know she's here."

"She evidently isn't," I said. "You can have some cake, though, if you like."

From elsewhere in the flat I could hear shouts of "clear". God knows what they were doing to my carpets. Two black-clad thugs opened the back door and went out into the garden.

The first man came so close to me I could count his nasal hairs, not that I wanted to.

"My name is DCI Rogan Court," he said. "You are going to tell me exactly where to find Clare, or God help me, you'll be getting arrested for obstruction."

"If she's not here, I genuinely haven't got the faintest idea," I said. Lisa appeared behind him, looking extremely stressed. "And

DCI Rogan Court? Is that really your name? It sounds like the first half of a sentence in which the second is 'the villains'. Ideally 'Camden's studio burglar bastards' but more likely 'not even a cold'."

He looked at me with a face like the Norse god Thor was winding up for a particularly big one. Then he poked a finger dangerously close to my face.

"I'm going to let DC Miller question you. We need to know where she is. Where she's staying. How she gets in contact. And you *will* tell us." He turned to Lisa. "DC Miller, she's all yours. We're going out to the streets."

This will be fun, I thought, as I watched the small army leave the way they'd come.

"What the hell was that?" asked Danny, looking at Lisa and sounding encouragingly furious.

"Are we having a lovers' tiff?" I said, which seemed to annoy them both. Not that I cared. Danny started shouting, and Lisa shouted back, and I thanked a non-existent God for the small mercies of domestic disharmony. We moved gradually in the direction of the front room as the altercation developed.

"Just because we're together doesn't mean I can renege on my duties," Lisa said at last, once the volume had returned to a semblance of normal.

"And is inviting armed police into my home classed as one of your duties?" he asked. Go Danny. Send her packing!

"No, of course not. But Clare is very much top of several wanted lists. And we need to find her. Urgently."

I'd heard enough by now.

"What on earth for, Lisa? If I can still call you Lisa?" I asked. "Clare is our friend. What happened to her special understanding? And where's Amy?"

"I don't know where DS Cranston is at this precise moment. And there was never a special understanding, as you put it. Not officially."

"Bullshit. She saved our lives. Repeatedly. And helped save your boyfriend from Graham March."

She gave me a look that bordered on pity. There was definitely an edge of condescension.

"You don't need me to tell you about all the other things she's done that haven't been quite as helpful," she said.

"Oh bugger off." I was getting into my stride. "She's more than redeemed herself. And more to the point, if you've got the resources to send a small army through my house - sorry, our house, given that Danny still lives here, unless you're also about to drop that particular bombshell - I assume that means you've caught the bastards who did over my studio?"

"What?" said Danny.

"Oh, your new girlfriend didn't tell you? I was keeping it quiet as I didn't want to spoil the mood of celebration, but seeing as that's well and truly fucked, I may as well give it both barrels. If that's not insensitive, given your history of getting shot."

"Anna!"

There was no stopping me.

"My studio was burgled. Cleaned out. Not just the petty cash box and any equipment I'd left lying around, but the whole lot. Even down to the carpet. It's a bare concrete shell, Danny, and apparently I wasn't insured even though I absolutely was. So, Lisa, can you please give me an update?"

"I'm afraid enquiries are still ongoing," she said.

"Funny that. But you'd much rather chase my guardian angel? It wasn't exactly a couple of local glue-sniffers looking for cash for a tube of Evo-Stik, though, was it? Can we at least agree on that? I may not be a crack detective, unlike your good self, but even I could deduce that was a pretty thorough, professional job."

"It looks that way." She looked to the floor.

"And when I'm living on the street because my entire livelihood has been wiped out, are you two going to invite me in for the occasional hot cup of Bovril to fend off the winter chill while you cosy up on the sofa looking like a pair of smug married lovebirds? Or are you going to send armed police to raid my cardboard frigging box?" My voice was getting ever louder.

Danny sank down on the sofa, clearly exhausted.

"Anyone for cake?" I asked. "I even made it in Sunderland colours especially for you. No? Good. I'll go to my room then. Bugger off the pair of you."

Which is precisely what I did, until long after I heard Lisa leave. I kept looking at the four familiar walls, as though seeing them for the first time, wondering how long they would be there to keep me safe, wondering just what I'd done wrong, and how things could have turned so bad so quickly. Danny knocked at the door. I pretended to be asleep and ignored him. I didn't want to speak to anyone. I couldn't. I didn't even want to be alive.

DCI Rogan Court was pacing around the room, furious.

"You had her in your sights, in the actual same room. You shook her bleeding hand, for God's sake. And yet still, somehow you managed to fuck it up."

"I'm sorry, sir," said DC Lisa Miller.

"With all due respect, she wasn't on duty," added DS Amy Cranston, in her junior colleague's defence. "She didn't have any back-up. If she'd tried to make an arrest it could have been extremely dangerous."

"We'll never know, though, will we. Because crucially that's the one thing she didn't do. Jesus. It's no wonder they've brought me in here, to instil a bit of professionalism."

"There's nothing professional about taking unnecessary risks when it's a matter of life and death," said Amy. "She called it in. She did exactly the right thing."

"You're as bad as each other."

Amy looked at Lisa in the chair next to her. They both knew their boss was being unreasonable, but equally that further discussion would be futile.

"At least we know she's in London," said Lisa.

"Wrong. She was. We were supposed to be using the element of surprise. But that's completely buggered. She could have taken flight. She could be anywhere. Absolutely outstanding work, detectives."

He stopped pacing for a moment, then leaned towards them over the back of a chair.

"First thing tomorrow, you go back, and you quiz this Anna Burgin. I didn't like her attitude and I don't believe her protestations of innocence. She knows where Woodbrook is. Don't leave the house till she's told you."

Chapter 9

EVENTUALLY, after giving Danny time to realise his colossal error of judgement, I gingerly returned to the front room. I'd tried to call Clare a dozen times, but she wasn't picking up. Danny was pretty much where I'd left him, hours before, looking shell-shocked. It wasn't quite the homecoming he'd been planing either.

He looked at me with real pain in his previously beautiful blue eyes. I'd tried to calm myself down to just below the threshold of raging fury, but I was still very far from happy.

"So, are you moving in with her?" I asked.

"No."

"And she's happy, is she, that you're living here with me."

"She understands our relationship - that we're great friends."

I laughed like a maniac.

"Right. Even so, though."

"Look, she doesn't see you as a threat."

"What?" I was immediately back on the cusp of fury.

"What do you mean 'what'? It's what I said."

"That I'm not a threat? She's a bit full of herself, isn't she? Who the hell does she think she is?"

He picked up a cushion and held it to his ribs. I wasn't sure if he thought I was going to throw something.

"Anna, you're being ridiculous. You're the one who bangs on about the futility of relationships. Life goes on. I can't spend my entire life waiting for you to see the light and change your mind. I'd like to be a grown-up and have a relationship and do grown-up things."

"What do you mean, waiting for me?"

"You know exactly what I mean. I love you. You know that. I always will. But you're the one who says it can never go any further. You may want to be single for ever but I don't. Okay?"

Oh, fuck.

"You love me but you're shagging some police floozy?"

"Hardly shagging. And she's not a floozy. I've been in hospital. They don't do conjugal visits."

"So you haven't, then?"

"What?"

"Shagged her."

"Not yet."

"But you're planning to?"

"Jesus. Do you want me to put an ad in the paper? Get them to write a news story when it happens?"

"When it happens? Not if?"

"When, if, whatever. I'll let you know. Okay?"

"You know what, I'd rather you didn't if that's all right by you."

For once in my life, there was a bottle of Champagne that I didn't fancy drinking. I wanted to make a cup of tea, but tradition would have dictated offering one to Danny, and I couldn't trust myself not to make it with one of the punishment Typhoo bags rather than a Yorkshire. The joyous Welcome Home banner was taunting me. It was time to change the subject to something marginally less depressing.

"So, it looks like my business is buggered," I said.

"You had insurance, though?"

"Apparently not. I don't understand it. They had a letter requesting cancellation a couple of weeks ago. I've lost everything. Equipment, my archive, work in progress, irreplaceable props. Do you want a cup of tea?"

"I'll make it."

Clearly he could read my mind, and knew not to trust me.

He was back within five minutes. He always made a nice cup of tea. It was his last redeeming feature.

"Do you have a start date back at the Echo yet?" I asked, in a calmer voice, when he was safely back behind the cushion.

"I've been thinking about that."

"And?"

"I'm not sure I want to go back."

"Wow. Okay. Because?"

"Because things have changed. Call it editorial differences. I was suspended, remember?"

I'd forgotten all about that.

"Of course, I remember. But they know that was all a stitch-up, so you were cleared."

"Not officially, as far as I know."

"But they will, surely?"

Danny looked thoughtful.

"Maybe. But I wasn't impressed by the way they dealt with it. They didn't want me to investigate Graham March in the first place, and when he tried to set me up, they didn't give me any support. It was like they couldn't wait to get me away from the place. As editors go, Mike Walker has always been a pain in the arse, but at least I always thought he was fair and respected his judgement. But something seemed to change."

"And who was the other idiot? The news editor bloke?"

"Who? Simon? Simon Oakley. Don't even start me on him."

"So what will you do?" On any other day I'd have been full of empathy.

"I could try to get a job on another paper. Maybe one of the broadsheets."

"Or go freelance?

"I'm signed off for another month so I've got a bit of time to think about it. Going freelance scares me. You know what it's like. It can take months to work on a story, and then months to get paid even after it's published. What am I supposed to do for money in the meantime? What if the stories don't come? I've got bills to pay, rent, car."

I knew that feeling.

"I'd normally offer to help but I think I'm going to be ultra skint."

"What are we like? I actually want to be planning for the future. Saving. You never know, hopefully one day buying somewhere to live, maybe starting a family."

"That all sounds terribly grown-up."

"It's just about being responsible."

"I thought she already had a child. So you're already going to be a daddy."

"Anna, come here." He patted the space on the sofa next to him.

"No."

"Please."

"Why?"

"Because I want you to."

"Make me."

"I made you a cup of tea."

"Oh for God's sake."

I joined him on the sofa. He put his arm around me. It was almost a hug. Obviously the arm was now tainted, and I'd need a shower, but despite my misgivings, it still felt good. We sat in silence. I counted the balloons, wondering what on earth had happened to Clare. I just hoped she was okay. The not knowing was the painful part.

"Is it good to be home?" I asked eventually, almost seeing the funny side of it.

"It's wonderful to be home."

"Really? It's like a war zone. Did you miss me?"

"Of course I missed you. Did you miss me?"

I flicked a balloon with my fingertip. The cake was still untouched. It was probably barely edible anyway.

"You know I did. You saved my life."

He pulled me closer.

"Thank you for everything," he said. "The place looked lovely. I'm sorry for the way it worked out. I didn't mean to hurt you."

"I know."

"Can you forgive me?"

I looked at him. At the floppy fringe and the wispy stubble, and the eyes and the mouth that I'd hoped to be kissing by now. I felt the embrace of his previously beautiful arms. I wanted to forgive him, I really did. I like to think I'm a nice person. Sometimes I think that perhaps I'm not.

"I wanted us to have a lovely day. I wanted to show you my new car. I wanted a hug without feeling like I'm in anyone else's space. But at this moment I just want to know what happened to Clare. I'm scared for her," I said, avoiding the question.

"Was that a yes?"

"I'll tell you what I'm going to do. I'm going out for a walk. I need to get some air. This is all a lot to take in."

To his credit, he didn't try to stop me.

I didn't have a clue where I was going. It was far too cold to be comfortable, but I didn't want to drive. I needed time to think, to clear my head. Clare sill wasn't picking up her phone.

Just two days ago, I'd been so happy. Everything was going well. Danny was coming home, I was working on the most lucrative commission I'd ever won. And Clare was coming to see me, for the first time since a drunken lunch in Venice in which she'd given me an insight into some of her darkest secrets. My admiration had only grown. I'd never understand why she'd turned to crime, nor how she could live with the thought of blood on her beautifully manicured hands. But as a person and as a friend she was truly something special.

I still had my health. That was one thing. And I still knew how to take pictures. Perhaps I could rent a studio somewhere and borrow a camera. Except I wouldn't be able to afford the rent unless I sold my lovely new car, and I probably owed more on the finance for that than it was currently worth. I walked and walked, thinking, trying to be rational, but hating life, and wondering if I'd ever be able to eat anything ever again. The chemicals in the brain that give feelings of euphoria in the happy times are also capable of producing the most horrible feelings of emptiness and despair.

I had two phones in my pocket. They were the mobiles Clare had given to me and Danny so we could always get in touch with her. I'd been guarding his with my life since he'd been in hospital. But then I remembered that there was another number programmed for emergencies. DS Amy Cranston was Clare's friend on the police. I pressed the button.

The number was disconnected. I suppose it made sense. If Amy and Clare were no longer on speaking terms, it was logical to cut the number.

I was torn. As if I didn't have enough to think about, I knew what Clare had said about the phones. They were my only link to her, but she couldn't have been more adamant. If there was ever any question of them being compromised, I had to destroy them immediately. If the police were no longer friendly it was a big problem. We couldn't pretend the phones didn't exist. Amy knew all about them and she was the straightest police officer I'd ever known.

I tried her one final time, but still she didn't answer. I tried from Danny's, too, with the same result. Then, with a heavy heart, I threw both into the canal. It felt wrong on so many levels, but it had to be done.

I'd felt desperately lonely while Danny was in hospital. But that was nothing. Now he was back, I was beginning to understand just how truly desolate real loneliness could feel.

Chapter 10

Sunday March 17th, 1996

EDEN Mills stood at the window of his penthouse office, looking out over the London skyline.

"It's getting out of control," he said.

"It's making me nervous," came the response from the other end of the line. "I'm sensing paranoia."

"You're not alone."

"The police think it's Clare."

"That's convenient."

"We need to find her and put a stop to it."

"We do. And in the meantime?"

"We all need to be very careful. Go back to your estate and lock the doors."

I was pleased to awaken without a crushing hangover, but rather less pleased to find that Danny still hadn't put right his heinous misjudgement and joined me in the night.

Immediately I regretted destroying the phones, even though it had been the right thing to do. My only option was to send Clare an email, but I knew in my heart that it would also go unanswered. Where was she? There's nothing more frustrating than deeply caring for someone, knowing that they're out there, somewhere, but not knowing where they are, and how they are, or even if they're safe. I was so tormented.

Was she out of touch because she couldn't make contact? Or because she didn't want to speak to me? Maybe she thought I was complicit. That I'd set up the raid to trap her. That made me feel sick to my core. Had everything changed? I had no way of knowing, only the fear that the wonderful sense of happiness and connection we'd shared was all just a terrible illusion. That I'd never have that sense of utter joy again. All wiped away through an awful, avoidable misunderstanding. All through no fault of my own, except for the crime of being alive and caring about someone so deeply that I'd give anything I owned just to hear her voice. Just for a two-word reply saying "I'm okay".

People are so unique. So valuable. She was irreplaceable. But so was Danny and I'd lost both of them on the same day, within a matter of minutes. How ridiculously careless was that? How was that even fair? I couldn't have felt more hollow.

Danny was up and dressed by the time I made it to the kitchen.

"Happy birthday," I said.

"You remembered."

"Of course I remembered. But I'm not making you another cake, before you start. You'll have to stick candles on yesterday's."

He laughed, but then his expression changed. He started to walk towards me, but stopped, looking uncertain as to how I'd react.

"I'm worried about you," he said.

"About me?"

"Yes."

"Why?"

"Because you don't look happy."

"I'm a big girl, Danny. I'll cope."

"Well, you're literally not. I could put you in my pocket."

Normally that would have made me smile.

"I'll make you a birthday cup of tea, though," I said. "I was going to offer to take you out for lunch but I don't know if that's still appropriate."

"Ah."

"What?"

"I'm actually going out already."

"Oh."

"Sorry."

"Where to?" But I already knew. "What time's she coming?"

"Shortly."

"Okay."

I pushed past him. I'd just make one for myself then. Actually I didn't even fancy a cup of tea. I'd just go back to bed. Bollocks to everything.

Lying on the bed, I tried again not to cry. I heard the front door close, and moved to the window. Danny was walking down the steps. I saw him climb into a grey Mondeo, then lean across and kiss the driver. The tiff was clearly over. I'd spent weeks planning how to make his birthday special. For so long it looked like he might never make it. Those dark days when he was lying in a hospital bed, in a coma, the victim of a deranged madman. A corrupt former policeman who'd fired two bullets into Danny's chest. But now the day was here, really, what was the point?

I tried to phone friends for a bloody good moan, but I don't really have many close ones. I have a good professional relationship with lots of people, but life and my career have been too hectic to really put the effort into nurturing friendships. That was a lesson learned. And for what?

Eventually, I decided the only way to shake off my despondency, and to stop myself pining, was to keep my mind and body occupied.

I tidied the flat, dusted the place, and felt genuinely heartbroken. Were they already having sex right now? Was Clare at this very moment plotting to kill me? I tried to eat but I couldn't even manage a slice of toast. And I love toast.

I began to make a list of clients that I'd need to contact, but my address book had gone the way of everything else. There wasn't time to add that to my long list of worries, though, because somebody was knocking on the door.

It was DCI Rogan Court.

"You're back again? Where's your private army? Hello, Amy."

DS Amy Cranston nodded in greeting but looked serious. The DCI was clearly the boss.

"Can we come in?" he asked, but didn't wait for an answer before pushing past me. Amy and I followed him into the front room. If he'd expected to find Clare lounging on the sofa, he was disappointed.

"I'd offer you a cup of tea, but only if you've caught my burglar," I said. "In fact, I'd even stretch to a biscuit."

"Miss Burgin," he said testily, "I don't think you understand the seriousness of your situation."

"I most certainly do. My entire career is buggered and all of my equipment is probably being hawked round East End boozers while you're standing here. I assume you are actually investigating?"

He ignored my question.

"You were harbouring a known fugitive. Should we add

obstructing an investigation? Perverting the course of justice? Aiding and abetting?"

"You bastards made a mess of my carpet so I think we're even." Where was this coming from? I wished I felt as brave as I was pretending to be. "Is that a 'no' on the burglar then?"

"I'm not here to talk about your bloody studio. Would you prefer we did this down at the station?"

"Oh good God. Spare me the clichés, please. So I presume this is about Clare? Fire away, anything you like." It was at times like this that I wished I smoked. I sat down on my sofa but immediately regretted it. Court and Amy towered over me. "Why the sudden interest in Clare? And have a chair, please." Both remained standing.

"We're investigating a series of incidents and we believe Clare Woodbrook may be able to assist."

"What incidents?"

"I am not in a position to divulge the details. What do you know of her recent travel plans?"

"Look, I don't know who you are, but I do know Amy. So bear with me a minute." I turned to his colleague. "Amy, you and I both know Clare has been back in the country and has, in fact, worked with you directly, in the same room, to sort out the issue with Graham March. And you've never wanted to arrest her. So please tell me what on earth is going on?"

She looked at her boss, who shrugged.

"There have been some developments," she said. "Certain things have happened that we think Clare may know about. We just need to speak to her. Urgently."

"Okay. Thank you. Not much more help, in all honesty, but why are you talking to me?"

"Because Clare was here yesterday, and we think that means you may be able to help us track her down."

I couldn't deny that part.

"You know her as well as I do," I said. "If she doesn't want to get found, she's quite capable of disappearing."

"Okay. But what can you tell us about her recent travel plans? Has she, for example, spoken about recent trips to Venice, Seattle or Frankfurt?"

I knew she occasionally visited all three, but I wasn't about to divulge that.

"You know what?" I said. "She turned up here yesterday to welcome Danny home from the hospital. Which, in case you'd forgotten, was quite a big deal, because one of your colleagues shot him. But before we had a chance to discuss where we'd each been on holiday, a team of commandos came charging through the house and she did what she does best: she disappeared. So no. She didn't mention trips to Venice, Seattle or Frankfurt."

"Where is she now?" asked DCI Court, regaining the initiative.

"I really have no idea. I genuinely wish I did."

"How does she get in touch?"

Amy, of course, knew how she got in touch, but her expression was a blank.

"She just turns up. Amy knows what she's like."

"What did you throw in the canal?"

"What?"

"Yesterday. You threw something into the canal. Two things."

"Oh that. Just two old phones. Why? Is there a law against that?"

"Yes, as it happens."

"Arrest me for litter louting then."

"Why did you throw two phones into the canal?"

"Why were you watching me?"

"Answer the question."

"It's a family tradition. Supposed to bring good luck, although there's not much evidence of it working."

He finally snapped.

"I'm warning you. Right now we need to speak to Clare regarding some very serious developments and you are the best lead we have. So if you're going to dick us around, we're going to take you in and keep you there until she comes to collect you. Am I making myself clear?"

"You're making yourself look an idiot."

"It is in your interests to cooperate."

"Well, I don't want to sound in any way reluctant to do that, but I'm not going to be much help if you lock me in a cell, am I? Can you even do that if you're not charging me with anything?"

"We'll charge you with plenty. Everything I mentioned, plus wasting police time and being a royal pain in the arse."

Despite myself I was enjoying the verbal jousting.

"There's no need to get personal. And if, as you seem to think, I am in some way in communication with Clare, I think you'd find I'd be more use to you out there on the streets."

Amy stepped in.

"So, she didn't mention any travel yesterday. I'll ask a different way. Are you aware that she's been abroad recently?"

"Clare is a law unto herself," I said. "She passes through closed doors. I don't know where she goes. I don't know where she lives. She doesn't consult with me on her travel plans."

That wasn't strictly true. I'd asked her about all those things in Venice and she'd told me.

"So she wasn't in Venice last weekend?"

I may have coloured up at that point.

"What makes you ask that?"

"Was she?"

"Like I said, she doesn't tell me."

"Where were you last weekend?"

"Now I *was* in Venice, now you mention it. I had a photoshoot, but I can't prove that because some bastard has nicked the pictures, so don't even start me on that."

I looked at Amy, who in turn was looking at Rogan, who in turn was looking at me with an expression that could burn skin.

"Let's talk about your studio," he said.

"Oh, thank heavens for that."

"Who do you think burgled it?"

"I was rather hoping you'd tell me."

"I'll tell you who I think burgled it."

"Please do. Then arrest them."

"Clare."

"What?"

"You heard me."

"You're just being ridiculous."

"And you're living in denial."

"Why would Clare burgle my studio?"

I expected Amy to be laughing at the stupidity of her colleague. But instead she had a very grave expression.

"We think she's trying to control you," she said.

"What?" I said again.

"Has she offered to help you sort it out? Suggested working together?"

"No." Actually yes, to both of those things.

"We think she will. Because she wants you in her debt. She needs you to hide behind."

"I'm sorry but this is madness." But deep down, the prospect, horrifying though it was, had hit home. I remembered how she'd once pointed a gun at me in Switzerland. I knew she could be ruthless and unpredictable. She'd been acting strangely. I knew from experience how she could clean up a room and leave it without a trace that anyone had ever been there. She'd done it in my lounge when she'd shot someone who was on the verge of raping me.

"So, for the avoidance of doubt," the DCI continued, "she does not deserve your loyalty. And that means if you're hiding her, or you have any information on her whereabouts that you're not disclosing, you're both being stupid and playing an extremely dangerous game."

"I'll certainly bear that in mind," I said. "Are we done?"

"For now."

I followed them both back to the front door. As I was showing them out, Amy turned back towards me.

"Be careful, Anna," she said. "We can't protect you unless you're honest with us."

She didn't wait for my reply before heading back to her pool car. I closed the door behind them.

She'd left a newspaper on the arm of the sofa. The headline caught my eye. A British woman was wanted in connection with the murder of a prominent hotelier in Seattle. What on earth was Clare involved in now?

Chapter 11

"DA-NEE do it. Da nee do it!"

Danny was playing with Jessica while Lisa was preparing a late birthday lunch, but now it was about to be served.

"How are you two getting on?" asked Lisa, as he joined her in the kitchen.

"I think we're bonding," he replied with a smile. "She keeps asking me to make her fluffy rabbit do voices."

Lisa laughed, then turned to her daughter, who'd followed close behind her giant new friend.

"Jess, can you go and put your toys away please?"

The two-year-old didn't look happy, but nonetheless went back to the living room.

"I'll do it properly, later," said Lisa. "Now, come here."

She embraced Danny, and they kissed. It was strange for both of them without the constant threat of interruption by nursing staff. Instead she was interrupted by the sound of her phone.

"Sorry, I've got to get this," she said. Danny went back to the living room to help Jessica with the tidying, and to give Lisa a moment of privacy.

In a few minutes, she called them both through.

"Welcome to the police life," she said. "I'm so sorry to do this on your birthday, but I've been called in. We're going to have to make it a very quick lunch. I'm sorry."

"Don't worry," said Danny. "Are you okay for childcare?"

"My mum was coming to take Jess anyway. I thought it might be nice for us to have a bit of alone time." The subtext was unmistakable. She sighed. "One of these days."

"Patience pays," said Danny.

"They asked if I could take you with me."

"Me?"

"They want to ask a few questions about Clare."

"What is it with Clare? What is she supposed to have done?"

"I wish I could tell you, but they'd fire me. We just need to find her, that's all."

"But is she in trouble?"

"Possibly."

Danny waited for more, but it wasn't forthcoming.

In the car, on the way to the station, Lisa was curiously quiet.

"Are you okay?" asked Danny.

She didn't reply immediately, her eyes fixed on the road. He reached out with his right hand and held her thigh. She let go of the steering wheel with her left, and squeezed it.

"I'm just frustrated, that's all," she said, at last.

"We'll get time. There's no rush."

"But this is what it's always like. I worry that you're going to get fed up with it."

"You shouldn't worry. I take it on board. I don't have any demands or expectations. It's just wonderful to see you when I can."

She let go of his hand to change gear through a roundabout.

"It's easy to say that now, but I think we need some ground rules," she said.

"Such as?"

The traffic ahead was slowing down, but she took the chance to move into the outside lane.

"It's not just about time. I know your job and you know mine, and we both know there could be conflicts of interest," she started. "So I'm not going to be able to tell you about things I'm working on, and I know that's going to get annoying for both of us."

"I'll try not to ask."

"It's not trivial, though, is it? I just don't want it to come between us. So I need you to promise me. If you ever get annoyed or frustrated or think I'm being unreasonable, you must please speak to me. Don't suffer in silence, okay?"

"Okay."

There was another roundabout. She indicated left and took the first exit.

"It's a delicate time. We've got a new DCI, who you met, who seems to be an unreasonable bastard. And the DSI, Joe Leyland, who we liked, and who should have been running things, has gone off on compassionate leave."

"That's not good."

"No."

Up ahead, a bus was pulling out, causing the cars in front to slow.

"How well do you know Clare?" she continued.

"Probably better than most."

"Did she ever visit you in the hospital?"

"Not this time. I hadn't seen her since the night on the rooftop, until we got home yesterday. I had no idea she was going to be there."

"Okay." She paused. "But I know you have history with Clare. I know you probably think you have a loyalty..."

"I do."

"... but I don't want this to come between us either, okay?"

"But you can't tell me why you want her?"

"I wish I could."

When they arrived at the station, Lisa parked up. Then they walked together to the entrance.

"I'm sure they won't want you for long," she said. "If I'm tied up, I'll get someone to give you a lift back home and I'll call you later."

Danny nodded. And then they hugged goodbye, just out of sight of the office windows. He took a seat in reception, awaiting his chance to help the police with their enquiries.

There's nothing quite like spending time on your own with a broken heart. Thinking of everything you've done. Every opportunity missed. Wanting to believe that the other person will be feeling the same and will call you and say they've been thinking about things and they miss you too, and they want you to forgive them so you have a chance to put things back together. But knowing that is just a fantasy born of a desolate, crushing sadness, and the phone won't ring, no matter how many times you look at it, and there's nothing you can do in the meantime without looking desperate.

But I was feeling desperate. And in the end, despite every part of me trying to resist, knowing it was the worst thing I could possibly do, I picked up my phone and called Danny. He didn't answer. I didn't expect him to. But was it because he was busy, or was he trying to avoid me? I tried not to imagine what he might be doing instead of answering my call. But there were crumpled bedsheets aplenty.

And then my phone rang. My heart leapt. Danny! But it was a withheld number. Clare, then? I wasn't expecting anyone else.

"Hi," I said, ready to pour out my heart.

"Anna Burgin?" said a female voice with the hint of some form of European accent. I couldn't place the nationality.

"Speaking."

"I've got a message for you from Clare Woodbrook." My heart leapt again. "She wants me to take you to her."

"Where is she?"

"I can't tell you that. I can only take you."

"Who are you?"

"A mutual friend."

"Why didn't she call me herself?"

"Because she's not currently able to do that securely."

Part of me was delighted at the prospect. But a bigger part was getting frustrated at the lack of straight answers.

"How is she?" I asked.

"She's fine. Doing well. Just being careful."

"Not in any danger?"

"No more than normal."

"What did you say your name was?"

"Just a mutual friend."

The frustration was growing. And the accent sounded increasingly fake.

"That's not technically a name, though, is it?"

"I can't give you my name."

"Why not?"

"Because if I don't give you my name, you can't accidentally give it away to the wrong person. Not that I think you would deliberately."

"Okay, but make one up then."

The line went quiet for a moment. Eventually she returned. But I was starting to feel uneasy.

"I'm not here to play games. Clare wants me to take you to a meeting point so she can talk to you."

"And you say you're a good friend?"

"A mutual friend. I'm not sure Clare has good friends."

I begged to differ after our bonding session in Venice.

"Prove it."

"I don't need to prove it. The proof will be when I take you to see her."

"Okay. Tell me when and where and I'll meet you."

"I'm outside your house now. Look out the window and you'll see my car."

My heart nearly stopped. It sounded so plausible I nearly fell for it. Once she'd seen me at the window, she'd know I was there.

"I'm not home at the moment, sorry."

"Your car is here."

"I know. I took the Tube." I never take the Tube. Her voice didn't falter. She clearly didn't know me very well.

"Where are you now? I can come and get you."

"I'm in Stockwell. Don't worry, I'll get the Tube straight back. It's direct. I'll be home before you're even south of the river."

"Give me the address and I'll send a cab to collect you."

"Really, it's no bother."

"I insist."

I had no idea. Why did I say Stockwell? I'd never even been to Stockwell. And then I counted my blessings. Inside my handbag was a mini London A-Z. I reached for it quickly.

"Let me just ask my friend," I said. I put my hand over the microphone to muffle the sound, and pretended to have a conversation with myself while I thumbed through to the right page.

"Apparently I'm close to the corner of Lingham Street and Crossford Street. I can meet you there. How long will you be?"

"There will be a cab in a few minutes."

"Okay. And the car?"

"The driver will recognise you."

"Okay, I'll dash now and wait on the corner."

I ended the call, and then was suddenly wracked with doubt. What if she was genuine? What if Clare really had sent for me?

I was desperate to look out of the window to see if there was any movement outside, but it was too big a risk. All I could make out from here was light and shadows, and there didn't seem to be any movement. Nothing that suggested a car driving away.

And then I was overcome by a sense of real fear. How long before the cab arrived in Stockwell and they knew that I'd lied? How long before they just broke in to get me? And if that was going to happen, what were the chances that I was already surrounded, and had no means of escape?

Chapter 12

"I EXPECT you know why you're here?" said DCI Rogan Court, once Danny had taken a seat. DS Amy Cranston was alongside him. She looked tired.

"Because you're looking for Clare," he said.

"Very good. And I don't suppose you're going to tell me where she is?"

"Right at this moment I've got no idea."

"Outstanding." The DCI's voice was showing signs of intense irritation.

"Danny," said Amy, "you know me. Hopefully you know you can trust me."

"Of course."

"Then please believe me when I say it would be better for everyone, including Clare, if we were able to talk to her. Urgently."

"In relation to?"

"Certain incidents of which we believe she may have knowledge."

"Clare has knowledge of all sorts."

"Quite."

DCI Court looked like he was about to butt in, but Amy put up a hand to stop him.

"Look, Danny, I know you've been in hospital but I also know she was at your house yesterday."

"It was as much of a surprise to me as anyone."

"I'm sure. But if she makes contact again, or you find out where she's staying, you must let us know. You can call me. Any time."

"Okay," said Danny. He looked from one to the other. "Is that it? You couldn't have done this on the phone?"

"I wanted to see your eyes to know if you were lying," said DCI Court.

"Why would I lie?"

"I don't know, Danny. Maybe you miss the confinement of the hospital, and you'd like a few nights staying with us."

"Wow, now you're threatening me." Danny sat back and folded his arms.

"It's not a threat. It's a warning."

"Well, the warning is duly noted. But I wouldn't hold out much hope. If Clare knows you're looking for her, I imagine I'd be the last person she'd contact."

The DCI leaned across the desk, and lowered his voice.

"Cut the bullshit, son. She contacts you, you contact us. Understood? Don't think you're going to get special treatment just because your girlfriend is in the next room, or things will get immensely unpleasant for both of you."

I'd never felt more on my own. With an ever-increasing sense of panic, I called Danny again, but there was no answer. Typical. He was probably deeply embroiled in the throes of passion just as I needed him most. Well, he'd just have to leave her alone for a moment. This was an emergency. I tried again. And again. He answered on the fifth attempt, sounding breathless. I was nearly sick picturing him with no clothes on. Which was a first.

"Where the bloody hell are you?" I said, and immediately wished I hadn't.

"Just leaving the police station. Why, what's up?"

I hadn't been expecting that. I nearly asked if it was 'take a pet to work' day, but managed to stop myself. Instead I rushed through an explanation about being questioned by Amy and then the mystery caller.

"I've just been getting questioned too. But that sounds serious," he said. "Don't, whatever you do, go to the window."

"They're going to be in Stockwell in a few minutes, and know I've lied, and come and get me, Danny." It was hard to keep the panic from my voice.

"Let me call Lisa."

"What? Danny, you cannot tell fucking Lisa, for fuck's sake. What if it's genuine? And we lead the police straight to Clare?"

"Credit me with some intelligence. I'll use discretion. But I'll ask her to make a call and get the nearest squad car to drive past, looking for anything unusual."

Ten minutes later, I had an overnight bag packed, and I could see flashing blue lights moving across my ceiling. I finally dared to look out of the window. A squad car was approaching. A dark-coloured car was pulling away in the opposite direction, pausing to let the police car past. Rochester Square is a dead end. The only reason someone would be driving in that direction was if they'd been parked up outside and were now driving away. I knew my neighbours' cars, and it wasn't one of them.

The phone rang again.

"You're not in Stockwell," said the voice.

I ended the call.

I had to get out of there.

Now was a good time, while the police were circling. I hurried out of the front door, double-locking it behind me, then down the steps to my car. Hands trembling, I fired the engine, clipped the kerb in an emergency three point turn, and floored the accelerator. I had no idea where I was going.

Chapter 13

Lisa pulled upside the flat.

"No, really, I think I should come in with you," she said. "Just to make sure everything's okay."

As they walked up the steps to the front door, she scanned the quiet street.

"Her car's gone."

"Do you know what's ridiculous?" said Danny. "She mentioned last night she had a new car. I wouldn't even know what it looked like."

"Dark blue SLK."

"Well, I hope it's a good thing that it's gone." Danny didn't know what to think. Did it mean she was safe? Or as safe as she could be, in an increasingly uncertain world.

Inside, they checked from room to room, turning on lights as they went. The house was empty and there was no sign of a struggle.

"It doesn't look like anyone's been here who shouldn't have been," he said.

They finished back in the front room. He tried calling Anna but there was no answer.

"I'm sorry I can't stay," said Lisa. "But if you're worried, I'd love you to come back to mine."

Danny thought for a moment, then shook his head.

"I'd love to, but I can't. Not until I know where she is."

"Okay."

He looked at Lisa, trying to read her expression. Was this the first big test? Prioritising Anna over a night together? She didn't sound happy, but that could have been one of a hundred things.

He sighed.

"You're going to have to tell me what's going on," he said.

"You know I can't."

"But it's getting serious now."

"I know, Danny. It's been serious all along."

Further protest was pointless. They hugged, and then Lisa left, having made Danny promise to call her as soon as he knew that Anna was safe.

***

"Any luck?" he asked.

"She didn't bite," she said. The soft natural accent was unmistakable.

"That's a shame. But the other one?"

"That's all done. Another one down."

"That's good."

"You'll hear about it tomorrow. You owe me."

"I know. I won't forget. You are the best, my dear."

"I'll be in touch."

"I'll look forward to it. Auf wiedersehen."

"Adios."

She ended the call.

My phone beeped. I'd missed a call from Danny as I was driving like a maniac towards the northern edge of London. I pulled into a side road and called him back.

"Thank God," he said. "Are you okay? Where are you?"

"I actually don't know where I am. But I'm fine. Told you, I'm a big girl."

"You're five foot one."

"And a bit."

"In shoes."

"I'm wearing shoes, so go me. I'm positively Amazonian."

He laughed. I didn't. I really wasn't in the mood.

"What shoes are you wearing?"

"My blue DMs. Why? Have you turned into a shoe pervert?"

"Stop it, I'm being serious. Are you coming home?"

I looked through the windscreen at the parked cars and street lamps of the unfamiliar urban landscape, and home seemed very appealing.

"I can't. I'd love to, but I'd feel like a sitting target."

"I'm here."

"Even so, Danny. I need to get away."

"Do you want to come to Lisa's flat? I can call her, you could pick me up and I'm sure we could stay there."

Had he gone completely mad?

"I can't do that," I said. "I don't want to visit the scene of the crime."

"What crime? I didn't know a crime had been committed."

"Not yet," I said, ominously. I couldn't guarantee I wouldn't be tempted to do one if I saw her with anything approaching post-coital radiance. "I'll stay with a friend."

"You don't have any friends."

That old chestnut.

"A hotel, then." Headlights flared in my rear-view mirror. A car had pulled in just behind me. It was making me nervous. "I've got to go. I'll call you." I disconnected, and floored the accelerator again.

I still had no idea where I was going. There were lots of lights in my rear-view mirror. Was I being tailed? I'd had enough of adventure. I just wanted to be safe and know where Clare was. I saw a sign for the A1 and followed it north.

Cars passed me. If I was being followed they were playing an elaborate game of tag. But why would I be followed? I wasn't involved in anything. Okay, so my friend had proved to have a rather deadly alter ego if you got on the wrong side of her, but she was no danger to anyone who played by the rules. It wasn't like she was some psycho halfwit who blew up random pubs and trains.

Clare had been a fearsome investigative journalist, until one day, in a moment of uncharacteristic greed and madness, she gave up her career for a rather more lucrative one as an international criminal. But that was all three years ago now. She'd since worked closely with friends on the Force - including Amy and the evil Lisa. Yes, she was technically still on the wanted list, but was more use to them running free bringing the really bad people to justice, albeit sometimes in a brutal and permanent way. So what had changed? Why had a firearms unit stormed my flat looking for her? Why now? And where the hell was she?

I hadn't been on the A1 since Danny and I had last travelled to Sunderland. The road was unfamiliar. Eventually, as I reached the outskirts of London, it opened out into a motorway. I decided to stop at the first major service station, keeping fingers crossed that there'd be a motel or something, so I could at least spend the night in relative comfort. At least I still had a credit card, even if no way to pay it off.

But as the miles passed there was no sign of a service station. Eventually I saw a Quality Hotel by junction 6 at Welwyn Garden

City and decided that would have to do. What on earth is a garden city? At the very least you'd expect flowers, water features and well-tended hardy perennials, and instead I got a motel by a motorway and copious traffic noise. The world was passing me by.

I parked up, headed to reception, and booked a room. And once I'd done all of that, and decided I didn't really want to ring Danny again after all, I realised that I hadn't eaten all day. The thought of food made me feel even more sick, but I knew I should try. So I dropped my bag, inspected the en suite, felt the first pangs of depression over what my life had become, and headed to the restaurant.

The wait for the waitress gave me a moment's calm for the first time in a very long time. I had a pang of nostalgia for my old life, before Danny, before running a business. Innocent schooldays, of back-combed hair and too much make-up, cheap wine and too loud music. Going to nightclubs for the sheer joy of dancing, and the first furtive glance at someone who was giving me the eye from the other side of the room. When life revolved around Top of the Pops, and the highlight of the week was the new edition of Smash Hits. Before leaving Manchester and moving to London. No pressures, no cares, no drama. Secrets shared with friends that amounted to little more than where the cigarettes were hidden.

And I could have all that again. First thing tomorrow I'd get my hair dyed purple, and blow the last of my money on Rimmel's finest, and be done with it. Everyone and everything else could just fuck off.

I browsed the menu, unsure whether to risk anything more than a very large glass of something inebriating, when I heard a familiar voice asking if the chair opposite was free. She appeared to have a new haircut, although it was largely hidden under a hat. But I'd recognise those hazel eyes anywhere.

"Clare! What the absolute... I am so happy to see you!" I

almost burst into tears. Standing up, I gave her the biggest hug I'd ever given anyone. "What the hell is going on?"

Chapter 14

CLARE took the seat opposite.

"How did you find me? Did you follow me?"

"What are we having? My treat," she said. I don't think I'd ever seen her dressed so casually. She was wearing jeans and a sweatshirt, and a pair of shoes that looked like a designer version of DMs. She clearly wasn't going to answer. I made a mental note to check my car for some form of tracking device.

"I've been worried sick. Tell, me, what is happening?"

She looked at the menu and then back at me.

"Will you believe me if I tell you?" she asked.

"Of course I will."

"Okay. Then I haven't got the faintest idea."

I almost laughed.

"What?"

"Trust me, I'm trying to find out. But the police turning up was as much a surprise to me as I expect it was to you."

"But you disappeared. Not being funny, but you were wearing heels that could have seriously impeded anything like a hasty getaway."

"I had a head start. Did you see the way Lisa was looking at me? Call it a sixth sense, but I knew from that moment that things weren't right."

The waitress turned up and took our order. I went for the all day breakfast. Even though it was deep into the evening, it would still be my first food of the day. And a glass of Sauvignon, obviously. I'm not weird.

"I destroyed the phones," I said. "But then I had no way of contacting you."

"You did well. I'm proud of you."

"But we had armed police searching for you. What have you done?"

"Nothing."

"That's not what they think. I've had a grilling. They keep asking me about your travel plans. They've questioned me twice."

She looked impassive.

"Yes," she said. "I thought that might be the case."

"Then I had a call from someone wanting to pick me up. Some foreign woman. Said you'd asked her to collect me, to take me to you. I didn't bite."

Her expression changed, to a look of real concern.

"That was certainly nothing to do with me," she said. "You did the right thing, but that worries me. What kind of foreign?"

"I don't know. She sounded European, but equally the accent could have been fake."

She frowned.

"And the lack of insurance. The police think..."

She put up her hand to stop me.

"I'm sorry, Anna," she said. "I'm sorting the studio out for you. I'm getting that put right."

"What does that mean?"

"It means you've got to trust me. I feel like I've let you down."

"What are you talking about?"

I was prepared to clutch at any straw, but she wasn't helping me understand anything.

"I was determined that you wouldn't ever again have to be part of my world," she said. "I don't mean as a friend, because I value that enormously, but just the dangerous parts. You've suffered enough already." I couldn't disagree there. "I thought that after what happened last year, I'd do everything I could to make sure you were left alone, to concentrate on running your business, taking brilliant photographs, and living a happy, safe life without me bringing trauma to your door."

"Yeah, well, I wouldn't worry about that. I don't have much of a business at this precise moment thanks to the burglars."

I wanted to tell her the ridiculous police theory that she was responsible, but she interrupted me.

"Please don't worry about the studio. I'll make sure everything is put back. And if it isn't, I'll pay for everything you need to replace it all."

"What are you talking about? I couldn't ask you to do that."

Clare appeared serious. But I could still hear Amy's voice. *Has she offered to help you sort it out?*

"Is there something you're not telling me?" I asked.

She took a deep breath, and refilled my glass.

"You said it yourself: it wasn't the average burglary. The police aren't going to fix it for you. I will. That's all."

"Clare..."

"Look, I've got a proposition for you."

I could hear Amy inside my head again. *Suggested working together?*

Clare went on. "I'll buy you the equipment but if that makes you uncomfortable, I could be a sleeping partner. Then it's up to you. Keep me on board as a partner or buy me out for something nominal. Whatever makes you happier. No rush."

"I... I need to think about that," I said, not wanting to consider the implications that were running through my head. "But it's very kind." It was almost exactly as Amy had suggested. But if Clare had arranged the burglary just so she could help me, to own me, to control me, then what did anything mean any more? And if I accepted her generosity, would I be benefitting from crime on a fairly industrial scale?

"Let's change the subject," she said.

I didn't want to change the subject. I wanted to tell her Amy's theory. Confront the issue, here and now.

"I think I'm becoming a liability," she continued, before I had a chance, her words betraying a vulnerability that rarely came to the surface, although I occasionally sensed it deep within.

I reached out and squeezed her hand. The beautiful hand with the Ceylon sapphire ring. The hand that looked so smooth and gentle, and yet which I knew had pulled the trigger that had ended lives. And which, judging by the police's enthusiasm to find her, might well be back to being as deadly as ever. Normally, her aura of calm control served to reassure me. But when she looked worried like this, I knew it was time to move my finger in the direction of the panic button.

"You're not a liability," I said, more out of hope than real belief. "You're the one person I can rely on."

"You can rely on Danny."

"Ha."

"All not well at home?" She raised an eyebrow, but it was pointless me explaining. She'd seen it for herself. There was a significant risk that I'd sound like some sort of petulant child who'd had her favourite toy removed.

"Let's just say that Danny is in the throes of an infatuation. It'll end in tears, obviously, but he clearly doesn't give a stuff about my feelings, so sod the pair of them. What happened with Amy, anyway?"

"How do you mean?"

This was one of Clare's most annoying traits - acting as though she was oblivious to something that was blindingly obvious to everyone else. Maybe she worked on a different plane to the rest of us, or maybe she enjoyed being deliberately obtuse.

"For the last two years she's been your friend, never trying to arrest you, even though she could have done any number of times. Now you're number one on her wanted list."

"I'm very selective about who I consider to be a friend," she said.

Sometimes I wanted to scream. But more than that, I wanted to know what on earth was going on.

"So, people, update me." DCS Paul Curtis sat at his desk. DCI Rogan Court, DS Amy Cranston and DC Lisa Miller had been called in to brief him on developments.

"We're still looking," said Rogan.

"Correct me if I'm wrong," his boss interrupted, "but is it not now two days since I said I wanted her in custody by nightfall?"

"It is."

"And?"

"We traced her to an address in London, but by the time we turned up to make the arrest, she'd vanished."

"I see."

The silence in the room was deafening.

"I called it in," said Lisa. "But by the time SO19 arrived, she'd made her escape."

"I understand."

And again, the silence.

"You'd better get to work, then," he said, eventually.

The meeting ended. It hadn't been a bollocking, but the unspoken menace was ominous.

"A word, ladies," said Court to Amy and Lisa as they left the room.

"Yes, sir?" said Amy.

"In here and shut the door." He indicated an empty office on the other side of the corridor.

Amy was last in, and closed the door behind her.

"That," said their boss eventually, "was embarrassing."

"We can't perform miracles," said Amy.

"I'm not asking you to perform miracles. I'm asking you to do your job."

"But we are doing our jobs."

"I'll believe that when you bring her in. This Burgin woman worries me."

"Anna?"

"Obviously Anna. How many others are there?"

Amy had to stop herself from making a potentially career-damaging riposte.

"Why does she worry you?" she said instead. "You think she's hiding something?"

"That, of course. But it's more than that. If Woodbrook is on a spree, then Burgin, by definition, is in danger. She's a pain in the arse, but I don't want her turning up on a slab. Have I made myself clear?"

"Crystal," said Amy. Lisa nodded.

"You heard the DCS," he continued. "You'd better get back to work."

Lisa followed Amy out of the room, and back downstairs to their office. It was strangely quiet, so Lisa took her chance.

"Can I borrow you for a moment," she asked.

Amy turned round, looking hassled.

"What is it?"

"If it's not a good time..."

"It's not really. Can it wait?"

"Of course."

Lisa watched as Amy headed towards the double doors to the lifts, then pushed them open with uncharacteristic force.

Chapter 15

THE plate of food arrived. I looked at it with trepidation. I felt better now I knew Clare was safe, but the underlying sensations of panic remained, and I still wasn't sure I could eat anything. But before I could pick up my cutlery to at least attempt it, my phone burst into life. Danny. I wasn't in the mood so I ignored it and turned the phone to silent. I wanted to get to the bottom of things with Clare.

"Don't worry about the police. It's nothing I can't handle," she said, stealing a mushroom from my plate.

"But what have you done?" I asked.

"Nothing. What did they say I'd done?"

"They wouldn't tell me, just that there had been some *developments* that you might have information about. But I suspect it's serious, given the way they trashed my house and the pressure they've put on me to tell them where you are."

She was looking longingly at my hash browns. I pushed the plate across.

"I think it's a bit of a misunderstanding," she continued, once she'd taken one.

"It sounds like a hell of a misunderstanding. You must know, surely?"

"Can I be honest with you?"

"Please do."

I was trying to read her expression but it was unfathomable. She took a tiny sip of wine before continuing, but it was barely enough to wet her lips.

"I've been investigating bad people. Some of them have died, but that's part of why I'm investigating them. And if the police think I'm involved any more than that, they're wrong."

"Wow. But you can see why they might want to talk to you, given your history?"

"Not really, because the irony is, I was working with the police on the investigation."

"What?"

"That's what makes me think something has gone badly wrong."

I pulled back my plate. I don't normally do fried bread, but I didn't think this was going to work on an empty stomach.

"I think you're going to have to go slowly with me on this," I said. I bit into a slice and immediately thought I was going to gag.

"It's not complicated," she said.

"There's a first."

She laughed, but the laughter didn't reach her eyes.

"Okay." She paused, as though trying to work out how to phrase things. She scanned the room, but we were the only diners. Nevertheless, she lowered her voice. "Three years ago, I was investigating Graham March, as you know. He was into all sorts that a policeman shouldn't be into, and I was working on an exposé, as you also know. Then I did what I did, in terms of going off the rails, which I accept was wrong, but forget that. I left the story with

Danny. Graham got suspended, and should have been fired, locked up, and ideally never released. But next thing we know, he's cleared by the inquiry and gets reinstated. It didn't make sense."

"You said he had friends in high places."

"Exactly. Which means there was corruption somewhere else - someone above him." She paused, checking the door for a moment before turning back to me. "I knew a Detective Superintendent, DSI Joe Leyland. We were good friends. Had been for years, from back when I worked on the paper, and before he got promoted. Yes, I was technically on the wanted list, or whatever the technical name for it is, but when it looked like Graham was going to get cleared, we had an off-the-record meeting. Once he'd given me a very stern lecture about all the things I'd done wrong, he suggested we could help each other. He was deeply concerned about corruption within his division."

"Specifically Graham March?"

"And whoever seemed to be sponsoring him. Joe knew that if he put me away he would probably get commended, but equally I could be a lot more use to him - finding out about March, keeping an eye on him, and ultimately putting a stop to all of it, and helping to clean up the division. He knew that I had contacts in Germany that he could only dream of, and he trusted me to find things out."

"Wow. Okay." I reached for the ketchup. Maybe I'd brave the bacon.

"He was determined to get to the bottom of it, but then he realised it was more than just one corrupt person in senior management. There was a whole network."

"Was?"

"What?"

"You said was."

"Was. Still Is. Joe offered me a deal. Use my contacts to continue investigating Graham and the network, and in exchange they wouldn't arrest me. At least not until it was all sorted, and then they'd give me a chance to disappear."

"Which explains why Amy wouldn't ever arrest you?"

She nodded.

"So what's changed now?"

"That's where it gets complicated."

"I knew it couldn't last. Why is everything always complicated?"

"Because we live in a complicated world. First, Joe's about to retire, so once that happens the deal is off. It was never official, anyway, so after that I'm on my own. And second, some of Graham's network have been turning up dead."

"Jesus. And they think you'd know who's killing them?" My voice had dropped to little more than a whisper.

"Looks that way, although I've got no more information than they have. I've been trying to get in touch with Joe but his phone seems to be off. So now you know about as much as I do."

"God. I don't know what to say. Can you not speak to Amy?"

"Apparently not. You know what she's like. She follows orders. She was happy to humour me as long as that's what Joe said to do. Actually, 'happy' is probably overstating it. But if she's had someone higher overruling that then no, I don't think it would be wise to speak to her."

"Try him again now."

"Joe? I've been trying since yesterday morning. He's not answering his phone."

"But he could sort it?"

"Yes."

"Give him a go then. Please. For me."

"I can't make a call from a restaurant. One moment."

She stood up and walked over to the till, then signalled for the waitress. She paid the bill then returned.

"When you've finished, we'll go outside."

I was having second thoughts about the bacon, so I arranged

the knife and fork, downed the wine in one, and stood up to follow. She led me outside to the car park, then opened the passenger door of a silver Audi. A moment later she was in the driver's seat beside me.

"It'll come through the speaker, but it'll go to voicemail," she said as she dialled the number.

But it was answered almost immediately.

"Leyland."

"Joe, it's me, I've been trying to call you. What's going on?"

"Clare, where are you?"

"I'm safe, but half the Met are looking for me."

"You need to turn yourself in."

"That's why I'm ringing. Why are they looking for me? I don't know anything."

"I'm being serious, Clare. Tell me where you are and I'll get somebody to collect you. It'll be in your interests to do this before it all gets out of hand."

It was hard to see Clare's expression in the near-darkness, but I sensed it wasn't good.

"Before what gets out of hand? What am I supposed to be telling you?"

"I can't talk to you now, Clare. But you know exactly what. Call Amy. Immediately. She'll come and get you."

"Joe, you're not making any sense."

"You knew the rules. It's time to stop this. Now."

"Stop what?"

"I've got to go. My wife is coming out of theatre any second."

"The theatre?"

"Operating theatre. Listen to me. Do as I tell you. Call Amy. Now. I'll be back in a couple of days and I'll make sure things are comfortable for you but I can't help you any more. DCS Curtis is running things now."

"Curtis?"

"I've got to go. Call her."

And with that, the phone was disconnected.

Clare turned to me, then leaned back against the headrest and closed her eyes.

"That could have gone better," I said.

Danny gave an exasperated, frustrated sigh. Where was Anna? Why wasn't she answering his calls? Was she trying to punish him? Did she not know he'd be worried sick? Of course she knew.

His thoughts were interrupted by the house phone ringing again, for the third time. He answered it just in case, but there was no one on the line. Again.

Then his mobile burst into life. He snatched at it. It was Lisa.

"Hey, Danny," she said.

He exhaled.

"Hi."

"How are things?"

"They're fine. All good. I'm just worried about Anna. She's not answering her phone."

"Shit. You still haven't heard from her?"

"She rang once. Said she couldn't come home. But she'd call me. That was about three hours ago. Someone keeps calling on the landline but it's silent."

"That's all we need. Listen." Lisa sighed. "Let me talk to my mum and see if she'll come and look after Jess. I could come and be with you."

"I can't make you do that."

"I'd like to. Unless you don't want me to."

Danny didn't know what he wanted.

"I'd love you to. But if she comes back and we're together, she's going to blow her stack again."

"I thought she told you she couldn't come home?"

It was a fair point.

"If you're sure?"

"Danny, I'd love to. I'll be there within the hour."

She ended the call.

Danny stood up. That should be just long enough to freshen up and make the place presentable. Deep inside, though, he knew that time spent with Lisa might never go quite as planned. He was about to head to the shower when the home phone rang again. And again there was nobody on the line.

Chapter 16

THE phone call to Joe seemed to change everything. Clare turned towards me.

"It's like they think I'm going round killing people. You've got to believe me - I haven't killed anyone, Anna."

That wasn't strictly true, but she looked so genuinely upset, I didn't want to argue the point.

"But do you know who it is?" I asked. "Any theories?"

"Who's pointing the gun? Or who the corrupt policeman is?"

"Either."

"No idea for both. I don't even know why someone would be killing them. As for the other, just that it's someone high up. Joe's a DSI. Once you get above that, you're into the Detective Chief Superintendents and Commanders and Commissioners. We thought we were getting close, though. Maybe that's what's triggered it. But it worries me. Although not as much as somebody phoning you, telling you they'd take you to meet me. I don't like the thought of somebody watching you."

I'd almost forgotten about that aspect of the afternoon.

"Where's Danny now?" she asked, winding down the window

and then putting a cigarette in her mouth, although for once she didn't light it.

"No idea. Embedded deeply within the local constabulary, most likely."

Clare smiled.

"You do make me laugh."

"What do you mean?"

"You do. You're acting like a love-struck teenager, jealous that he's two-timing you. But Danny would have done anything for you. If you'd wanted him, you could have had him at any time for as long as I've known you."

"Yeah, well, I didn't, so can we change the subject? Are you going to give me one of your cigarettes?"

"No."

"Fair enough."

"You don't smoke."

"I think it's time to start in earnest."

"Believe me, it isn't. So, seriously, where's Danny now?"

"At home, last I heard, but he could be anywhere."

I checked my phone. There were eight missed calls.

"Oh," I said. "He's been trying to call me."

"Call him back. He'll be worried sick."

"I will in a minute."

It wasn't that I didn't want to. It was just that I didn't know what to say. I went to press the preset, but Clare reached out her hand to stop me.

"I don't want to burden you with everything, but I'll do you a deal, okay? We'll meet with Danny in the morning and I'll explain everything to both of you. Tell you everything I know about the network. I'm not asking for help. My number one objective is to make sure you're safe and then it's to find out what's going on. The priority for tonight is to make sure we both stay out of trouble."

"I'm not sure it's wise to discuss this with him, whatever it is."

"Why not? You'd trust Danny with your life."

"I would, but I do worry about a conflict of interest."

"I don't."

"Why not? You're the one that has everything to lose if he says the wrong thing to the wrong person."

"Because I think we both know him well enough to know that he would never do that. And I think that you're just grumpy at the moment because the arrival of Lisa put your nose out, but in your heart of hearts you know, as well as I do, that the three of us are a team. And if it came to a question of loyalty between you and Lisa, or even between me and Lisa, I'm a hundred percent convinced that she would be the one that misses out."

"Maybe," I said. But I wasn't sure I shared her confidence. I was cold, tired, confused, and hungry, although still unable to contemplate food.

"Can we at least go inside?" I said. "I don't know about you but I'm freezing. Come on."

She put the cigarette back in the pack. We both got out of the car, then walked back towards the reception.

"Where are you sleeping tonight, by the way?" I asked, when we arrived back at the bar. I didn't expect her to tell me. But it was beginning to get late and I knew she could disappear at any moment.

She looked at me as though tortured, trying to decide whether to confide in me. And then I realised it was something more than that. It wasn't that she was reluctant to tell me but that she didn't know herself.

In recent times I'd had a window into her world, and I was now seeing an expression I'd rarely seen before. She was scared. For the first time her vulnerability seemed stronger than her skills of self-preservation. For all the money, and all the contacts, and all the mystery and intrigue, she was a woman alone in the world and the vultures were circling.

"Are you going to call Danny?" she asked, changing the subject.

"I should." I made no effort to reach for my phone.

She reached out and put her hand over mine. Her skin felt cold, but her touch was reassuring. She squeezed my hand and I placed my free one on top to return the gesture.

"I get the sense there are things you want to say," I said.

She nodded, with a look of real sadness in her eyes.

"I've got a kettle in my room if you'd like a cup of tea," I said, with a smile. Sometimes it was the small acts of kindness that had the greatest effect.

She squeezed my hand again and then rose from the table.

"Lead the way."

The room was tiny but functional. Aside from the bed there was a small desk running along one wall, with a portable TV in the corner, a kettle with two cups next to it, and a pot of assorted tea bags and pots of long life milk. I filled the kettle from the bathroom tap, not confident that it would boil with any degree of haste. The teabags weren't an encouraging brand, but I was determined to do my best.

"You can stay here with me, if you want," I said

"Oh, Anna. That's a lovely thing to say but I can't put you out."

I smiled at her.

"You know what? Given how things are going, and if it's true what you said about somebody watching me, then frankly I'd be glad of the company. Especially you, given that you've already proved your credentials as a bodyguard of repute."

Clare laughed.

"What's funny?"

"It's just ironic. I've spent the last three years periodically arranging accommodation for yourself and Danny, finding it amusing to book you double rooms, because I've been desperately keen to encourage the two of you to get together."

"I knew it!"

"And here we are and now I'm grateful for the expertise in platonic bed-sharing."

"That's a valid point actually. You do have a history of touching my leg."

"Only in gay nightclubs."

"Quite. But I'm not sure there are many of those in Welwyn on a Sunday."

"Well, you should be okay then."

I put a teabag into each cup.

"Do you have a suitcase or anything?"

Clare nodded.

"You make the tea and I'll pop out to the car and get it."

I wasn't having that.

"Not being funny, but I'm not letting you out of my sight. It's bad enough that people are watching me, but God alone knows who's looking for you at the moment."

"I'll be fine, honestly."

But I think she could see real concern in my expression.

"Come on then," she said, beckoning me towards the door. I switched off the kettle and followed.

There were a fair few cars in the car park. Certainly more than I'd have expected, given the lack of customers in the restaurant and bar. Maybe they were all staff? That would be a lot of staff.

"I'm still nervous," I said. "If you're being watched, they could swoop down on you at any minute."

"Look, if you're worried, follow me."

She led me down the rows of cars, looking in every one. There was nobody in any of them. We doubled back to her Audi. She took an expensive-looking leather holdall from the boot, and then we made our way back to my room.

"What did I say the last time we were in a hotel room together?" she asked.

"Five minutes ago or in Venice?"

"Venice."

"You said all sorts. It was fascinating."

"God, did I? That's your fault for getting me drunk."

"Me?" I laughed. "On wine you suggested we should order and then paid for?"

"The idea was for you to get drunk so you wouldn't remember what I told you."

"I know." I smirked.

"But you do remember?"

"Yup. All of it."

"Ah. Well, that's gone badly."

I couldn't keep the smile out of my voice.

"What, specifically, were you referring to?"

"The bit about me having a career change."

"Ah, yes. To summarise: you're going straight and are now something of a philanthropist, doing good wherever you go, and no longer doing dodgy deals and shooting people."

"In a manner of speaking."

"And you expected me to believe that?"

She pointed two fingers at me and made a clicking noise as she cocked her thumb.

"Maybe one for old times' sake."

Luckily, she was smiling. I reached for my phone.

The Holborn police station was largely deserted. Cleaning staff were moving through, and a skeleton night staff had taken over, but Amy knew she would have to be careful not to arouse suspicion.

She made her way to DSI Joe Leyland's office. The door was

unlocked. With a final look to check the coast was clear, she slipped inside. She didn't turn on the light.

She moved to his desk and checked the drawers. They were locked. Kneeling down, she shone a miniature torch underneath the desk, hoping to find a spare key taped to the surface. But there was nothing. It was always so much simpler in the movies.

Movement in the corridor caused her to extinguish the torch. She could hear talking. Two voices, both male. They stopped just outside the frosted-glass door. She held her breath, listening, trying to recognise them, but she couldn't. Her heart pounded in her chest. Discovery now would mean an end to everything. The talking stopped, and the shapes moved on. She tried the drawers again, pulling harder, but still they wouldn't give.

She wiped her fingerprints from the handles, then stood up. Forcing the drawers would arouse suspicion, and suspicion was the last thing she needed. It was imperative that the focus remained on Clare. She listened carefully to make sure the coast was clear, then left the room, and hurried to the lifts and then out into the late London evening.

***

Danny didn't seem in the best of moods when he answered my call. Perhaps it was another tiff.

"Where the hell are you? I've been worried sick," he said.

"I told you, I'm staying with a friend," I said, looking to Clare, who nodded.

"You said you'd be in a hotel because you didn't have any friends."

"Ah. Well, two birds, one stone. Because I'm in a hotel but with a friend, so it's a classic double whammy. There's nothing to worry about. Anyway, you've got your girlfriend to look after you. How's your birthday, by the way? I thought you were supposed to be out with her?"

"For the afternoon. I was always planning on coming back here this evening."

I didn't believe that in the slightest, but let it pass. Definitely a tiff. Result.

"Have you had a nice day?" I asked.

"It's been okay, but it just feels a bit weird, being back here on my own."

"So where's the lovely Lisa?"

"She's at work."

I wasn't sure I believed that either. I pictured her lying next to him on the sofa, tiff or not.

"Nothing to do with Clare?"

"Almost certainly. Which friend are you with?"

"Nobody you'd know. I do have friends of my own, you know."

"Right."

"I did manage to track down Clare in the end, though."

"Excellent news. How? How is she?"

"She's fine. I just bumped into her."

Clare stood up, and bumped into me. I gave her a look, trying not to giggle. It was all the encouragement she needed. I felt a finger prod me just below the ribs, causing me to gasp. I grabbed her finger before she could do it again, and bent it back slightly, giving a look of warning, while trying to keep a straight face.

"What are you up to?" asked Danny.

"Nothing. I've just got something irritating me."

Clare pulled her finger free. She was clearly up to something. I locked myself in the bathroom.

"But you're sure you're safe?" he said.

"Definitely."

"Brilliant. I'll let the police know. Everyone has been worried about you."

"By the police, you mean Lisa?"

"Yes, obviously Lisa. Get over yourself."

Charming.

"Fine. Nothing to get over," I lied. "Anyway, I managed to speak to Clare. She wants to meet us both, tomorrow. So she can tell us what's going on. Are you free, and can you do it without getting a lift from your girlfriend, as that would kind of defeat the object?"

"Where are you? It sounds echoey."

"Nowhere. So can you?"

"Of course. When and where?"

That was a good point. I should have checked.

"I'll give it some thought and let you know. Okay?"

"Okay. I'll look forward to it."

"Perfect."

"Have a lovely evening."

"You too."

That was enough stilted conversation. I ended the call, left the bathroom and turned back to Clare.

"You are a pain in the arse! You know that?"

She winked.

"How was Danny? Can he meet us?"

"Yes, but we need to tell him where."

"I'll think of somewhere."

I looked at the double bed.

"So are you staying?"

"If you're sure you don't mind."

"I'd prefer it."

"Okay then. I'd be delighted to."

"As long as you don't snore."

"Obviously I don't snore."

"You smoke a hundred fags a day. You're going to snore."

"Well, A: I don't, and B: I'm not. But if it's a problem I can smother you with a pillow."

I folded my arms. It needed to be said.

"Clare, can you stop joking about murdering me? It would be funny, but you've got previous."

"I promise I'm not going to murder you."

"You did once point a gun at me, though."

"Oh come on. It obviously wasn't loaded."

"Does that make a difference? It was just as scary."

"I promise never to shoot you."

"Or smother me?"

"Or that. Can't rule out poisoning, though."

"Christ. Just go to bed."

It felt strange to have someone alongside me, albeit with a big gap in the middle. With the lights out, the room was only faintly lit by the ambient light from outside. I could hear intermittent traffic noise from the busy A1 motorway, but was pretty sure it wouldn't keep me awake. Everything else that was on my mind would see to that.

I turned over, eventually, to face the middle, and was surprised to see Clare looking at me.

"Hello," she whispered.

"I thought you were asleep?"

"I am. I've just kept my eyes open."

I could almost believe it.

"I've been thinking about things," she continued.

"And?"

"I don't want to sound morbid, but there's only one way to fix this."

"What do you mean morbid?" I was instantly nervous.

"I'm planning on being dead in the very near future, and I would be deeply honoured if you would attend my funeral."

Chapter 17

Monday March 18th, 1996

WITH every day that passed, the briefings were getting earlier and increasingly more tetchy.

"Three days on from me giving you a deadline, and still no progress," began DCS Paul Curtis. "Sorry, people. Substantially far from good enough. Can you please tell me what I should say to the Commissioner to stop you all getting fired?"

Amy had never seen him look so angry. But DCI Rogan Court's expression wasn't much better. It wasn't even 8am and already the day was turning sour.

"What do we have? Any movement at the borders? DCI Court, an update please, and make it significant."

"There are no reports of her entering or leaving the country," said Rogan. "At least not under her own name, or any of her known aliases. We've interviewed her friends, Burgin and Churchill, but neither have given us anything."

"Well, that's worse than useless."

The DCS turned to Lisa.

"Are you still in a relationship with him?"

"Danny? Yes, sir," she said. "Although it's early days and we haven't had much time together."

"Spend more. Get closer. Shag it out of him if that's what it takes. Next?"

Amy gave Lisa a sympathetic glance.

"We've been looking into her links overseas, trying to find a motive," said Rogan. He clicked a button on a remote control, and a wall screen lit up with images of two men. "She was known to be close to a German national who was living in London last year. Went by the name of Otto, although we're making enquiries on that to find his real identity. Either way, he's lying very low. She was also close to a Bulgarian national, out of Sofia, by the name of Georgi Stoyanov."

"Either linked to the victims?"

"Not as far as we know."

"For fuck's sake. So pointless then?"

"We're exploring all avenues."

"Any actual progress?"

Rogan clicked the remote again and the image changed.

"We've compared the reports from Frankfurt and Italy. Frankfurt was made to look like suicide, but Venice was a shooting. A Zastava CZ99."

"That rings a bell."

"Exactly." Rogan nodded to the screen. "That's Miroslav Nikolić. Serbian gangster, arrested late last year. Currently on remand, but a stash of Zastavas were recovered from his house in Lancaster Gate. CZ99s, M57s mainly."

"Are we saying Woodbrook got a weapon from him?"

"It's possible. We know they had at least one meeting in December. It could have been more."

"Thank Christ for that. Find out where this Nikolić is, speak to him. Offer some sort of deal if you need to."

"Already on it."

The screen changed to a terraced house.

"This is a property in Farringdon," Rogan continued. "Rented under the name of Charlotte Sadler, which is a known alias of Woodbrook. We know she was staying there last year, but we've searched and there's no sign of recent habitation. We are, however, keeping a watch and we've installed monitoring equipment in case of movement."

"That's progress," said DCS Curtis. "Anyone else she knows? Family? No? Known associates? Boyfriends? Girlfriends?"

"We're still following leads."

There was a knock at the door. A uniformed officer entered.

"Sir, may I have a quick word?" he said, looking nervously at the DCS.

"I'm in the middle of briefing. Can it wait?"

"I'm afraid it's urgent, sir."

DCS Curtis sighed, then stood and left the room. But before Rogan had a chance to impose himself on the others, his boss returned.

"Looks like she's in London," he said, grimly. "There's been a fourth victim."

Clare had already been in the shower and was immaculately dressed by the time I woke up. Even though she was still wearing largely the same outfit as yesterday, she looked effortlessly chic and perfectly made up, while I knew I'd resemble a mad-haired zombie. There was a knock at the door, which Clare answered, and a moment later she returned with a tray of breakfast things which she put down on the bed beside me.

I could get used to this.

"I'm afraid I'm probably not looking my best," I said. "What time is it?"

"It's all right. I'm not going to try to date you, given your record. Just gone nine."

"Really?" I felt like I had so much to do, although I had no idea where to start. I couldn't lie around in bed all day. But the breakfast did look lovely so I made a tentative start, as Clare disappeared into the bathroom and then returned with a toiletry bag that she packed into her holdall.

"Have you thought any more about what I said last night?" she asked as I was finishing up.

"I have. You're still bonkers."

"Why?"

"Because you've already been killed once in a helicopter crash that didn't happen, and I think it's fairly common knowledge that you made it up. You're looking very well for someone who died three years ago. So if you do it again, first and foremost nobody is going to believe you, and secondly, you can't just have a funeral without a body because I'm pretty sure that'd be illegal. Not that that's ever stopped you doing things in the past."

"But I could really do with organising a funeral."

"What on earth for? Are you feeling unwell?"

"Let's wait till Danny turns up."

We had just over an hour to vacate the room or risk missing the checkout cut-off. I asked Clare to pass me a towel from the bathroom, then wrapped it around myself and put the breakfast tray on the desk. But before heading into the shower, I needed to get this off my chest. Clare had opened a window and looked ominously close to lighting a cigarette.

"Am I missing something?" I asked.

She gave me a look that was somewhere between benevolence and pity, then lit a cigarette and blew smoke into the crisp morning air before turning back towards me.

"One won't hurt. Regarding?"

"Anything. Everything. The funeral."

"You shouldn't worry about the details," she said.

"Of course I worry about the details. I've had previous experience of getting involved in your plans and they usually involve being captured or shot at. And in Danny's case, the bullets actually connecting. And you're not supposed to have secrets from me any more."

"Who said that?"

"You did. When you were drunk in Venice."

"Can we have an amnesty on everything I allegedly said in Venice? Agree to never mention it again?"

"No."

"Please?"

"No. And stop changing the subject."

She laughed.

"Danny said *you* always change the subject when you're in the midst of something awkward."

"You're doing it again."

"You should be getting in the shower."

I stood, unmoving.

She took a deep breath.

"Look, some things are better kept private. You can't get in trouble if I don't tell you about them."

I still didn't move. And so she told me and it still sounded bonkers.

Chapter 18

BEFORE leaving the hotel, I called Danny and asked him to meet us on the top floor of a multistorey car park above a shopping centre in Barnet, north London. Clare's instructions were clear. He had to take the Underground but swap trains several times to make sure he wasn't being followed. Even then there was a risk he'd get picked up on CCTV, so the meeting would have to be brief.

I asked if he'd spoken to Lisa, and Clare told me off for apparently being horrible to him. I'm not sure why she thought that. I'm pretty sure I've never been anything less than entirely cordial.

We left my car in a residential cul-de-sac in Welwyn, just in case my number plate was being traced, and instead took Clare's anonymous hire car.

"Are you sure they're not going to be able to find you through your driving licence?" I said, as we pulled away.

"Believe me, if I can't do something as simple as hiring a car without being traced, I've got bigger problems than being found by the police," she said, mysteriously.

Danny was there before us, looking relatively smart, with a

bag over his shoulder. He gave Clare a hug, which would have caused me problems in previous years, but now I just hoped she squeezed him hard enough to make his scars smart. We got back into Clare's car. Danny took the front and I leaned through from the back.

"First things first," said Clare, "I've got you both a present." She reached into her holdall and then gave us each a new phone, together with a charger. "Same as before, but guard these with your lives. And Amy's not on this one, for obvious reasons."

We took the phones, then Danny was the first to speak.

"What's going on, Clare?" he asked. "Why are the police mobilising small armies to arrest you?" He wasn't pulling any punches.

The worried expression was back. She explained about the deal with DSI Joe Leyland to investigate DCI Graham March. Then the murder of three members of March's criminal network, and how the police seemed to think she would know who was doing it.

"Why would they think you'd know?" he asked.

"Because I know more about the network than anyone else, I suppose. The original plan was for me to disappear once Graham had been brought down, but then Joe thought I could still be useful to him. Although apparently that's changed in the last couple of days."

"Useful as a grass?"

"What?"

"An informer?"

"I know what a grass is. I'm just shocked you'd ask that." She sounded offended. "I've got standards. I don't betray people who trust me. I'm an investigator. It's what I do, and I've got access to contacts he doesn't have."

"So what's changed?"

She shrugged. Her expression changed from worried to something more closely resembling sadness. She was staring out of the window, as though looking for the answers somewhere in the sky

"I'm trying to work that out. I know Joe's about to retire. There's a huge reorganisation going on within the Met and he was offered early retirement. That was always going to change things."

"But he hasn't yet?"

"Not quite."

"So what, then?"

Clare paused, collecting her thoughts. It was back: that vulnerability I was beginning to see more often.

"Are you okay?" I said, when she still didn't speak, thinking now might be an excellent time for a hug, if it wasn't so logistically difficult. Eventually she nodded.

"I wish I knew. We absolutely nailed March with the original investigation. And yet after a period of suspension he got back. How did that happen? It could only be because somebody was protecting him."

"His friends in high places," said Danny.

"Exactly. So even before he came back, I started investigating. I spoke to Joe. He started investigating too. He took it personally. But investigating police corruption is a dangerous and delicate thing, even at DSI level."

"Presumably the further you go up, the smaller the pool of potential suspects?"

"Precisely." She turned to look directly at Danny. "But equally, the better they are at hiding things. So we started to look at Graham and the people he associated with. And between us we started noticing patterns, similarities, and weird things, and started putting connections together. Did I tell you that after I saved his life in that warehouse, he tried to have me killed in Sofia?"

I think our expressions suggested she hadn't. There was so much in her world I never wanted to be part of.

"That was his show of gratitude for you," she continued. "He knew I was still onto him, and he knew I wouldn't give up until I'd put him out of action."

Clare paused again, looking thoughtful. Her next words took us both by surprise.

"How are you on Greek mythology?"

"Greek mythology?" I said. "Somewhere between utterly clueless and absolutely no idea. Why?"

"So you're not familiar with the Lernaean Hydra?"

"Never heard of it. Something to do with water?"

She gave a faint smile.

"Not exactly."

"What then?"

"It was a hideous, vile, multi-headed serpent monster that lived at the entrance to the underworld. It had poisonous breath, and even the scent of the thing was deadly."

"Sounds like Graham, apart from the multi-headed thing."

"Quite. But its other main claim to fame was that every time someone chopped off one of its heads, two more grew in its place. Eventually it was killed by Heracles, but it took a bit of doing."

"Okay. And this is relevant because?"

"Because if I'm right, we might be dealing with the modern equivalent."

Chapter 19

I WAS more confused than ever. I looked at Danny. He didn't seem to be any wiser than me.

"I'll tell you what we know," Clare continued. "There's some sort of network, almost a cabal. Rich, powerful, influential people, all looking out for each other."

"Like the Masons?" I said.

"Far worse than the Masons. But they've set themselves up as some kind of mysterious society, helping each other get up to all sorts of dubious mischief, and somewhere within it there's someone high up in the Met."

"Sorry, you're losing me," said Danny. "I'm struggling to think of Graham as a rich, powerful, influential person."

"No, he was far from it. And that was one of the earliest mysteries. If this thing exists, how come he was involved? But then it became obvious he was a kind of foot soldier, doing some of the dirty work. Someone else in the police holds the power but he was the one on the ground."

"Bear with me," said Danny. "I'm going to have to write all this down, or I'm going to get lost." He reached into his bag and withdrew a spiral-bound notebook. Clare offered him a pen but he found one of his own at the bottom of his bag. "Okay, but who is involved in it? And what do they actually do?"

"That's the big question. We think it started as a few friends doing each other favours and then expanded from there. And they were doing all sorts of deals to help each other. So one ran a hotel chain, for example, and if the others needed somewhere discreet to do a dubious deal, or even just somewhere for a dirty weekend away from the wife, they'd have a free room, with nothing on a card statement to trip them up. Another was into high finance, so if you needed funding for something high risk, she could bypass the traditional banks and get the money with very few questions asked."

"It's not actually illegal, though, is it?" I said. "I'd have thought a weekend away with your mistress was par for the course in that world."

Clare frowned.

"Yeah, but it was more than that, and a lot of it is a lot more sordid. The same hotels were also being used by prostitutes trafficked by one of the others. Another was an arms dealer, so if you needed a handgun, he was your go-to man."

"God. So who are they?"

"Again, that was difficult. They don't use their real names. They gave themselves code names that mean some variation on the word 'secret'."

"Really?" I said. "Are they like ten-year-old schoolboys or something?"

Clare laughed.

"If only. It's a lot of pretentious nonsense really. March was Keme which means secret thunder. The hotel man was Nihan which means concealed, secret and undisclosed. I'd hear names on the grapevine but didn't know who they all were, so I started making a list. Hassiba, the secretive and reserved woman. Asrani, secretive, hardworking and ruthless. Draca, an interesting person with a secret desire. The list goes on."

"How many are there? Or were there?" asked Danny, writing in furious shorthand. Ever the reporter.

"Ah, now you get to the crux of it. There were twelve of them but of late there have been a few fatalities."

"And that's what the police think you'll be able to help with?" he said.

"I expect so. The only reason I can think of is that every time I identified a new one I went to see them to confront them, and then they'd immediately turn up dead."

"Jesus."

"Exactly. It's like there's someone following me round, cleaning up every time the secret comes out."

That caused us to stop for a moment.

"You told me they'd turned up dead. You didn't mention it was just after you went to see them," I said at last.

"No." If I was expecting a longer reply it wasn't forthcoming.

I could see Danny thinking.

"How do you know there are twelve of them, and how have you worked out who they are if they all use code names?" he said at last.

"We only think there's twelve. We're not sure but it looks that way. As well as the ridiculous names, we've found occasional evidence of pretentious symbolism. You're aware of the symbolism of the number twelve?

"Not really," I said.

"It's the symbol of cosmic order. The number of space and time. There are twelve signs of the Zodiac, twelve Greek gods on Mount Olympus, twelve months of the year, twelve days of Christmas."

"Twelve disciples," I said.

"Exactly. And going back to mythology, twelve labours of Heracles. In the Bible you've got twelve gates of Jerusalem, guarded by twelve angels, and they're named after the twelve tribes of the sons of Israel."

"Wow."

"There's loads more. If you want to get specific about it, Mary Magdalene is mentioned in the Bible by name exactly twelve times. Even the Brussels bureaucrats are at it. The flag of the European Union has twelve stars because twelve is considered the number of completeness and perfection."

"Even bigger wow."

"The clincher, though, was something I saw at Graham's funeral."

"Hold on," said Danny. "You were at Graham's funeral?

She gave him a look as though to say, why wouldn't I be?

"How did you manage that? Wasn't that a bit risky?"

"It was the week before Christmas, I was in the country, and I wanted to see who else was there to send off the old fraud. But I'm coming back to that in a moment. The thing I spotted was something that looked like a playing card on the floor by the coffin. But when I got close, I realised what it was. A tarot card. Not just any, but the twelfth. The hanged man who symbolises self-sacrifice and meditation. Unless you reverse it, when it represents selfishness."

"That's weird."

"It gets worse. Because there's been another one left with each of the bodies."

———

DC Lisa Miller stood next to DS Amy Cranston while DCI Rogan Court was talking to a forensics officer. Somebody else in a white coversuit was photographing the body. And the tarot card lying next to it.

"Who was he?" she asked.

Amy bit her top lip before answering.

"Eden Mills. Have you heard of him?"

"The newspaper guy?"

Amy nodded.

"More than that. He was the owner of the Echo. Which is your link with Clare from the outset."

Lisa hesitated. She needed a moment to process that. This was a rich and highly influential media owner. The ramifications would be unthinkable.

"But why would Clare kill the owner of the newspaper she used to work at?" she said at last.

"Why does Clare do anything?" said Amy.

Rogan came over.

"Time of death is estimated as yesterday afternoon, between two and four," he said. "The housekeeper found him this morning."

"How is she?" asked Lisa.

"In a state of shock, obviously." His expression suggested he thought it was a ridiculous question.

"The murder weapon?" asked Amy.

"Looks like a small calibre handgun."

"Zastava?"

"Could be. We'll know when we get him back to the lab."

He sighed.

"We are so in the shit. We *have* to stop her. Because if we don't, we may as well be pulling the trigger ourselves."

Chapter 20

THE windows of the car were starting to steam up. Clare edged one open, to let in fresh air, but that just served to make it colder.

"How did you go to Graham's funeral?" asked Danny. "Presumably you couldn't just turn up?"

"There was an element of disguise," said Clare.

"You're either mad or fearless. Or both."

"Think about it - in one sense, it's the last place anyone would have expected me to be. And it was a good excuse to dress up."

"What did you go as?"

"I couldn't decide between distant cousin and elderly aunt, so I went as a taxi driver."

"What?"

"All I had to do was park the cab, then walk through the church just before the service to see who was there, then wait outside in the cab, taking pictures as they all emerged."

I had to credit her ingenuity. Not for the first time.

"So how was it? The funeral?" I asked.

"Interesting."

"In what way?"

"Because aside from a smattering of family, colleagues and no end of lowlife, there were a few others who seemed genuinely upset. It looked like a cabal day out. I took the pictures to Joe and we identified a few of them. There was one who I immediately recognised."

"Which one?" asked Danny.

"Axel Meier, the boss of a German energy company, which was extremely weird in some ways as he was so out of place. Why was a big German industrialist at the funeral of a bent copper in London? But I'd come across him before in Germany. Have you heard of him?"

"No. Should I have done?" asked Danny.

"He made the papers in January but you'd have been in no state to read them, I expect. His body was found in Frankfurt. Shortly after being caught on video taking cocaine in a brothel. Apparent suicide."

"Sounds awkward," I said.

She nodded, looking thoughtful.

"It was. National scandal. But contacts of mine in Germany had already been watching him, and they'd asked me to take an interest and get close to him. What you've got to understand is that I've done work for some pretty influential Germans. They're not always on the side of the angels, but they're fundamentally legal. So I'd been to see him that day. I'd heard about the video. I thought I'd have a bit of fun, make him squirm because I knew he'd done some bad things and it was good to see him mortified. But the next morning he was dead."

"But presumably not a suicide?"

"It was too much of a cliché. I mean, sleeping pills and the bottle of Jack? Really? It was too textbook. It looked staged. And then a few weeks later I heard that a tarot card had been found in his room."

"Hanged man?"

"Exactly. I didn't tell Joe I'd been to see him, initially, because

I didn't think it was relevant at the time, and I wasn't exactly proud of myself, but he heard about it after the death."

"Okay. So back to the funeral. Any others?" asked Danny.

"Yes. Then we identified Nils Bengtsson. Until recently, the right-hand man of Olof Lindberg. You've heard of Lindberg?"

"I've heard the name."

"He was the CEO of the Hamra Hotels group. Until he was found dead a couple of weeks ago, in a suite in one of his own hotels, in Seattle."

"Just after you'd been to see him, too?" I asked.

Clare looked shocked.

"How do you mean?"

"The police asked me about your recent trip to Seattle."

She shook her head, and her shock seemed to clear.

"I haven't been to Seattle. Not recently. I love it. It's my favourite American city, but I've not been for about eighteen months."

That was strangely reassuring. I wished I'd known that so I could have put Amy's mind at rest.

"I'd been to see Bengtsson, but that was in London," Clare continued. "Then next thing you know, he's vanished, presumably back to Sweden, and Lindberg is dead."

"Murdered?" asked Danny.

"Apparently."

"And there was a tarot card?"

"There was. Joe heard about the murder and was immediately interested because of the links to March, so he spoke to the Seattle police. They mentioned the card, but that's all I know."

"There's a definite pattern, then."

"There is. Because the third we identified was Marzia Neri."
"Who's she?"

"She was the high-flying financier from Italy. She worked between London and Frankfurt, so there was always a potential connection with Meier. Until she was found dead in a hotel in Venice last week."

"Card?"

She nodded.

"Three bodies. All with cards. And all just after I'd been to see them, or somebody close to them."

I could see why the police wanted to talk to her.

"It's amazing people agree to meet you," I said.

"They don't." She gave me an ominous look.

"But you can understand why the police want a word?"

"In one sense. But it's not me they want to be looking for. It's the person who's following me around. And the fact that he's leaving a card - assuming it's a he - needs to be looked into too, because that's a message to someone. Is it a warning to the rest of the group? Is it someone within the group punishing members for something? A betrayal? Or maybe a rival trying to close them down, sending a warning?"

"Why didn't you just speak to Joe?" asked Danny.

"I tried to. But when I got back from Venice he was away on leave, sorting out his new house in the Lake District. And now he's back up there after his wife's car crash. Did Lisa tell you about that?"

He nodded. We paused for a moment to process all this information,

"Is that it?" asked Danny, eventually. "Or were there any others at the funeral?"

"Two. Eden Mills."

"*What?* Our Eden Mills?"

"Who's he?" I asked.

"He owns the Echo," said Danny.

"I imagine he was there at the request of the police," added Clare. "Although it could explain why they tried to shut down your investigation. And then Lukáš Mäsiar."

"Who's he?" asked Danny.

"He was the arms dealer, from Slovakia. But he's an interesting one."

"Is he also dead?"

"That depends on your definition of dead."

"Technically, you're dead," I said. "Although, as I said, you're looking very well for it."

"Thank you."

"A bit pale, maybe."

"I've been working too hard. Anyway, yes, I suspect this is similar."

"How?"

"He was in the UK last week, but suffered a fatal heart attack on Friday night."

"So he is dead?" said Danny.

"Maybe. The body was found on Saturday morning, but by the time the coroner turned up, it was already on a private plane back to Slovakia, so we've only got the word of the hotel chambermaid and his bodyguard. Which means it's one of three things. Either his next of kin were obsessed with privacy. Or they had something to hide. Or, I suspect most likely, he faked his own death, because if I had to point the finger at anyone it'd be him. And if he was assumed to be dead, then he could carry on killing people without arousing suspicion. He's certainly got the means to do it."

At last it felt like we were getting somewhere.

"Can I ask a possibly stupid question?" I asked.

"Of course."

"Don't take this the wrong way, but why are you getting involved? I appreciate the journalistic instinct but what I don't get is why you don't just disappear for a bit, keep out of danger and let the police investigate. What do you actually have to gain?"

"Because until the real assassin is stopped, people are getting killed. And I suspect that they'll then be coming for me."

"All the more reason to go into hiding, then," I said.

"But Anna, you don't get it, do you? Remember the phone call? Also, until they're stopped, you and Danny are going to be in danger too because they're always going to see you as the gateway to me. I'm not having that."

Danny's face had lost some of its colour. I expect I was much the same.

"So what do we do?" he asked.

"We invite everyone to my funeral," said Clare.

———

DCS Paul Curtis walked into the room, and shut the door behind him.

"Number five?" said the man he'd come to see, with a raised eyebrow.

"Signed and sealed."

"I think this calls for a drink." He reached down to his bottom drawer, withdrew a bottle of single malt and the two crystal glasses he kept for special occasions.

"What do we do now?" asked Curtis.

"We do what we've always done," he said, pouring liquid into the two glasses, passing one across and then raising his. "Cheers."

Chapter 21

"YOU'RE not still banging on about your funeral?" I said. "Tell Danny."

He looked as bewildered as me.

"Another funeral?" he said.

"I'll paraphrase. Clare thinks that because everyone turned up to give Graham a send-off, she should follow in his footsteps, so that whoever is doing this pops along to pay his, or her, respects. At which point we'll know who it is."

"I haven't fully thought it through yet," she said. "It needs a bit of fine-tuning."

"Well, I have. And although I'd be the first to admit that while you normally have a decent plan, even if it's sometimes unconventional, this one, to put it bluntly, is shit."

She looked at me with something approaching hurt.

"First of all," I continued, "you've got previous for this, so nobody would be naïve enough to be taken in by it. Even assuming you could find a vicar mad enough to risk his reputation by burying an empty coffin."

"It'd be the church in Staverton. The vicar's a family friend.

Do you know how many times that churchyard has been used to film TV dramas? It's very picturesque. If anyone asks, it's a dress rehearsal to test the logistics before the camera crew turn up."

"And does he know about you?"

"How do you mean?"

"Well, without trying to be too brutal, the fact that you're an international criminal and wanted murderess?"

"It was self-defence."

"It wasn't, but whatever."

"No, it's not something we've ever discussed over a cup of tea and a fondant fancy."

I felt like I was making my point.

"So there'd only be me and Danny there anyway, and the whole thing would be a shambles."

"It's not a question of who turns up, so much as who is watching who turns up," she said.

"So let me get this straight: you want to turn up to watch the people who are watching the people who turned up? That makes my head spin."

"In essence."

"But what if nobody turns up?"

"They definitely would."

"They definitely wouldn't. And isn't there a law against burying an empty coffin? Don't you need a licence? Presumably you need something. Otherwise anyone who wanted to commit a murder could tip the wink to the local priest and they'd have a foolproof method of body disposal."

"Stop it, you're giving me ideas!" She had a twinkle in her eye that was both funny and deeply unsettling.

"Clare?"

"What?"

"I love you dearly but are you actually completely stark raving mad?"

"Not any longer. All you have to do is sit in the church with Danny and look tearful at the sad bits, when they say what a lovely person I was, and how I'll be sorely missed, and keep an eye out for anything unusual."

"And where will you be?"

"In the coffin."

"What?"

"I'm joking. I'll be up the street, watching."

"Well, I think it's bonkers. Danny?"

"Agreed."

"Fine, spoilsports. Scrap the funeral."

I didn't know which was the bigger surprise. The fact she'd come up with a ridiculous idea in the first place or that she'd been talked out of it so easily. This was not the Clare of old. But before I could say anything, Danny's phone rang.

As he listened, his face drained of all colour. It didn't sound like good news.

"Jesus," he said.

"What?" I asked, getting annoyed that he didn't just tell us.

"Eden Mills. He's been found murdered."

Reacting to that, Clare's expression was strange - not as shocked as I'd imagined. Her eyes were unreadable. It was almost as though she'd been expecting it.

"I've got to go in to the Echo," said Danny. "There's an emergency staff meeting."

I looked at Clare.

"I think we're done anyway," she said. "I just wanted to tell you both everything I knew."

"So what happens now?" I didn't have the first idea.

"I've got a few things to attend to," she said. I raised an eyebrow. "Danny: you're going to the Echo. Anna, why don't you go home, pack a bag and grab your passport, in case you want to get away from it all. I'll call you both later."

I couldn't imagine where I could go, but agreed anyway. I didn't want to think about what she was up to.

I hugged Danny goodbye, momentarily forgetting how much he'd annoyed me. I said I'd see him later that night. How wrong I was.

Chapter 22

THE Daily Echo building was simultaneously familiar and unsettling. Danny didn't recognise the new security man behind the desk at reception, and it was strange to have a visitor's pass when he was still on the payroll. But officially he was still suspended and his swipe card remained disabled. Some of the staff had changed, too. Packing crates were arranged in stacks, presumably ahead of the imminent move to a new building, whenever that might be. Would Danny move with them? So much had yet to be decided.

"Hello Danny, howyadoin buddy?" came a familiar voice, as Danny walked across the main open-plan editorial area, towards his corner office. Derek Hughes was a long-serving sub-editor and the closest Danny had to a trusted colleague.

"Derek," said Danny, turning and extending his hand. "Great to see you. Are you still getting up to mischief?"

Derek smiled.

"The usual. How are the wounds? Are you back among us?"

"I'm getting there, but no, not yet. I'm not sure they want me. I've just come in for the meeting."

Derek frowned.

"You've heard, then? It's been a massive shock. Half the news desk is out chasing the story, but God knows what'll happen now. Do you need somewhere to sit and wait?"

"I was going to head to my office for old times' sake."

"Ah."

"What?"

"I'm not sure that's going to work. It's been requisitioned."

They both turned to look at the far end of the room. The door to the Special Investigations Department was closed, but through the window Danny could see boxes piled high where once he'd stood with Clare, discussing whatever story they were investigating.

"Maybe I'm not coming back, then," he said.

"Oh, I'm sure they could move everything. We need you."

There was just enough time to visit the canteen for a drink before the meeting. Derek said he had to get back to work, so Danny left him and made his way on his own. He hadn't got far when he felt the glare of news editor Simon Oakley. Danny returned the look as he crossed the office. Simon, he was sure, was partly responsible for his suspension. Someone had planted evidence of phone tapping, and Simon had certainly had the opportunity, and quite possibly the motive. He had also, Danny knew, had links to Graham March. The news editor had tried to close down his investigation before that fateful night when March's crimes proved his final downfall.

None of the usual rooms was big enough to hold the meeting, so editor Mike Walker asked everyone to gather around desks in the editorial space. He relayed the events of the morning as best he could. Eden Mills, the newspaper's owner, had been found murdered, although the police hadn't released many details. Reporters were investigating, and preparing background pieces and a suitable obituary.

The police were now openly talking about Clare Woodbrook as a suspect. There were audible gasps around the room. For all her misdemeanours, most of the staff knew her and respected her journalism - even if her reputation had been tarnished by her turn to crime. Danny listened attentively. He couldn't equate the vision of a murdering psychopath with the woman he'd left behind only an hour or two before.

"They're following leads, but don't be surprised if they turn up here, asking if any of you know her whereabouts," Walker continued. Danny felt the outline of the mobile phone Clare had given him, in the pocket of his jeans. He knew exactly how to get hold of her. Simon Oakley was still staring at him as the editor spoke.

"What does it mean for us? And for the move?" someone asked. Danny didn't recognise her.

"Everything continues as normal as far as we're concerned. Obviously, things may change over the next few days but at the moment it's business as usual."

Eventually the meeting disbanded and everyone returned to their desks. The atmosphere was surreal. The shock tainting everything. One of their own, potentially killed by another one of their own. Even for the staff of a big daily newspaper, used to reporting on world atrocities, the ramifications were hard to fathom.

Danny headed back towards the lift, but he was stopped as he passed his editor's office.

"Come in for a moment, Danny," said Mike Walker. "And shut the door behind you."

Danny did as directed, and then took a place on the small sofa opposite the editor's desk.

"How's the recovery? You're looking well."

"Small steps," said Danny. "It's good to be out of the hospital."

"That's good. I don't think I ever had the chance to talk to you about Graham March."

Danny shrugged.

"I don't like to say I told you so, but, well, I did."

But if he was expecting praise and a fulsome apology, he was about to be disappointed.

"I told you not to pursue it."

"You did, but..."

"There are no fucking buts about it, Danny. I told you to stop. You didn't and you got yourself shot. Which is precisely how much fucking use to anyone?"

Danny took a breath. Some things never changed.

Clare dropped me at the High Barnet Tube station. I gave her a look of horror. She said it was only ten stops to Camden Town. I gave her another look of horror. She told me to stop looking horrified and get over it, and that the Tube was entirely safe. I thought about explaining that it wasn't my safety I was worried about. Just the thought of speeding through a tunnel in a tin can driven by someone who'd spent too long playing with a train set when they were little. Which kind of amounts to safety in the macro sense, but just seems unnaturally weird, and in any case takes a distant second place to concerns about hygiene.

Ten stops later, I emerged into the comparatively fresh air of a polluted Camden and made the short walk home, trying to decide what I was going to do with my life. Was I even safe going home? Should I be phoning Danny and asking Lisa to give me a police escort? So I could show her some photographs of him being irresponsible under the influence of alcohol and clearly not marriage material?

I needn't have worried. Amy and DCI Rogan Court were

standing on the steps waiting for me when I turned the corner into Rochester Square.

"Morning," I said, trying to sound more cheerful than I felt. The last thing I needed was another grilling, but it could be fun.

"I was hoping I'd find you," said Rogan with something approaching a sneer. "Where's Danny?"

"He had to pop into the office. You've heard about Eden Mills?"

"Are you going to invite us in?" he asked, ignoring my question. "Or do you want the neighbours to hear what we've got to say?"

I looked up at the other houses. I liked my neighbours. At least the ones I'd met.

"I suppose so," I said.

I unlocked the door, kind of hoping my potential kidnapper would be lying in wait so they'd get arrested and fix at least one of my issues. But the flat was empty, and felt cold.

"Are you stopping for a cup of tea?" I asked.

The two detectives exchanged a glance.

"That won't be necessary," said Rogan.

I led them into the front room, and indicated to the sofa. This time they both sat down and I remained standing, which was a minor victory.

"Sit down," said Rogan. And something about the way he said it made me think I should probably not try to be clever. He was clearly on edge. I sat down. "Where have you been?"

"Shopping," I said. "Is that illegal?"

"What did you buy?"

"This and that."

"Funny, because you don't have any bags with you."

He had a point there.

"It was a Greggs steak slice, if you must know. And a chicken and mushroom one. I couldn't make my mind up so went for both. I kind of regret it now, though. I'm sorry I didn't bring the paper bags back, but if you check the bins near the station, I'm sure you'll find them."

His face was turning steadily more florid.

"Can you just cut the crap?"

I shrugged, feigning innocence.

"I don't suppose you've found my burglar yet?"

"Have you seen Clare?" he asked, ignoring me again.

"No, not since Saturday."

"Really?"

"Yes, really. But you know all that. She was here for Danny's homecoming. I assume she thought she had some sort of understanding with the police, but then an armed response unit turned up and made a mess of my carpets."

"How well do you know her, Anna?" asked Amy, speaking for the first time. I turned to look at her.

"Reasonably."

"Look, you need to be careful. I'm saying this professionally but also as a friend."

"You've changed your tune."

"She can be your best friend and absolutely dependable."

"Yup."

"But it's a bit like the parable of the fox giving the hen a lift across the stream. She can turn. She's ruthless. How do you think she got in this mess in the first place? She had a business arrangement with two people in the art world. Everything was going well. They probably thought she was their best friend, too. But in the blink of an eye she killed them."

"I'll bear that in mind."

Amy looked to Rogan as if for permission to continue. He gave a slight nod.

"Maybe we should have a cup of tea," she said.

"Okay."

I was back in five minutes with two Yorkshires and a Typhoo. I liked Amy, even if she was acting strangely.

"Let me share something with you," she said. "We're investigating four murders now, all over the last few weeks. In Seattle, Frankfurt, Venice and now London."

"You've added Eden Mills to the list, then?"

"We have. You've heard about that?"

"Danny told me. And you think Clare may know who's doing them?"

She pursed her lips.

"It's really, really important that I speak to her. And believe me, it's better that she speaks to me than any of the others that are looking for her. I'd be a lot more sympathetic than most of the people I work with." Her eyes darted towards Rogan, although her head didn't move.

"Okay. Well, if I do speak to her at any point, I'll certainly ask her to contact you."

"If you speak to her, you just tell me, okay? Tell me where she is, so I can go to meet her."

"Meet her? Like some casual chat?"

Amy looked thoughtful, as if debating what she could say. She turned to her colleague.

"Sir, can you give us a minute? Go and wait outside in the car?"

He very nearly snarled, but nevertheless stood up. I made a move to show him to the door, but he pushed past me and showed himself out.

When it was just the two of us, Amy's voice softened slightly, but her serious expression remained.

"Anna, I know you're lying, so I'll also tell you what else I know."

I didn't speak.

"I got to know Clare fairly well last year when we were investigating the bank murder and working out what Graham March was up to. She can be sweet and charming and very persuasive. She can make you believe everything she says, because she looks to all intents and purposes like a super-intelligent, successful woman. But do not be taken in."

"Okay."

"I know about DSI Joe Leyland. I know about the deal they had. I know they were working on a project together."

"How is Joe? How's his wife?"

"You know about that?"

"Danny mentioned it to me." Did Danny even know about it? I couldn't remember.

"He was holding up, the last I spoke to him, but she seems in a bad way. But in the meantime, the case is being handled by DCS Paul Curtis and - let's just say, he's a lot less benevolent."

"I'm not a big fan of your man Rogan, either, in fairness."

"No."

I thought I'd found a point of commonality.

"I'll tell you what I know about the project," she continued. "It's a secret group of fundamentally influential but corrupt businesspeople all pulling favours for each other. There are supposed to be twelve of them. I know they use code names that mean 'secret'. I even know some of the names. Graham was one of them, ensuring a blind eye was turned if anything crossed his desk. And the murders we're investigating are linked as part of the group."

"Is this public?"

"None of this is public. But it is all being investigated."

"Wasn't Clare investigating it all with Joe? If she's investigating this as well, wouldn't it make sense to pool resources rather than try to arrest her?"

"Oh, Anna. Be absolutely honest with me. This is off the record. I promise you it will go no further. Were you with Clare yesterday?"

"I..."

"Please say yes. Honestly, it will be the best news I could possibly hear."

I took a deep breath.

"Yes."

"Thank God."

"Only late last night, though. I stayed in a hotel because I'd been spooked by a phone call. She turned up."

"I heard about the phone call. What time did she meet you?"

"I don't know. Maybe eight-thirty?"

Amy sighed deeply, and I thought I detected a very un-Amy-like swear word under her breath.

"What's up?"

"Look, you've been honest with me, so I'll be honest with you. Primarily for your own good, okay?"

"Okay."

"How did she seem? Clare? Has she done anything out of character?"

Yes. But I didn't want to mention the funeral plan because it still sounded ridiculous. She was definitely behaving erratically. It was not the calm, rational Clare of old.

"Not that I noticed," I said.

Amy nodded.

"You asked if I was going to pool resources with Clare? Let me tell you something else I know. Someone is going round killing members of the group. It's a clean-up operation."

"Precisely. That's what Clare's looking into."

"Oh, Anna. Of course that's what she told you. But you don't get it, do you? You know about the Germans Clare's done work for?"

"She's mentioned them."

"She probably didn't mention that they were sworn enemies of Graham's network. It's a classic old-school gangland feud, just played out across borders. Clare isn't investigating the murders, Anna. Clare is still working for them. She may be pretending she's your best friend and protesting innocence and bewilderment, but she's the one doing the cleaning up."

Chapter 23

"WITH all due respect, Mike, I was suspended because someone fitted me up," said Danny. "So, irrespective of you telling me not to look into Graham March, I wasn't technically working for the Echo when he nearly killed me. And I still don't understand why you told me to leave him alone. The evidence was there. It was still a great story."

"Okay." Mike Walker sat back. "What does it say on my door?"

"On your door?"

"Yes, the wooden thing right behind you."

"Mike Walker. Editor."

"Exactly."

Danny looked puzzled.

"And the point?"

"The point is, Danny, I'm the editor of one of the biggest national newspapers in the country. And the reason for that is because I'm good at my job. I pursue stories that readers like to read. I don't need to have my experience, or judgement, questioned by junior reporters."

"Technically, I'm not a junior reporter though, am I? I was running Special Investigations. My job, unless I missed something, was precisely to uncover that kind of corruption."

The editor's eyes narrowed. He sighed.

"Have you thought about what you're going to do now you're fit again?"

"I'm signed off for another month. Then it's up to the doctors."

"So you're still thinking you'd like to come back?"

"If I'm passed fit to continue." It probably wasn't the time to reveal his doubts about the idea.

"Interesting."

"Why interesting?" Danny crossed his legs, while waiting for a response. Eventually the editor spoke.

"You're a good journalist, Danny."

"That's kind of you to say."

"But just because you got injured while off duty, and we're all very sympathetic, it doesn't change the underlying facts. You were suspended because of evidence that pointed to significant misconduct..."

"Evidence that was entirely fictional."

"Significant misconduct that still needs to be investigated."

Danny laughed.

"So you're saying I'm still suspended?"

"That's exactly what I'm saying."

"Even though the so-called evidence was cooked up by March and somebody who works on this newspaper specifically to discredit me, to stop me investigating."

"That's a very serious accusation."

"Yeah? Is it?" Danny stood up. "Okay. I'll tell you what I'll do. I'll take part in whatever it takes to clear my name. Whatever shambles of an inquiry. And then we'll discuss our options, shall we?"

"Danny..."

"And in the meantime, I apologise in advance if my evidence, the evidence I'll be giving to whoever is looking into it, implicates you or anybody else who works here. Fair enough? I'll wait to hear from you."

Danny didn't wait for an answer. He left the office and slammed the door. It probably wasn't his wisest career move, but enough was enough.

I gaped at Amy. What she was saying didn't make any sense.

"She can't be. She's changed," I said. "Trust me. I know Clare. She doesn't do that any more."

Amy sighed.

"I wish that were true. But we've got her on CCTV at the hotel in Seattle, plus a hair recovered from the room that matches her DNA. We've got DNA evidence from a cigarette in Italy and an eye witness report of a visitor to the victim's room, a woman who matches her description. We know she's had dealings with the victim in Frankfurt and was due to to see him around the time he died. And now Eden Mills, who she used to work for, has been killed as well. That's a lot of links to a lot of murders, Anna."

"Wow." But she'd told me she hadn't been anywhere near Seattle? "I'm sure there's an explanation."

"There is. She's killing them."

But then a thought occurred.

"When was Eden Mills killed?"

"His body was discovered early this morning but it happened yesterday."

The relief was palpable.

"That's not Clare, then," I said. "She couldn't have done it. She was with me all last night."

"I'll pretend I didn't hear that. But it wasn't last night. It was the afternoon. Was she with you all day yesterday?"

"No."

"That's why I asked. I was desperately hoping you'd give her an alibi. Believe me, I don't want it to be Clare any more than you do, but we've got to face the harsh reality. What do you know about the group she's affiliated with in Germany?"

What did I know? She'd hardly mentioned them. I'd met the mysterious Otto last year, when we were closing in on Graham March, and he seemed to be quite influential, but not much apart from that.

"Not a lot," I said. "They're in Cologne, possibly. She said they weren't angels but nothing too bad."

"Okay. Let me put you right there, then. They're nasty bastards. They're linked with all sorts of crimes all over Europe. You know she was brokering deals between Bulgarian factories and German investors?"

"Yes."

"Well, let's just say they didn't exactly pay full market price, due to the way they were negotiated. I don't know much about Bulgaria, but you'd have to be either brave, stupid, or very sure of your physical strength to take on Bulgarian gangsters and win."

I'd visited Bulgaria. There were some scary-looking people in Sofia.

"Do you actually know all of this?" I asked her. "Or is it all supposition?"

"I know what Joe told me. And do you know what the last thing he told me was? That Clare was in London, trying to broker something with a Slovakian arms dealer. God alone knows what on earth that was going to lead to. Then I've heard reports that on Friday night, just three days ago, they met, had dinner, went back to his hotel. On Saturday morning his body was discovered by room service."

"That's not quite how she explained that to me."

"Wake up, Anna!"

This was all a bit much to take in. I took a sip of my tea, but it didn't bring its usual reassurance.

"She's trying to get this network disbanded, presumably at the behest of her German friends," Amy continued. "And she was trying to do it peacefully by feeding us intelligence so we could place people on the watch list and hopefully one day bring them all to justice. But then, in the last few weeks, something changed. Ever since Graham's funeral."

"Apparently a lot of the group were there to pay their respects," I said.

"They were, or at least their henchmen. And I think they took the opportunity to have a meeting, deciding to take revenge on Clare and her group because they believed that she and they were responsible for the loss of Graham. Suddenly there was a degree of urgency. Stakes were upped and she was sent to sort it out."

"And again, is this what Joe told you?"

"It is. He said it didn't stack up. That there was something fundamentally missing in the information she was giving. Like there was something big that he couldn't see. So the next thing you know, we've got dead bodies."

"She was definitely in Venice." I couldn't believe I was saying it. It sounded like a betrayal, but Amy sounded so convincing, my loyalty to Clare had wavered. "I was there on a photo shoot. Clare turned up at the hotel. We spent an afternoon getting drunk."

"When was this?"

"A week past Friday."

"And did she say what she was doing out there?"

"No. Just that she had a couple of free days. She'd heard I was out there so she'd come to see me, to check I was okay."

"How did she seem?"

"Okay. Clare's Clare. You know what she's like. Actually she seemed more relaxed than normal, now I think about it. Why?"

"Because Marzia Neri was killed the day before."

"Shit."

I didn't want to think about this.

"Indeed. And now Clare's back in London and already we've had another murder. And a dead Slovakian arms dealer that she left in his hotel room."

It was unbelievable. But equally, the way she explained it, she made it all sound so logical.

"So be careful, Anna. Please. I don't think she means you any harm, but we still think she was behind your studio burglary so she could ingratiate herself with you. Tell you she was looking after you. Offer to help get you back up and running so you'd be in her debt. I think she arranged the call on Sunday to freak you out. To scare you into thinking she would protect you. I don't think she wants to kill you, but please believe me: despite the fact she'll try to pretend she's your best friend, remember she doesn't do anything without an agenda. And she wouldn't be averse to using you as a human shield if the going gets tough."

I started to feel very nauseous. I put down the tea. I didn't know that I'd ever be able to drink tea again.

"Look, this conversation is just between us," Amy continued. "I'll continue to investigate, but I'm going to have to go now. Rogan will wonder what we're talking about. But my advice to you is to steer well clear of her. And, for your sake above anything else, get her to turn herself in. Please."

I was trying to get my head round it. It had to be wrong. Surely. I knew Clare. She'd changed. She told me she didn't do that any more. That she was having a career change and planning to do lots of charity work. But if she was back to her old tricks, then the studio clearance made sense. It was a professional clean-up. I knew she was good at that. It was too horrific to contemplate.

"Are you absolutely sure about this?" I asked, in one final, desperate attempt to discount it.

"A hundred percent."

"But she seemed so - I don't know - so vulnerable. As though she was desperately trying to put things right, trying to help you - Joe - to fix things. To get to the bottom of it all."

"And you believed that?"

"It was very convincing."

"Anna, please. She's an actress. She's ruthless. She long ago abandoned the values that people like you and me live by."

"But she wouldn't lie to me."

"Wouldn't she?"

"I don't think so."

"The same woman who dragged you to Geneva and pointed a gun at you? What are you doing now?"

"I'm supposed to be packing a bag for a few days away. I don't know where I'm going, though. I've still got to work that out."

I didn't dare tell her I was supposed to be meeting Clare again later to discuss it.

"Take my advice. Please. Make your mind up very quickly and get as far away from here as possible. If Clare gets in touch again, let me know. I know you thought she was your friend, but believe me, she isn't. She's incredibly dangerous and we have to stop her. Understood?"

I nodded.

Amy made her way to the door.

Then, as she was leaving, she turned and said one final thing.

"You can't argue with DNA, Anna. Please don't place your trust in someone who wouldn't think twice about killing you."

Chapter 24

DANNY was almost at the lift when he heard someone calling his name. He turned. Simon Oakley, the news editor, was approaching. The man Danny was sure had been complicit with Graham March in planting the evidence that may well have ended his career.

"Danny, I'm so glad to catch you," he said, arm extended. Danny didn't want to shake hands so he ignored it. He turned back to the lift and pressed the call button.

"I know we haven't always seen eye to eye."

Danny bit his lower lip. Would punching someone harm his chances of clearing his name?

"And I was wrong about Graham. I apologise," Simon continued. "Can I buy you a coffee?"

"No," said Danny. "I'm just leaving. So maybe you could just, like, fuck off?"

"Hey, look, it's an olive branch. That's all. I heard about the suspension. It's a massive injustice."

"Really? And what have you heard? That some bastard who works here tried to fit me up?"

"I don't know about that, Danny. But seriously. Let me buy you something."

The lift arrived. Danny got in. Simon stood against the door so it couldn't close.

"No thanks," said Danny, pressing the button for the ground floor.

"Okay, mate, I understand." Simon took a step back. "I'll call you and we'll have a catch up then."

Danny's reply was lost in the closing of the door.

When Amy left, I returned to the front room, wanting to scream. I couldn't believe it. Refused to believe it. But it all sounded so plausible that I couldn't do anything other than accept the truth. I lay on the sofa, closed my eyes, and thought back to that wonderful time in Venice, just ten days ago. Everything seemed so good. Now my two best friends - my only true friends - had both turned into lying, deceitful psychopaths. Admittedly Danny hadn't actually murdered anyone, and his only real crime was a catastrophic error of judgement, but the effect on my heart was every bit as deadly.

I had to get away. I didn't care where. But where can you go when you haven't got much money? My passport was up to date, so I thought of heading straight to the nearest travel agent and booking a cheap fortnight somewhere sunny, but then thought better of it. I don't like the sun. It makes my nose peel.

I decided to wait till Danny got home from the Echo. Maybe we could go somewhere together. Second thoughts, that wouldn't happen. Unlike me, he had his own police protection in the form of the lovely Lisa. And that made things even worse.

Nor could I even get in my car and drive somewhere, because my car was abandoned in a cul-de-sac in the middle of nowhere. What were the chances of finding it? That would just be the final straw. The only option was to reverse all my strongly held views on religion and immediately join a nunnery and give all my worldly possessions to the church, although I wasn't sure they'd give me the best of rooms for a box and a half of teabags. I did actually scream, but silently. I didn't want the neighbours to think I was being murdered, and then assume it was another false alarm when - if - it ever happened for real.

First and foremost, I had to find the car, assuming it was still even there. I looked up the travel information number for Kings Cross and found out the times of the trains. It was less than half an hour to Welwyn and there were trains at least every hour. I set off with an overnight bag, unsure how long I'd be away for, but equally not sure if there was anything worth ever coming back for. I wanted to find the car and then just drive to however far it would take me, on what was left in the tank.

The train pulled into Welwyn Garden City. I got off, assuming I'd find a taxi rank, but instead the station opened out into the middle of a shopping centre. Once I found a taxi, I gave the driver the name of the street. Nothing looked familiar, but eventually we turned into a residential cul-de-sac and there it was. My lovely car! And not even vandalised. I paid the driver, plipped the locks, put the bag into the boot and got in the driver's seat. Then closed my eyes, lost in the moment, wanting to fall asleep and be looked after, and for someone to take all the pain away.

I came to with a start when a person opened the passenger door and started to climb in beside me.

"Going somewhere?" asked Clare.

I was momentarily speechless. I had to get out. I opened my door and stood on the street, wanting to run but knowing it would be futile.

A moment later she came to stand beside me.

"What's up?" she said. "You look terrible."

"Oh, piss off," I replied. "Is it any wonder?"

"What's happened?"

"What do you mean what's happened? What's happened is I've found out you've been lying to me. How could you? You of all people. I trusted you."

"I haven't lied to you."

"Oh, stop please. No more, Clare. I'm done. I'm out of here."

I started to walk to the other side of the car to get away from her. She reached out and grabbed my arm.

"Anna. What is it?"

"You want me to tell you? Where should I start? Oh yes. Your Slovak arms dealer friend. Faked his own death, did he? Buggered off back to Slovakia? You conveniently missed out the bit where you quite possibly killed him."

"I haven't killed anyone."

"And again, piss off."

"Jesus. Look, we had dinner. He started to feel unwell. He asked me for help to get back to his room. I thought he was making it up in an attempt to lure me back and try something sordid, but then he really did look very ill. I helped him back, he assured me he was okay. Then I left. He was alive when I left him."

That sounded plausible, but I still knew she was lying.

"So why didn't you tell me that?"

"Because I was trying to simplify things. There's an awful lot to take in."

"Okay. Where were you on Sunday?"

"You know where I was. I was with you."

Her eyes seemed to be pleading for forgiveness, but I knew that behind them lurked the ruthless mind of a killer.

"Before that."

"Before that I had a few things to sort out."

"Like murdering Eden Mills?"

"What?"

"That's what the police reckon."

"That's just ridiculous."

I shook my arm free.

"Listen, Clare, I would like to believe you, honestly, but you seem to inhabit a world of your own in which your version of events becomes the truth because it's what you sincerely believe. But other people looking at the same facts draw different conclusions. Do you know what I mean? I hate to be the one to point this out, but I'm a simple person. I'm severely pissed off about the fact my studio has been burgled and even more pissed off about the fact the man I love has fucked off with some tart in a uniform."

"Technically she's plain-clothes," said Clare. It didn't help.

"But I've been talking to the police," I continued, ignoring her, "and they tell me that you burgled my studio, so you can own me, and that you've ratcheted up murders in Seattle, Venice and London times two. And I'd discount all of that and take your word for it, on the basis that I like you as a person, I really do, but you're lying to me by your own admission, and you have a previous track record of killing people, which is massively fucking weird in the world in which I live. So if it's all right by you, I'd really rather just pick my car up and disappear off somewhere until either you've sorted this out, or you've been arrested. And I'm really sorry if that's disloyal but I'm really not in my most jovial frame of mind right at the moment. I'm sure you understand."

"Wow."

She stood looking at me. I'm not sure if I was aiming for more of a reaction, but either way it wasn't forthcoming.

I gave in.

"All right. You win. What do you mean, wow?"

"There's no subtext. I admire your passion and I respect your point of view."

"But?"

"But? You tell me. What else do you want to add?"

"I suppose that I'd really like to thank you for everything you've done for me, and I'd really appreciate it if you didn't kill me too. I don't think you will because you're my friend and we've been through a lot, but who knows with you any more. And I'd like to help you - honestly, I really would - because I think deep down there's a decent person in there somewhere, but you've been badly affected by something that I just don't understand. It's a whole other world to me. And if you're doing deals with weapons dealers and you've turned back into some sort of international assassin, then it's a pleasure to know you, but you're not the sort of person I want to hang around with. Partly because I don't believe in killing people, and partly because it's too bloody dangerous."

"Do you think I need help?"

"Yes. I really do. I don't know what's happened to you, but I think it's a tragedy because you have so much good in you. But the killing thing kind of takes the gloss off."

She stepped back.

"So that's it then?" she said.

"What?"

"You're just going to get in your car and drive somewhere?"

"Pretty much."

"Okay."

She took another step away.

It nearly broke my heart.

"What?" I said.

"Nothing."

"Oh, don't turn into a teenager on me. What's up?"

"Nothing. You go. Somebody has obviously got to you. If you believe them rather than me, then there's not much I can do to stop you."

I moved back to my driver's door. She followed me.

"Say it," I said.

"Say what?"

"Whatever you want to say."

"There's nothing I want to say. I just thought we understood each other. You know more about me than anyone else in the world. And I really mean that. You probably understand me better than I understand myself."

"I'm not sure that's true. Clearly."

"But I think you do. And what did I say to you in Venice?"

"You said lots of things. One of which was that you thought it was an excellent idea to get a third bottle of wine."

"I still maintain it was."

"My head the following morning would tend to disagree."

"But it loosened us up. We had fun."

"We did."

"And do you regret having fun?"

"No. The only thing I regret is that you lied to me and that you're still lying to me. Because if I think about that, it makes me wonder if anything you told me was true."

I put my hand on the door handle, ready to open it. All I had to do was get in and turn the key and then everything would be behind me.

"Come here," she said.

"Why?"

"Because I want to give you a farewell hug."

"Promise you're not going to stab me."

"Do you think I want to stab you?"

"Oooh, you're infuriating. You know that? Stop asking bloody questions. Promise me I'll be alive at the end of the experience and I'll willingly give you a hug."

"Okay. I promise."

I stepped forward. And then she grabbed me with considerable force and threw me to the ground, just as a bullet ripped into the side of my car, directly behind where I'd just been standing.

Chapter 25

A SECOND bullet tore into my car, smashing the window. Clare grabbed my arm and dragged me through a bush, into somebody's garden. And then we ran, down the passageway between two houses. Anywhere just to get away from whoever was pulling the trigger.

We climbed over a fence into another garden. She pulled me to the ground, her finger to her lips, urging me to be quiet so we could listen. Eventually she let herself exhale.

"What the fuck was that?" I said.

"That, I'm afraid, is proof that I'm not lying to you."

"How did you see it? And who was shooting at us?"

She frowned.

"I caught the reflection in your window. And clearly someone who's not a very good shot," she said. "Apart from that, I really don't know at the moment."

I closed my eyes and rested my head on the fence.

"I can't go back out there. But that's my car. It's the only thing I've got left."

"I'll look after you."

"Clare I don't want you to look after me. You're going round killing people."

"Will you stop saying that. I'm not."

"God, my head hurts. All right. You said you hadn't been to Seattle for eighteen months. They've got you on CCTV there from three weeks ago, from the night the hotel bloke died. And before you say mistaken identity, they've also recovered your DNA from the room. Explain that, then."

For once she didn't have an immediate answer.

"Who's got DNA evidence?"

"The police, obviously. Amy."

She shook her head.

"They can't have. That's impossible."

"I didn't get the impression she was making it up."

She stood up. I half expected her to get her head blown off, but thankfully she didn't.

"Give me your car keys and I'll get your car. Drive it somewhere safe and then pick you up," she said.

"You can't do that. If you go near it someone's going to kill you."

"Which is why I'm going rather than you. I think they'll have gone. They're not going to hang around. The police will be getting called any minute, so there is, however, a sense of urgency."

"Fine. We'll leave it here then."

"But I still need to get your bag from the boot."

Before I could protest again, she reached into my pocket, grabbed the keys and disappeared.

A couple of minutes later she was back, dropping my bag beside me.

"Told you," she said, with a smile.

I sat next to Clare in her hire car, watching as she navigated the outskirts of Welwyn Garden City and then headed back in the direction of the A1.

"How did you even know I'd be there?" I asked.

"Of course you were going to get your car," she said, as though it was the most obvious thing ever. "I was a bit concerned about where you would have gone next, though."

"I was just going to drive. Anywhere."

"Exactly."

"So what now?"

"You can't go home," she said, joining the slip road for the motorway.

"Neither can you."

"No, seriously. It's not safe. There are people being killed. Connected with me. I don't want you being next."

"The evidence suggests being with you significantly increases the risk."

"So how do you explain the call on Sunday? Someone saying they'd take you to me?"

"The police reckon that was you as well."

She laughed, but didn't deny it. I didn't know what to think any more. What if she was still lying to me? What if she had done the murders? What if she did burgle the studio? What if she was behind the phone call just to scare me, so I'd be more amenable to her suggestion of protection? What if she only wanted me as a sort of elaborate human shield as she plotted her getaway?

Her next suggestion only intensified my fears.

"You're going to come and stay with me so I can look after you," she said.

I was torn. Part of me wanted her to stop the car so I could make a run for it. Part of me remembered how she'd saved me before. And yet there was the DNA evidence to consider. Could I ever really trust her? And what if the only person you can trust is the person who is plotting to kill you?

Chapter 26

BELGRAVIA is one of the most affluent and exclusive areas of London. Situated between Buckingham Palace and the famous department store of Harrods in Knightsbridge, it's home to the seriously rich and mysterious. Of course that's where Clare lived. Everything seems so obvious when you know the facts.

She reversed into a space in Lyall Street, between a Bentley and an exotic sports car, and led me across the road to the huge black front door of a very expensive-looking terraced house. It was a little bit like the house Danny and I shared in Camden, except five times the size, and probably about thirty times the price. I followed Clare up the stairs to the top floor flat. She was hardly out of breath, which was impressive, given the smoking. The front door opened into another staircase, which in turn led to a huge living room that was dominated by two giant horseshoe-shaped leather sofas. Everything was black or cream. Even the floor was covered in spotless, glossy black tiles. There weren't many personal artefacts, but it was immaculately tidy. It was just on the tasteful side of ostentatious, but only just. At the far end there was a giant open-plan kitchen.

"Wow," I said, trying to take it all in. "Whose is this?"

"Mine."

"How much did this cost?"

"Impolite question."

"But have you actually bought it? Do you rent it?"

"Bought it. Property is a good investment." Clare put her keys on a giant circular dining table to the right of a staircase that seemed to disappear into a glass ceiling.

"That's what people say when they're trying to buy a semi in the suburbs. How much money did you make?"

"And another impolite question. Anyway, I already told you in Venice."

"You did, but I doubt even that would be enough for this."

She shrugged.

"In fairness, you only asked me what I made from the art thing."

She smiled and I laughed.

"Well, it may be terribly un-English but I'm not consumed by envy. I salute your achievements. Just don't quote me on that if it ever gets to the witness box."

She took my coat and hung it on the back of a dining chair.

"We'll be safe here while we decide what to do," she said. "There's food, drink, everything you'd need. I am honoured to have you as my house guest."

I stood for a moment, sizing her up. She didn't look happy. And something about the sincerity in her voice betrayed a sense of loneliness at her core.

Clare made some sort of grated-cheese-and-water-biscuit arrangement, with chilli flakes and sliced cherry tomatoes, topped with a splash of balsamic vinegar. It was the perfect snack. I hardly dared touch it in case I made a mess on the cream sofas, but she encouraged me to tuck in.

"So what's our plan?" I asked, as she joined me and reached for one of the water biscuits.

"Our plan is to keep you safe and for me to find out who is really behind this," she said.

"Not just run?"

"I can't just run, Anna. I'd be running forever. I want this to be over so I can lead some semblance of a normal life."

As she said this, she looked so much younger and more vulnerable than she had at the height of her criminal misdemeanours. The hard edge had gone.

"You see, that's interesting," I said.

"Is it?"

"Yes." I took a bite, then had to wait to finish it before continuing because it's impolite to talk with your mouth full. "What for you constitutes a normal life? I can't see you sitting at home on a Saturday night, watching Gladiators, getting stressed out by a pile of ironing that you can't be arsed to tackle, and going to the shop, worried that if you buy something nice for your tea tonight you may run out of cash to buy any kind of food before the next payday."

She reached for another water biscuit.

"I just mean: put this all behind me. Live without fear."

"But you do remember, and I hate to bring up a delicate issue - but you did actually kill people. So the only way you're going to live a normal life is if you go to the police station, turn yourself in, do probably a twenty-stretch in Holloway and come out an old lady, but at least free to pick up your bus pass without needing to watch over your shoulder."

That made her smile, although it wasn't one of her warmest.

"I'm not even thirty-four till next week, so I'd still have to wait for the bus pass," she said. "Anyway, that's not happening because I don't want to go to prison, and even if I did, it'd never get that far. You saw what March was like and how he was willing to apply his own form of justice. That's my experience of a certain faction within the police force. I'd never live long enough to see a trial."

"You really believe that? Have you spent too long talking to former members of the Stasi while you've been in Germany? This is England."

"Trust me," she said. "I'd be made to disappear."

It was such an alien world.

"So how do we find out who's really behind this?" I asked.

"*We* don't. You stay here; I'll have to go out and talk to some people."

I put the plate on a coffee table, then turned to face her, crossing my legs.

"Ignoring your assumption that I'd be willing to stay here, rather than helping you, isn't that peculiarly high risk? Actually going out while people are looking for you? Assuming whoever you'd be talking to knew anything, they'd be getting watched, or they'd know the police, in which case they may also be getting watched. Because aside from the police, we're not even sure who's looking for you, are we?"

"I think I do."

I had to think for a moment.

"The Hydra? But specifically who?"

"The head of it."

"You said it had lots of heads. Isn't that the entire point of it being called a hydra?"

"Jesus. No wonder Danny doesn't want to marry you. Okay, then. The beating heart."

"I've never asked him to marry me, so your point is pointless. Who's the beating heart?"

"Someone who goes by the name of Agadhi. Which translates as one who is indescribable, mysterious, mystifying, secretive and enigmatic."

"Also known as?"

"I'm working on that. I just need to make sure I manage it before they find us."

Chapter 27

DS Amy Cranston couldn't quite quell the feelings of paranoia. The situation was delicate. The pace was gathering. She'd need to stay focused, alert, think laterally. Rely on her survival instincts. There was no margin for error. No room for sentiment. It would be brutal, but with a single-minded intensity she was determined to see it through.

"Are you coming for a drink?" said Lisa as the office started to empty. Amy shrugged and indicated to the pile of paperwork on her desk.

"I'd love to but I've got to finish this," she said. "You go on and I'll try to join you in an hour or so."

"It was only a quick one. I won't be stopping."

Amy turned back to her desk, but Lisa hadn't finished.

"Are you okay? You've been looking stressed."

Amy took a deep breath and remembered to smile.

"Yeah, I'm all right. Just lots to do. I'll be better once we've found Clare."

"Okay." Lisa looked thoughtful. "If you're sure. I'll see you in the morning, then."

Amy waited for Lisa to leave, and then gave it an extra few

minutes to make sure she had the office to herself. When she was sure she wouldn't be disturbed, she made her way back to DSI Joe Leyland's office. This time she'd be able to pick the desk drawer locks. It wouldn't take long.

Thankful that the corridor was empty, she tried the door. It gave. She moved to the desk and knelt on the floor, heart rate accelerating. A moment later, the lock was picked and she was riffling awkwardly through the drawers, the torch in her other hand. She had to know if there was evidence. Anything that would give the game away. Just for her own peace of mind. So she could continue with one fewer thing to worry about.

But there was nothing. She double checked, not sure whether to be relieved or more paranoid than ever. She placed everything back as she'd found it. She wouldn't be able to lock the drawer, but by the time that was discovered, she'd be well out of the frame.

"What are you doing?"

Amy's looked up in shock. Lisa was standing in the doorway, a dark silhouette.

"What are you doing here?" Amy rose to her feet, her heart pounding.

"I came back to find you."

"Well, now you have."

"But what are you actually doing in Joe's office?"

"For heaven's sake. What is this? I was looking for his address, if you must know. I wanted to send flowers. Is that all right with you?"

"Sorry, I'm only asking."

"Yeah? Well, now you know."

Amy came out from behind the desk and joined Lisa at the door, then continued to the corridor. Lisa followed and Amy closed the door behind them.

"What did you want me for, anyway?" she asked, hoping that her complexion wouldn't betray her sense of panic.

"Nothing hugely urgent. I just wanted to talk to you about Danny."

"Really? Can it wait?"

"I suppose so, but..."

Amy sighed. "I'm sorry. Go on." She stopped walking.

Lisa hesitated, but then found the words.

"I just don't feel comfortable spying on him," she said. "It's like a massive breach of trust."

"You're not being asked to spy on him. Just keep your ears open. If he says anything that makes you think he may know where Clare is, you can pursue it. But I'm with you. I don't think she'd be that blatant."

"You heard Curtis. 'Shag it out of him.'"

"He's a dinosaur. Ignore him."

"That's easy to say when it's not your career."

Amy rubbed her forehead. Sometimes it was so frustrating.

"No, you're right," she said. "But look. Keep your head down. We'll find Clare. Then we can make a complaint about Curtis and his attitude, and we can drag them kicking and screaming out of the 1970s. But don't worry for now, okay? I've got your back."

"Cheers, Amy," said Lisa.

"I'll tell you what, let's go for that drink, okay? Put the world to rights."

"If you're sure."

"Never more certain."

Amy smiled and led the way back downstairs.

But as she waited for her colleague to get her coat, something else was troubling Lisa. Why would you search for an address by torchlight?

By the evening I'd had the guided tour. The rest of the flat was just as impressive. Downstairs there were three huge bedrooms with exposed brick walls, each with luxurious en suite bathrooms. Back upstairs, the state-of-the-art kitchen looked as though it had never been used. A sliding glass panel gave way to the roof terrace, from which we had simply incredible views across the city.

But despite the amazing surroundings and obvious sense of privilege, I didn't feel like I could ever belong. I couldn't imagine ever mixing with the neighbours, always wondering just how rich they were and how they'd managed to get hold of the money. Was everyone who lived here a master criminal? Or just good in business? It was lovely and luxurious in so many ways, but I was still homesick for the simpler pleasures of our little flat in Camden. I missed living across the road from a garage that sold milk and biscuits.

Clare made pasta with typical efficiency, but once the plates were cleared, she announced that she had to pop out for a while. She was absolutely insistent that I should stay behind. I was equally insistent that I shouldn't, so she threatened to handcuff me to the bed. It would have been an intriguing suggestion, coming from Danny, before he turned traitorous, but coming from Clare, it had an edge of menace.

When she left I lay on one of the sofas, watching the TV, with the sound reverberating from the huge walls. I gave up on that after a while, and decided to test the impressive-looking music system instead. It would be fascinating to discover Clare's tastes in music. But despite the high calibre of the equipment, there wasn't a CD in sight. In fact the whole flat seemed curiously devoid of personal possessions. The perils, I supposed, of an itinerant lifestyle. And possibly the need to scarper at a moment's notice.

I like to think I am a decent person. I like to think I am kind and trustworthy. That I do the right thing, am respectful of others, and that I go out of my way to be helpful. But if you leave me in your house of an evening there is a reasonable chance I will - at some point - make a cup of tea and go in search of a biscuit. And that point had arrived.

I walked through to the kitchen, and found the kettle easily enough. And I even worked out that there was a separate tap for filtered drinking water. The tea bags and biscuits were in the first cupboard I opened. I was on a roll. I should have known it wouldn't last.

All was going well until I returned to the living room and put the mug on the coffee table but then knocked it over, causing tea to spill all over the floor and the mug to smash to pieces on the tiles. I was horrified. It had looked like a nice cup of tea. And then, further horrified by the mess, I ran to the kitchen, grabbed a roll of paper towels, and managed to soak up the tea, but my efforts to clean up the remains of the porcelain resulted in a cut to my finger, which subsequently started bleeding. If ever there was a time for a cup of tea, this was it. The irony wasn't lost on me.

I ran my finger under the tap, and then wrapped it in more kitchen roll to stop it bleeding. But what I really needed was a plaster. I had no idea where she would keep those. I went to my bathroom and checked the cabinet, but it was empty. That made sense, I suppose. She thought of everything, but she couldn't be expected to foresee the rank clumsiness of her houseguests.

Then I had a moment of conscience. Would Clare be really annoyed if I looked in her en suite? Could I justify it? It was a moral dilemma. She'd already showed it to me on the guided tour so it wasn't really a breach of privacy, and I didn't want to drip blood on the cream leather sofa. So, tentatively, I knocked on her bedroom door, even though I knew she was out. The door to the en suite was immediately on the right.

I was in luck. There was an open packet of plasters on the middle shelf. I eased off my ring, put it on top of the cabinet for safekeeping, and then carefully wrapped a plaster around the cut. Mission accomplished, I returned to the living room. Via the kitchen for a second attempt at tea.

This time I was much more careful and put the cup on the floor. Not wanting to risk any more drama, I picked up my secret Clare phone and sent an SMS to Danny.

Are you alone?

A moment later my phone burst into life.

"Hi," he said. "How are you? Where are you?"

I didn't know what to answer to that.

"I'm okay," I said eventually. "Clare arranged somewhere for me to stay."

"What happened? I came home and it looked like you'd gone."

"Oh, Danny." I gave him a brief recap of my attempt to pick up my car, and getting ambushed, trying to play down just how close the bullet had come. Danny was shocked, but once I'd reassured him everything was okay, he told me about the meeting at the Echo, about still being suspended, and being approached by Simon Oakley.

"So essentially we're both buggered, then," I concluded.

"I'm sure it'll all get sorted," he said. "You'll be back up and running. I'll get a job. It'll be like the old days. Starting out."

"But back in the old days we at least had each other."

"We've still got each other."

"Really? You've moved on, Danny. So unless you're about to discover polyamory, and then persuade both of us to join you, and then promise never to see Lisa again, it's *not* going to be like the old days."

"Don't be like that. We've not even had a proper date yet."

"You've kissed her, though."

"I'm not discussing this."

"But you have."

"I'm not discussing it."

"I don't want to discuss it either. In fact I didn't want to discuss it first, so technically I win."

"You're such a child." He laughed, and I couldn't stop a smile from forming. He could always make me smile.

"I'm worried, Danny," I said eventually, once it had faded.

"Because of the burglary? Or the call? Or because we seem to be getting immersed in something bad again?"

"All of those." I couldn't tell him of my lingering doubts about Clare. But then I thought: this is Danny. He's my best friend. We've been through so much. So I told him.

"She said she was going straight, but the police have CCTV and DNA evidence. What if it is her? We know she goes to Seattle. She was even with me in Venice. But she denied it. Said it was impossible."

"Of course she did."

"You don't sound convinced."

"You know what she's like."

"But she said she'd changed. I want to believe her. But then there's this man Lukáš. What if it's him?"

I explained about the Slovak arms dealer, his apparent heart attack, and the missing body.

"It's a bit Agatha Christie isn't it?" said Danny. "Faking your own death so you can go round murdering people."

"Clare's done it. And she was suggesting she did it again with the funeral madness. Oh God. I don't know what to think any more."

"Why don't you come home. Or let me come and get you. I've got friends in the north - we could go back there."

"You can't do that. You're supposed to be recuperating. And not being funny, but won't Lisa think it's odd if you bugger off with me? Maybe you should stick close to her. You may learn something."

"I can't leave you on your own."

"I could go back to my mum's in Manchester." What was I saying? For the avoidance of doubt, I couldn't go back to my mum's in Manchester. That wasn't even on the agenda. Jesus, what a mess.

"The police are adamant that Clare did over my studio, so she could control me," I continued.

"That's ridiculous," said Danny.

"I know. That's what I keep trying to tell myself. And yet..." Danny didn't know about the dead body she'd cleared from our flat. Somebody who she'd stopped from killing me with a bit of his own medicine. My last serious date.

"Who was it who tried to lure me out on Sunday then? The police think that was Clare as well."

"God knows," said Danny. "Clare didn't have any ideas?"

"She was vague, which didn't help. But you know what she's like."

"I do. You know, I think it's like this. Graham March was part of a network. Whatever it was, there are former associates who want Clare and will stop at nothing to get her. Both they and the police are trying to track her down."

"But if they're doing that, why are they killing each other? And what about Eden Mills? Surely he wasn't in cahoots with the old scumbag."

"I don't know."

Neither of us did. We ended the call, and I drank the tea and then decided that, as Clare still hadn't returned, I may as well get ready for bed. I was starting to get concerned. What if she didn't come home? Would I end up staying here forever?

I was lying in bed, all sorts of thoughts running through my head, when I finally heard the front door. But before I could get a chance to get up and say hello, I heard the shower running in Clare's en suite. Then I had a moment of panic. A picture popped into my head: my ring, still sitting on top of the medicine cabinet. What if she saw it? She'd know I'd been in there.

The shower stopped. A few minutes later I heard her bedroom door close, and then noises from the kitchen on the floor above. I decided to join her, but sneak into the bathroom first to retrieve the ring.

What I saw nearly made me throw up. There were clothes on the floor of the bathroom. Covered in blood. And peeking out from the corner of her jeans pocket was an open packet of tarot cards.

I went straight back to my bedroom and locked the door.

Chapter 28

Tuesday March 19th, 1996

ONCE again, I didn't sleep very well. Eventually, I gave up and decided to have a shower and get dressed before heading to the kitchen. And I packed my overnight bag. I wasn't planning on staying. By the time I arrived, Clare was at the dining room table reading a newspaper. She gave me an inappropriate smile.

"Good morning," she said, full of equally inappropriate cheer. "Can I make you breakfast?"

"I'll just make tea if that's okay," I said. I knew my voice sounded as sullen as a teenager's, but how could I explain what I'd seen?

My hands were shaking as I tried to fill the kettle. I felt faint. I wanted to sit down, but I didn't want to sit next to Clare. I wanted to reinvent myself and start all over again. Coping with a broken heart was bad enough without all of this utter mayhem. I was done. All of my instincts were telling me to run, and never stop running.

"Are you okay? You don't look too good," she said.

I imagined I looked far better than I felt.

"I'm sorry, but I broke one of your mugs last night," I said. "I'll replace it."

"Don't worry. I saw the remains in the bin. Did you throw it against the wall?" I think she was trying to make a joke. I wasn't in the mood.

"No, I knocked it over. I'm sorry."

"Hey, don't worry."

I could feel she was watching me while I made the tea. I didn't speak. I didn't know what to say any more. Eventually Clare broke the silence.

"What's the matter?"

"With me? Nothing." How could I say that for the first time, I felt a real sense of fear while in her company. At least, for the first time since she'd last pointed a gun at me. I wanted to mention the blood but I didn't want to run the risk that she'd tell me the truth. I was in a twilight zone. Maybe I could blank out the reality by denying the facts to myself. But the facts were now inescapable.

"Did you sleep well?" she continued, voice still full of cheer.

"Not bad." I'd lain awake most of the night, half expecting to be murdered, working out how best to escape. But I'm not sure that was what she wanted to hear. "Is that the Echo?"

"Yes." She passed it to me. The front page, as I'd have guessed, was dominated by a picture of Eden Mills, with ten pages of further coverage promised inside. The double page spread on pages four and five stopped me dead. "Who is Clare Woodbrook?" read the headline, and beneath it: "Hunt goes on for chief suspect as net closes in."

She saw me looking.

"Have you seen this?" I asked her.

"You can hardly miss it."

"Jesus, Clare." I started to read. It was a potted history of her career and subsequent misdemeanours. Several were news to me. "The whole country's going to be looking for you."

"Admittedly it's not going to help."

"But all these things?"

"Not entirely accurate, but the standard of reporting has gone downhill since I left. That's Simon Oakley for you."

I couldn't stand it any longer. I had to confront it. Whatever the risks.

"Where were you on Sunday afternoon?"

"I was here, in this flat."

"Can you prove it?"

"Why should I have to prove it? Of course I can't prove it. I was here, on my own, and then I came to see you."

"So you didn't kill Eden Mills?"

"Of course I didn't. Seriously, why do I keep getting accused of killing people?"

"Because the police have got evidence, Clare. Lots of it. And you've got previous. It's what you do."

She looked slightly offended by that, but I was only speaking the truth.

"The weird thing is that half the Metropolitan Police are looking for you," I continued. "And here you are, bang in the middle of London."

"It's the last place they expect me to be. The population of London is twice the size of Denmark's. It must be possible to hide somewhere."

I was beginning to find her joyful tone irritating.

"You enjoy it, don't you?" I asked.

"In truth? No. Did you bring your passport?"

"Yes. Why?"

"Good."

I rolled my eyes. I was beyond pissed off. Fuck it.

"Where were you last night?" I asked.

"I was here, downstairs. In the room next to yours."

"I mean in the late evening. You went out. I heard you come back, about three hours later, then I heard the shower running. What had you been up to?"

"You're quite the investigator."

"I've hung around enough of them."

She smiled, again, and I was beginning to find that irritating too. I couldn't remember when I'd been in a worse mood in a morning without an accompanying hangover.

"I had to go out to see someone," she said when I continued to look at her. "It was unrelated. Honest truth. Just sorting something out. And having a shower helps me to sleep. Okay?"

"No, not okay. I saw, Clare."

"Me in the shower? You should have joined me."

"Will you please piss off? No. The blood."

"Blood?"

"Yes. On your clothes. On your bathroom floor."

Suddenly the smile disappeared.

"Were you spying on me?"

"No. I went in to retrieve my ring which I'd left there when I was getting a plaster. What was it?"

"I cut myself."

"Really?"

"Yes."

"What the hell with? I cut my finger last night but I didn't end up looking like that. It was a hell of a lot of blood for a graze. Show me."

She looked offended again. I didn't care.

"Of course I'm not going to show you."

"Just bloody show me if you want me to believe you."

"Fine."

She removed her sweatshirt. There was a scratch on her arm.

"Happy now?"

"Not completely. Again, that was a hell of a lot of blood for a graze. And if you were wearing long sleeves I don't know how it ended up on the front of your shirt. So again, where were you last night?"

"There are some things it's better not to ask."

"Fuck off then."

Now she really did look offended. I didn't care any more.

"What's got into you this morning?" she asked.

I poured the hot water into a mug. And made a mental note of the location of the knife drawer as I was fetching a spoon.

"I need to know, Clare. Because you came home last night covered in blood. And because Amy came to see me and she is adamant you're going round killing people. And if you are, that's fine, I can live with that, weird as that bloody sounds. I can help you. Seriously, get you professional help. But the thought of you lying to me is substantially more painful."

"You can help me?"

"Yes."

"How? By holding the gun?"

"Stop it. Not funny."

I removed the tea bag, and added milk from the fridge. Tea is magical but the thought of anything passing my lips was back to making me feel nauseous.

"Have you finished now?" she asked.

"I've hardly started."

"Well, park it for the time being. We're going to Bratislava."

"What?"

"You and me. We're going on a trip."

"Where the fuck is Bratislava?"

"Slovakia. We're going to find Lukáš."

I looked at her as though she'd finally gone mad. Maybe it had happened years ago.

"No, no," I said, shaking my head. "I'm going to have to stop you there. We're not changing the subject. Clare, please. Just answer the question."

"Okay, I was seeing someone from a former life. Okay? Nothing to do with this, I promise you."

"And the blood?"

"He had a nosebleed."

"Oh, bullshit."

"It's true. Admittedly because I hit him in the face. We didn't see eye to eye over something, but it was nothing. Okay? I promise you."

"I don't know if I believe a word of it."

"I'm not lying to you, Anna, honestly. You have my absolute word. Now, can we discuss Bratislava?"

"No, we bloody can't. Clare, I care about you. I really do. But Amy's got evidence. DNA evidence. And I know you've lied to me."

"Such as when?"

"Such as when you told me about Lukáš. You said he'd been found apparently dead in his room. You neglected to tell me that you were the one who went there with him. And so do I believe that he really faked his own death? Or did somebody kill him? Because if it's the latter, then I'm really sorry to say this, but I am struggling to pin it on anyone else."

I sat down at the table, but kept my distance.

"I told you, we're going to Bratislava to find him," said Clare.

"Will you just shut up for a minute? We are not going to Bratislava." I slapped myself in the face. Maybe it was all a dream. It wasn't. "Let's discuss my studio, okay?"

"Okay."

"I've seen how you clean things up, which is remarkably efficient, with no trace left behind. So when Amy suggested that you'd arranged for my studio to be cleared out, I thought it was ridiculous at first. But then the more I think about it, the more I realise I've got no bloody idea what you're playing at any more."

And then she gave me a look I'd never seen before. Her eyes

seemed to change. To harden. She stood up and walked towards me, then knelt down, her face inches from mine.

"You're very brave, you know that?"

"What do you mean brave?" I said, feeling anything but.

"I mean you're here, with me, now. When you clearly think I'm a killer."

"You are a killer."

"Were."

"Oh come on, Clare."

"Okay, so we'll add delusional to that as well, shall we? You think I'm a delusional killer on a mad spree of death and destruction, with some unquenchable bloodlust. And yet you haven't made a run for it. I think that's very brave. Or maybe you're just too terrified to run, in case I reach out and pull you back and cut you into a million pieces. Is that it?"

She was getting closer.

"Clare, you're scaring me."

"Oh, am I?" She stood up and leaned against the sink. "Well, let me tell you something, Anna. I don't want to scare you. But if that's what you think of me, then you should be scared. Because it's a big vicious bastard of a world out there. And for some reason I have taken it as a matter of personal pride that I should protect you. Why? Because I know I've done bad things. And I know you have been affected by them. And because, despite the fact that you clearly think I'm some sort of insane psychopath, I do still care about you. So make your mind up. Which is it to be?"

"What? Between saying I believe you and being cut into a million pieces?"

"No, between actually believing me or ending our friendship right here and now. Because if you don't trust me - you of all people, after all we've been through - then frankly I'm going to suggest you walk out of here and you will never see me again. It's time to make your mind up."

I looked at her. I didn't know who she was any more.

"You know what? I'll go," I said. "I'm done. I just want to go home and you can call me when everything is over."

"You don't want to go home."

"I really do. Watch me."

I made to get up but Clare gripped my arm, more firmly than strictly necessary. It was borderline painful.

"Let go of my arm."

She squeezed harder.

"The plane is booked."

"Well, enjoy your trip and safe flight, and send me a postcard if you get a moment, but..." I shook my arm free. "If I've got a bruise I'm not going to be very happy."

"You're not going home."

"Oh, I think I am."

"You can't."

"So you said. But I think you'll find I absolutely can."

I stood up as well. The tea would have to go to waste.

"I don't want to fall out with you," she said.

"Stop behaving like a prick, then."

"Fine. Go."

"I will."

"But just to be completely clear on this, I won't be there to protect you. I'm going to be in Bratislava, finding Lukáš and getting to the bottom of all of this. So when your mysterious caller comes back for a second attempt to kidnap you, please be aware that you are very much on your own. Understood?"

"Understood."

"Because it isn't me, Anna. It isn't me going round killing people. It isn't me that burgled your studio. It isn't me that's threatening you. And evidently it wasn't me that shot at you when I was standing next to you in Welwyn, but it was me who made sure the bullet didn't hit you. But no, that's fine. You go. If you think you're better off on your own, you just go and wait in Camden until they come back and add you to the list."

"I wouldn't be on anyone's list if I didn't know you."

"I'm sure Danny will persuade Lisa you're a priority."

I don't often lose my temper but I was on the verge of violence.

"Do you need change for the bus fare?" she asked. That nearly tipped me over the edge.

"Fuck off."

"I will. Take care, Anna. Be lucky."

I grabbed my jacket. Clare sat back at the table and played with a packet of cigarettes, watching me. I was desperate to say something clever before I departed, but the sound of the bullet hitting the side of my car replayed through my brain with ever-increasing volume. I felt my bravado evaporate the closer I came to the door. By the time I was turning the handle, the reality was sinking in: the reality of just how alone I was in this mad, chaotic world.

"I take it you're going to try to stop me," I said, turning. Clare shrugged. She knew how to piss me off, but suddenly the thought of losing her was worse than the thought of a monumental climbdown. "You weren't actually going to just let me go, were you?"

Rather than answer, she sat back and threw the cigarette packet spinning up into the air, and then caught it on the return.

"It's just that if you did have any final word on the subject, now would possibly be a good time to mention it," I continued. I opened the door. "Bye then," I added, poised on the threshold. And a moment later I was walking downstairs, grabbing my bag from my bedroom, and out through the front door of the flat. And as that door swung closed behind me, I didn't have the first idea what to do next.

Chapter 29

THE morning conference at the Daily Echo was more sombre than usual. Surrounded by the heads of department, Mike Walker occupied the editor's chair at the table's head.

"It's an embarrassment," he said. Everyone was listening to him, but news editor Simon Oakley was the one under the spotlight.

"With all due respect," Simon replied, "it's a bloody good, in-depth story."

The editor's expression was unmoved.

"I'm not talking about the frigging story. I'm talking about Clare Woodbrook. If anyone should know where she is, it should be bloody us."

"And again, we're looking for her. But so are the police. If she doesn't want to be found…"

"Fuck her not wanting to be found. Of course she doesn't want to be bloody found. So find her."

As the conference ended and everyone left the room, Simon Oakley called up a number on his phone. There was a lot he could say when the time was right, but it was time to speak to Danny again.

———

Detective Chief Superintendent Paul Curtis was standing behind his desk, on the verge of a full-blown rage.

DCI Rogan Court stood opposite, flanked, as ever, by DS Amy Cranston and DC Lisa Miller. If there was blame to be apportioned, he was going to make sure it was shared around.

"It's Tuesday and I want her head on a plate today," said the DCS. "If not then I'll be ordering two more plates, so I've got one for each of you. Do I make myself abundantly clear, people?"

"You do, sir," said Rogan. "And we are making progress. We've traced the manufacturer of the tarot cards and we've got a list of the places in London that sell them. We're asking for CCTV."

"*What?*"

"If we can find out which shop she's using, we may be able to narrow down the search area."

"And what exactly do you hope to achieve by doing that? So we get her on CCTV buying cards? We already know she's buying cards. We already know who's doing it. And while you're pissing about, she's going round killing people and laughing at you. Laughing at all of us. DC Miller. The latest with Danny?"

"He doesn't know where she is," said Lisa.

"Bollocks. Get him in, threaten him with obstructing the police."

"I honestly think he doesn't know, sir."

"And I honestly think you're deluded. What about the other one? Anna, is it?"

"Bit of an issue there," said Amy, dreading what was coming next. "But I think she'll let us know if she hears from her."

"You *think?*"

"She will. But she's disappeared as well at the moment. She wasn't home last night."

"Oh, fucking outstanding."

"It's actually worse than that. Her car was found abandoned in Welwyn Garden City in Hertfordshire. There were bullet holes. She hasn't been seen since. There's no CCTV in the street but we're running ANPR checks on vehicles on roads in the vicinity."

"This gets progressively better. And by better, I mean exponentially fucking worse. Remind me. Didn't she also allegedly have a phone call on Sunday, from some potential abductor?"

"She did."

"Are they connected?"

"It's a line of enquiry."

The DCS swore again and then turned to look out of the window, giving the three detectives a moment of respite. When he turned back, his voice was slightly calmer.

"Okay. Aside from losing our potentially most important lead, what else is new? The latest on Eden Mills? Any links, aside from the card?"

"Maybe, sir," said Rogan. "I've spoken to his housekeeper. He had a visitor on Sunday afternoon. A woman."

"Description?"

"It fits. I showed her pictures of Clare. She gave a positive ID."

"Good. Did she see her leave?"

"No. She only works half days on Sundays. Woodbrook turned up just as she was finishing."

"And the time of death?"

"Some time in the afternoon, within a couple of hours of Clare arriving."

"Do we know what the meeting was about?"

"We don't but it fits the profile. He was at the funeral."

"That's good enough for me." He paused. "But when I say

good enough, what I really mean is very far from good enough. Get out there now and bring her in. Dismissed."

The three detectives left the office and took the lift back down to their floor. As the doors opened, Rogan walked off but Lisa paused for a word with Amy.

"I'm not sure about him," she said.

"Who?" Amy looked reluctant to talk, and kept walking. Lisa followed.

"Curtis."

"Is this the dinosaur thing again?"

"No, it's more than that."

"What then?" There was definite irritation in her voice.

"Can we go somewhere quiet?"

Amy sighed. She nodded in the direction of the ladies' toilets. Lisa followed. After checking they were alone, Amy spoke.

"So?"

"We know March had someone here looking after him."

"We do."

"Curtis gave the eulogy at the funeral, didn't he? And suddenly he's in charge of this. He seems adamant it's Clare..."

"We're all adamant it's Clare."

"I know but he just, I don't know, seems obsessed by it. It's like he's not interested in the evidence. He just wants her at whatever cost. What if he's the person who was looking after March and this is some sort of vendetta?"

But if Lisa was expecting empathy, she was about to be disappointed.

"There's one thing you need to learn on this job," said Amy, "and that is that we follow orders. Curtis is obsessed with finding Clare because he's getting pressure from above. She's high profile. She's killing people at will. So put your conspiracy theories to one side for the moment, if that's okay with you, and just do your job, okay?"

"But what if he's the one?"

"So what if he is? It doesn't alter the facts. And when Clare is caught, as she will be, she can have her day in court, and if she wants to make allegations about Curtis then let her. But until then, we do our best to find her. Understood?"

"Understood," said Lisa. Amy left the room. Lisa stayed for a moment, looking in the mirror, wondering if the only straight person on the Force was the one staring back from the glass.

It took nearly three minutes before Clare opened the door to let me back inside.

"You're coming in, then?" she said.

"No, I'm just thinking, admiring the paintwork."

She went back inside, but left the door on the latch. After another half minute or so, I followed, padding upstairs to the kitchen. She'd already made me a cup of tea. I was kind of impressed by the thoughtfulness, but also irritated by the presumption. I re-took my seat opposite, and looked at her with a grumpy teenage scowl. I was twenty-frigging-six. She passed across a packet of biscuits.

"Will you promise you won't kill me?" I asked, then pointed to the mug. "There's no actual poison in this, is there?"

"I promise I won't kill you. But if you don't start trusting me, I may as well do, because somebody else will." The thought of that was chilling. "When did you last speak to Danny?"

"Last night. I texted him and he called me."

"Did you delete the message?"

"How do you even delete messages you've sent? Short of throwing another phone into the canal, I'm not sure how you do that. And I'm not normally a litter lout. This is all new to me, Clare."

"Okay, so what did he say?"

"He suggested running away together."

She laughed.

"Wow, that's very romantic."

"I'm being serious!"

"I know. Sorry. Does he think that I did it?"

"Everyone thinks that you did it."

"Do I look like someone who would go around murdering people?"

"That is rather the point, Clare. No, you don't. But equally, you have actually got form in that respect."

"I told you, that's all in the past."

"The police don't think so."

"And what do you think?"

"Christ!"

I took a Digestive from the packet and dunked it before continuing. I needed the sugar.

"I'll tell you what I think," I said, "although there's a good chance you won't like it. I think you inhabit your own world with your own sense of reality. You're a game player and you've got a plan. And I'd love to trust you, but I don't think I can, because I still don't think you've been honest with me."

I looked up, straight into her hazel eyes, trying to read them. She held my gaze for a few moments but finally reached for a cigarette and tapped it on the table.

"I haven't," she said.

"Haven't what?"

"Haven't been completely honest with you."

I waited for her to continue. It took a while.

"I did go to Seattle," she said eventually, lighting the cigarette.

"So why lie?"

"Because I don't like being accused of things I haven't done. Call it an automatic defence reflex if you like. I deny things. Not because they're true but because they're irrelevant, and they'd only confuse the issue."

"Okay, anything else you've lied about?"

"I don't think so."

I sighed. Took another biscuit.

"Talk me through Seattle."

Clare flicked ash, inhaled and then stubbed out the cigarette surprisingly early.

"Yes, I was in Seattle and yes that will be me on the CCTV. I went to see Olof in his room. I was trying to warn him."

"That someone was trying to kill him?"

"No. That it would be in his interests to stop doing bad things. He was letting his hotels be used for trafficking. I said it had to stop."

"Okay, so who killed him?"

"I don't know, but clearly it was someone happy to let me take the blame."

We were finally getting somewhere.

"And Venice? I know you were there. They have DNA evidence on a cigarette butt."

"It's ridiculous. All that means is that someone saw me, and picked up a cigarette and left it there. Would I really be stupid enough to leave evidence like that? Not that I'd go round killing people in Venice. I did go to see Marzia. I told her it would be in her interests to stop financing criminals. But again, I didn't kill her."

"Fine, whatever you say."

It was almost convincing. But then I remembered the blood on her clothing. It looked like a lot of blood for a nosebleed. And if she was lying about that, she could be lying about everything.

"Bratislava, then. First time you've been?" she said, cutting off my train of thought.

"I don't even know where it is."

"I told you, Slovakia."

"That's not helping. I've only heard of Slovakia in terms of Czechoslovakia, but aside from it being in eastern Europe I'm not much further forward."

"For starters, it's in central Europe, rather than the east. Bratislava is just down the road from Vienna. I presume you've heard of Austria?"

"Are you taking the piss?"

"I'm just checking."

"I'm not in the mood, if it's okay with you. I'm having a bad week."

"Noted."

As if to accentuate the point, the third biscuit snapped off in my mug and floated in the tea, taunting me. The first food I'd actually fancied in days, and it had turned into a shambles.

"How are you even going to get to Bratislava? Presumably the police are watching the ports and airports, and even if you're a master of disguise, then I'm not. Not that I'm going."

"Leave that to me. I'm going to have to sort out the logistics this afternoon, but I suggest we get to bed early tonight. We've got an early start tomorrow."

"Have you?"

"We have."

"How early?"

"Early."

"You do know I don't do alarm clocks."

"I will shoot you with my water pistol."

"What the fuck is it with you and shooting people?"

"Old habits." Her smile was infectious. "Meanwhile, I'll look after you today and make sure neither of us comes to any harm. We can have a return chess match later, if you want to take your mind off things."

"I'm well out of practise."

"Good. That means I might stand a chance."

She had a habit of letting me beat her at chess when she wanted me to do something, but this time I was wise to it.

Chapter 30

DS Amy Cranston switched off her engine but made no move to exit the car. She took her phone out of her coat pocket and pressed the number for DSI Joe Leyland.

It rang six times and then voicemail kicked in.

"Hi boss, Joe," she said. "It's just me with an update. I hope all is well there. In truth, though, there's not much to tell. Investigations are ongoing. Nothing to worry about, but we're not much closer. Curtis is blowing his stack and Rogan is a pain in the arse, but I probably shouldn't say any of that." She laughed. "Anyway, just so you know, we're thinking of you. I'll call you if there's anything more."

She pocketed the phone, then gazed out of the window, looking for answers in the clouds, beginning to feel that she was way out of her depth and things were spiralling out of control.

Danny tried to call Lisa but her phone went to voicemail. It was getting frustrating, never knowing where she was, or how she was, or whether she was any closer to finding Clare. But that was the least of his worries at the moment. Where was Anna? What was Clare playing at? What would Clare do now if she was sitting at home, asking the same questions of someone else?

He'd learned his trade as an investigative journalist under Clare's tutelage and it had served him well. But sometimes even that training led to feelings of helplessness. It would come with time. Each year, each headline, and each award gave confidence, but there was no substitute for an all-knowing mentor to turn to in times of doubt. But where was she? Physically and mentally? If Clare was on the verge of a breakdown, Anna could be at serious risk. The body count was already critical.

Danny took a notepad to the sofa, and started to think of ways he could resolve this. Could he find Anna? Find Clare? Speak to them both. Could he persuade Clare to confront her demons? To come clean and turn herself in? To seek the help she so clearly needed?

His phone rang. Unknown number.

"Danny, mate, it's Simon," said the voice. It took him a moment to place it, but then he had an overwhelming urge to end the call.

"What can I do for you, Simon," he said instead.

"I want to take you out for coffee, mate. Bit of a catch up."

Again, the word "mate". It grated.

"I appreciate the offer but I'm busy."

"I thought you'd say that, but I'm asking as a favour."

"Because you want to know if I've got any secrets on Clare? I've seen your piece this morning."

"No, listen, forget that. That was just background fluff Mike asked me to cobble together."

"I'd hardly call it fluff."

Simon laughed.

"You know how it is. But look, I'm on your side, mate. The police are looking for Clare. I want to help you."

"Help me do what exactly?"

"Clear her name."

Danny wasn't expecting that. He didn't believe it either.

"We can help each other," Simon continued. "I'll be honest with you. I know we haven't got on but we understand each other, yes? We both understand the news. We chase the story. Occasionally that means pissing people off, and I know I've pissed you off, so I apologise."

Danny could feel his temper rising.

"I'm sorry but that's bollocks. I was onto Graham March last year and you did your best to stop me getting the story."

"I know, but I want to explain that to you. Explain the bigger picture. Meet me for coffee and I'll tell you everything."

Danny was still reluctant.

"I'm in Camden," Simon continued. "A ten-minute walk away. Come on, mate, it'll do you good and there are things I want to tell you."

Half an hour later Danny was looking at Simon across two cappuccinos. The coffee shop was bustling, Elastica on the radio, the windows steamed up, obscuring the view to the street. The scent of roasted coffee permeated the air. A young woman arrived with a baby in a pushchair and sat down, two tables away.

"So, enlighten me. Why did you try to silence the March story?" said Danny.

"I'll be completely straight with you, Danny. Everything I'm going to tell you is gospel," said Simon. "I was working on something bigger."

"Bullshit."

"Look, I know you don't trust me - you probably think I'm the last person you want to be speaking to at this moment - but let me be honest with you."

"That'd be a first."

"Let me tell you what I know about Graham, and why I tried to stop you."

"Go on then." Danny sat back, his face etched with cynicism.

"I knew Graham was bad. That was never in doubt, but I suppose the best analogy is that of the undercover police department tracking an international drugs gang. They're on the verge of busting the entire network, but some local detective comes along and arrests one of the gang members for something minor, and the entire bigger investigation collapses."

"That's a flattering analogy. I assume you're the international spy master while I'm the local plod?"

"No, God, I don't mean it in that way. Only that I knew there was a bigger story than just March getting up to a bit of mischief."

"It's funny how you describe trafficking, corruption and loan-sharking as 'a bit of mischief'. Are you actually in touch with reality?"

Simon sighed.

"I'm sorry, I'm not very good at this. That's not what I meant either. Can we start again?"

"Go on."

"You know March was involved in some sort of network, yes?"

Danny nodded.

"Well, that was what I was looking into. But it was incredibly sensitive because of who owned the paper."

"Eden?"

"Yeah. We all know about Robert Maxwell, so we know that newspaper owners aren't always squeaky clean."

"And again the understatement."

"Just bear with me, Danny, please, and for fuck's sake see it from my point of view. I was looking into the network and started to think that Mills was a part of it. Yes, there was high-level police as well, but if the Echo's owner was involved then it was going to need incredibly delicate handling. It's a massive story but the Echo wasn't going to run it. For obvious reasons."

Danny lowered his voice.

"And you're sure you're not just saying this now because he's dead?"

"I'm absolutely saying it now because he's dead. Robert Maxwell wasn't outed until he fell off the boat. Could you see the Mirror exposing him while he was still in charge? I know the public has a low opinion of journalists but we're not stupid. But I was investigating. I was in the perfect place to do that as long as nobody realised what I was up to. I could get access to his office, try to overhear conversations when he was in the building. Follow hunches and try to back them up with evidence, so that when the shit did eventually hit the fan and I got fired for it, I could take the story to one of the other papers and blow the whole thing wide open."

"So essentially what you're saying is, you were thinking of your own career, and stuff the rest of us?"

Simon looked frustrated.

"No, not in the slightest. What I'm saying is that if Eden Mills was part of some corrupt network, the story needed to be told. I wasn't looking to leave the Echo. But I had to be aware that if I brought it up at a morning conference, the very least I could expect would be to be escorted from the building, and at worst possibly find that I was floating face down in the Thames. And either way, running a story designed to take out Graham March wasn't going to help. I'm sorry I couldn't discuss this with you at the time, but hopefully you can see how impossible it all was."

"Okay." Danny still wasn't convinced. But it did sound kind of plausible. "But who else was in the network?"

"That's what I've been working on. I think we both know there was police involvement. Someone higher than March. And obviously we know there have been a few murders that are being linked to it all. But some of it, I'm still in the dark."

"But you don't know who in the police?"

"I've got some ideas."

"Do you have a name?"

"Not for definite. But we could start by looking at who is the keenest to find Clare and pin it all on her."

"Curtis."

Simon leaned forward, lowering his voice as well.

"Exactly. Look, I know about Clare's deal with DSI Joe Leyland. And I know Leyland is off the case because his wife had a car crash."

"News travels fast."

"It does. But I'm struggling to find the cause of the crash. I don't have the contacts in Cumbria. But what if it wasn't a crash? What if Curtis arranged it so that Leyland would have to be taken off the case? Joe's coming up to retirement anyway, so what's the problem with speeding it up a bit?"

"Unless you were the one in the car?"

Simon nodded.

"Obviously that. But what I'm saying is, what if Curtis needed to be in charge so he could set about finding Clare? He would have known of her agreement with Leyland, so if he's trying to pin everything on her, it stands to reason he'd want Leyland out of the way."

"It's possible."

"It's more than possible. Because look, I don't think Clare did this. We know she's not an angel, but suddenly going on the rampage? I don't see it."

"The police seem to think they have the evidence."

"They do. But that means if they get so much as a sighting of Clare, they'll shoot first and ask questions later. As far as they're concerned, she's armed and dangerous. She needs to be taken out."

"But why pin it on Clare?"

"Because she was working for the other side, for one thing.

And because they know that she's good at investigating things herself. If she started looking into this, then things could get extremely uncomfortable for anyone involved."

Danny found himself nodding, despite his obvious cynicism.

"But she could still tell everything she knows even if she was arrested," he said.

"Yes, if she was arrested and had her day in court. But do you think it'd ever come to that? She'd get taken out long before that happened. Look, let me run something by you. This may freak you out."

"What? The thought of you actually being something other than a conniving shit?"

Simon laughed.

"Danny, you're right to have that impression of me. Given how things have gone between us. But trust me, I'm good at what I do. You have to be tough at times. That's news. And I know I can sound... brusque. Is that the word?"

"One of them. And I'm not saying I'm believing a word of it, but go on, try to freak me out."

"It's March."

"Go on." Danny sat back.

"Specifically the night he was killed."

"I know. I was there. Do you want to see the scars?"

"I know you were and that's why I'm trying to be sensitive. But I'll tell you what I think."

"Enlighten me."

"I think he was deliberately killed. They could have shot to disable him. My theory is that he was becoming an embarrassment. He was out of control and getting unpredictable. So somebody who was controlling him took the opportunity to wipe him out."

Danny tried to cast his mind back, but his memory of the night was vague. Two bullets could have that effect.

"It's an interesting theory," he said.

"It's more than a theory. I've tried to find out exactly what happened that night. Who pulled the trigger. Who authorised it. The records just aren't there."

"They must be, surely?"

"There are records, of a kind. But there are details missing. So I think if we can find out who gave the order, we find out who the main man in the police is. And if we can work out that, everything comes together."

"And in the meantime?"

"In the meantime the police will be going all out to pin it all on Clare."

"Which, of course it could possibly be."

Simon took a sip of his drink, then added sugar and stirred it in.

"It could. I'm not saying all the police are corrupt. They'll be following orders. But if they've already killed one of their own, do you really think they couldn't manufacture a situation in which Clare had to be stopped as she was deemed to pose an 'imminent threat to life'?"

"You know a lot of stuff."

"It's my job, Danny."

"But how do you know it?"

"Sources. And following hunches."

"And do your sources know where Clare is now?"

"No, but they think you do."

Danny laughed at the irony.

"So they've asked you to be my new best friend so I'll tell you?"

"No, of course not. But if you could arrange for me to speak to Clare, it could be extremely useful. For all of us."

"You and the police, maybe. Would you believe me if I said I didn't know where she was?"

"I'd believe you. But I think you have a way of contacting her. And you know what? You're going to have to be careful, because the police aren't going to stop going at you till you tell them."

"This isn't the 1970s. They don't just beat people up."

"I think it's going beyond police. National security, if you know what I mean."

"MI5? For Clare? What the fuck for?"

"Because she's made quite an impression."

Danny downed the cappuccino, to give himself a moment to think.

"I've got a problem with all of this," he said, eventually.

"Okay. Tell me."

"Someone's going round killing various members of the network. The police, Curtis, whoever, think it's Clare. But if Curtis was a member of the network, why on earth would he be trying to frame Clare for it? Surely he'd know he was at risk too. So, yeah, I get it if he really thinks it's Clare. Take her out and save himself. But if he doesn't and he's just trying to pin it on her, that means that the person who is responsible is still out there. And Curtis must know that, and know that he himself would be in serious danger. It doesn't make sense."

Simon clicked his fingers, as though getting to the point.

"It does, but only in two scenarios. One: he thinks it is Clare, in which case he'd better hope he's right. Or two: he knows exactly who's doing it and he's in on it. Because if it's Clare, then agreed, it could be some kind of gangland feud and it's kill or be killed. But if it's Curtis himself doing the clean-up, it's altogether different. It's all about saving his own skin."

Danny let out a low whistle. Reluctantly he could feel himself getting interested.

"Okay, but I don't know what use you think I can be," he said. "I don't know where Clare is. I'm officially still off sick, and even if I wasn't, I'm also officially still suspended."

"I don't need you to do anything. Just eyes and ears, okay? And be careful what you say to the police. Any of them. We don't know who we can trust. I gather you're quite friendly with one of the detectives?"

"News does travel fast."

"I'm not prying into your personal life, mate. But you never know, you may hear something. Not necessarily something she tells you, but something that jumps out as being odd. But be careful what you say in front of her. And of course if you do speak to Clare, I'd love to meet with her."

"I'm not sure she's your biggest fan either."

"I get that. But let's catch up later. Okay? I'm going to keep working on this. And thanks, Danny. You could have just told me to piss off."

"I did think about it."

Simon reached across the table, and this time Danny did accept the handshake. They stood up to leave, and said they'd keep in touch. As they left the café, the young woman followed a moment behind.

Chapter 31

BY mid-afternoon I could sense Clare was getting restless.
"I don't like it," she said.

I'd never watched her in action from such close quarters before. She disappeared into one of the bedrooms a couple of times, and I could just about make out the sound of a phone call, but the walls and doors were too well insulated for me to make out the words.

"Everything okay?" I asked when she came through to the kitchen. It was an asinine question, but I felt powerless, as though as I was just taking up space. And yet she seemed to actively want me there. I was trying to process so many things. Was I safe? Was I mad? Was I going to get arrested for colluding with a criminal? Or more accurately, being looked after by one? Or were people looking for me right now, assuming I'd been kidnapped. Maybe I had been.

"Can we get in touch with Danny again?" said Clare. "I want to ask him about Eden Mills. And make sure he's okay. Obviously."

"You've got the secret phone."

"I'm nervous of using that. He could be in an interview room."

"Understood, I'll try him on mine."

I dialled his number. He picked up on the third ring.

"Danny," I said, putting it on speaker. "It's me, how are you? Where are you?"

"I'm okay. Walking back up Camden Road. Everything seems louder after a few months in hospital. Where are you?"

"I'm not completely sure. Are you on your own?"

"As much as you can be on a street in London. I'm not walking with anyone, if that's what you mean."

"Good. I've got someone here who wants to talk to you."

"Hi, Danny," said Clare.

"The elusive Clare. How are things?"

"I'm fine. We both are." She looked at me as though for confirmation. I just raised an eyebrow.

"Where are you?" asked Danny.

"Still in London. I need to talk to you. About Eden. About all of this."

"It's chaos at the Echo. They're in meltdown."

"I can imagine."

"You seem to have an unlikely ally, though."

"Who?"

"Simon Oakley."

"Simon? Why's he getting involved?"

Danny explained about his conversation. I'd heard of Simon. He'd always been Danny's nemesis within the paper, so it seemed strange that they were now best of friends. But Danny had gone mad on the friend front recently, so it was less of a surprise than it might have been.

"And he's sure Eden was involved in the network?"

"Seems to be. He's desperate to speak to you, though."

"I'm sure he is."

Clare paused for a moment, frowning.

"Danny, there's something you need to know. Both of you."

"That sounds ominous." It was as though Danny was speaking my mind for me.

"First of all, you have to believe me. I didn't have anything to do with the murder of Eden Mills."

"Glad to hear it."

"But I did go to meet Eden on Sunday."

"Jesus, Clare."

"I had my reasons, okay?"

"Your reasons?"

"Yes."

"Which were?"

"There were a few. I'd had my doubts about him. It bothered me that you were told to lay off Graham. I know Mike Walker. He's a good editor. If there's a story he'd be all over it, so it didn't make sense. I thought there may have been pressure from above."

"I'm not sure about that. Simon was involved in that too. He admitted it. He thought it could mess up the bigger story."

"That could be true. But Simon couldn't get you suspended. March planted evidence against you and he needed inside access for that. I know Simon can be a bastard but I never thought he'd stoop that low. Mills was also at Graham's funeral, and that seemed really weird. And more than any of that, I wanted to clear your name."

"You wanted to do what?"

"You're nearly ready to go back. So I wanted to talk to him. Ask a few questions. Make him see the logic in lifting the suspension."

"Christ. And the next day he's dead?"

"Exactly. So what does this tell us?"

"It tells me yet again that it's bloody dangerous to be in your presence," I said, chipping in.

"It does," said Clare. "But it also tells me that there are people out there watching. They're not watching me, because if they were, they'd know where I was and they'd just kill me. And if they're not watching me, that can only mean that they're watching the people I've been going to meet. Word gets back and then, bang."

"So who's doing it? Who's behind it all? Who is at the head of this?"

"I don't know yet, but it's escalating. But why? Why now? And there's something else I need to tell you."

"What?"

"In the interests of full disclosure, I also went to meet someone else. On Friday morning. A Chris Stokes. He was also at the funeral. He runs an international haulage company."

"Don't tell me. He turned up dead the next morning?"

"No. He hasn't turned up dead anywhere."

"That's a relief."

"Not necessarily. He disappeared that evening and hasn't been heard of since."

"I'm losing count."

"You're not the only one. My guess is he'll turn up before too long."

"So, Clare..." Danny paused.

"What?"

"Can you do me a favour? Keep out of this for a bit? Don't go to see anybody. Let the police investigate."

"Paul Curtis?"

"You know him?"

"I know him well enough to know that he has an agenda."

"Simon's thinking along those lines too."

"That's kind of reassuring." I could see Clare thinking. "Danny, stick close to him. And Lisa." That raised my hackles. "See what you can find out about Eden Mills and his involvement. And any links to Paul Curtis. We're going to get to the bottom of the Lukáš Mäsiar situation."

"You said he'd been flown back to Slovakia."

"Officially, but nobody saw the body. It could be that he's still over here, causing mayhem. We need to meet him, to rule it out. Or not as the case may be."

"It's a mess."

"It's bloody dangerous. Watch your back, please?"

"I will. And you too. And make sure you look after Anna for me."

"I am here, you know," I said. "I'll make sure she does."

But I had a feeling we'd be looking after each other, and our success in the endeavour could quite literally make the difference between life and death.

The woman stopped pushing her baby for a moment, once she'd entered a quiet side street. She dialled a number. DCS Paul Curtis answered. She gave him a summary of the conversation she'd overheard.

"Okay," he said eventually. You've done well."

"Next?"

"Keep following Danny. Put the frighteners on if you need to."

It was time to start planning for the end-game.

Chapter 32

DS AMY Cranston watched Danny turn into Rochester Square, and got out of her car to meet him.

"A word?" she said.

"Of course. Come in."

Danny led her up the steps to the front door and then through to the kitchen.

"Would you like anything to drink?" he asked.

"No, I'm not stopping. I just need to know if you've heard anything from Clare. Or Anna."

Danny looked up, calculating the risks.

"I've had a call from Anna. She's fine. She's just lying low for a few days. I've got no idea where Clare is."

Amy's expression hardened.

"If you're lying to me, Danny, you don't even want to think about the consequences."

"Seriously, I'm not lying to you. Stick me on a polygraph if you like. You'll get the same answer."

He took a chair at the kitchen table, wincing slightly with the pain from his scars. Amy remained standing.

"We've had a positive ID for Clare visiting Eden Mills," she said.

"How positive?"

"The housekeeper identified her from a photograph."

"Is that proof? She could have got it wrong."

"It's proof enough." Amy paused, apparently waiting for a reaction.

"Okay. Anything else?"

"Where have you just been?"

"At a coffee shop in Camden with a colleague from the paper."

"Can you prove it?"

"I can prove I was at the coffee shop. I've got a receipt. I can't prove who I was with. Call Simon Oakley, though. He'll confirm it."

"Simon Oakley who wrote a profile on Clare?"

"That's the one. He wanted to know if I knew where Clare was too. I gave him the same answer. Believe me, I wish I knew."

"Okay, Danny." She turned to leave. Danny stood to follow.

"If I hear anything, I *will* let you know," he said.

"You make sure you do." She opened the door, but then turned back.

"One more thing. I know you're seeing Lisa."

"Not really seeing at the moment. She's working all day and night."

"Get used to that. But no, I mean, I know about the relationship. Just treat her well, okay? She's a good person. Be tolerant over the hours. She works hard. She's under a lot of pressure. We all are."

"I know."

"It's never easy having a relationship in this job. Especially at the moment. It's a very difficult time for us. Take care of yourself. Of both of you, okay?"

"I will."

Danny closed the door. And reached for his phone.

· · ·

"Simon," he said when it was answered. "Are you still in Camden?"

"Just heading back, mate."

Danny let the "mate" pass.

"I've been thinking about what we discussed," he said. "Do you know the Royal Scot Hotel at Kings Cross?"

"I've heard of it."

"I'm going to book a room there for a couple of days. Can you meet me there later? In the bar?"

"Sure. It'll be good to be working with you."

"I don't know if I'd go that far, but it would be good to have a chat, I think."

They arranged a time. Danny ended the call and started to pack an overnight bag, then called the hotel and booked a room. He didn't want to stay at home, not without Anna. Not knowing where she was and if she was safe. And not knowing who might come to the flat looking for her.

Within twenty minutes he was ready to leave. He locked the front door and then set off in the direction of the bus stop. It was about a ten-minute journey. But as he walked, he could feel someone right on his shoulder. He turned, but hardly had time to register the face before being pushed hard against a wall.

"Where's Clare?" spat the man. He was perhaps mid-thirties and muscular.

"I really don't know," said Danny.

"We don't believe you. Do we have to hurt you?"

"I don't bloody know."

"What about Anna?"

"She doesn't know either."

"That's not what I meant. I meant, do I have to hurt Anna? Would that make you tell me?"

Danny tried to shake himself free, but he was pinned. He was in no condition for a street brawl.

"I don't know who the fuck you are, but you don't go

anywhere near Anna," he said. "And I don't know where she is, either, before you ask."

"Oh, we do," said the man, menacingly. He gave Danny one final shove and then walked away, turning immediately into a side street and out of sight. Danny was too shaken to follow. He called Anna. It went to voicemail.

"Anna, it's me," he said. "I don't know where you are, but get out of there, okay? Immediately. You're not safe. I've just been stopped in the street by someone who threatened to hurt you unless we tell them where Clare is. He said he knows where you are, and he looked serious. Amy's been back again too with ever more evidence. I'll be at the Royal Scot at Kings Cross. Come and meet me. Soon as you can. Please."

I finished listening to the voicemail message and turned to Clare.

"That was Danny. He's spooked."

"What happened?"

"He got accosted on the street."

"Is he okay?"

"I don't know. But whoever it was said they know where I am, and they're coming to get me and they're going to hurt me until one of us gives you up."

Clare sat back on the sofa. The chessboard was between us. My position, as predicted, was looking good.

"That's impossible. Nobody knows where you are. You don't need to worry about that. They're just trying to smoke us out. Where's Danny now?"

"Heading to the Royal Scot at Kings Cross. And I don't want to annoy you, but Amy has been around again. I don't know what she said to Danny, but apparently there was even more..."

"Evidence, yes. I get it. Which would be funny if it wasn't so utterly ridiculous. But you know why they've got all this evidence against me? Because I'm being set up to take the fall. Wipe out a bunch of corrupt bastards and pin it on the one person that they all want to catch anyway, because suddenly I'm flavour of the month again and I'm an easy route to a medal of commendation. Despite letting the real bastard go completely free."

"But Amy wouldn't do that."

"You think?" Clare raised an eyebrow.

"She wouldn't deliberately spread false evidence. She's the straightest, least corruptible person I know. You know that as well as I do."

"Is that what you really think?"

"Of course it's what I think. She was the one determined to bring March to justice. You said it yourself: she was working with Joe Leyland to keep you onside and out of prison. She embodies anti-corruption."

"Right." She shook her head, looking intensely disappointed in me.

"Oh, come on," I said. "You're not seriously suggesting..."

"What do I always tell Danny?"

"Lots of things, probably. Never to assume anything?"

"Correct. Never take anything at face value. Question everything."

"Okay, but surely you don't doubt Amy."

"Right at this moment I'm doubting everyone. Let me run this by you." She took a deep breath and adjusted her position to face me before continuing. "Amy is anti-corruption, yes? I think we agree on that. So what's this all about? Some maverick hitman - or woman - wiping out an entire corrupt network. It's one way of getting rid of it."

"You're not suggesting Amy is killing people rather than trying to arrest them?"

"You said it, not me. What if she's been frustrated by the lack of justice? What if she's decided that it's time to take the law into her own hands? Amy is the one person besides me and Joe who knows who is in this cabal. Joe's out of action in some Cumbrian hospital, and now he's out of the way, she no longer needs to protect me. Convenient, that. Because I'd make the perfect fall guy."

"Yes, but even so..."

"Even so what? Ask yourself when the police started making connections between the murders. As recently as last week, when the Italians got involved and brought it to their attention. But Amy knew those connections going back to last year. She knew who was at March's funeral. She'd been keeping a watch on all of them. So are you seriously suggesting she didn't spot a link when Olof got murdered? Of course she did. She had to. So why did she hide it? Suppress the evidence of a connection?"

That stopped me.

"And who do you think is amassing the evidence against me?" Clare continued. "Forget that it's all utter bollocks. It doesn't exactly need to stand up to scrutiny, because everyone knows I've got form. So the CPS and the jury are going to give it the merest once-over and decide that I'm guilty, while the real killer laughs all the way to hell."

"But it's still not Amy." Although in truth I didn't know what to think any more.

"Anna, you're not listening to me. I'm saying this to you because I'm trying to prove a point. Amy would be the perfect person to be behind all this. You might think she's beyond reproach, but let me give you one final bit of information that could just change your mind. Do you think I've been sitting around over the last few weeks, waiting till the day they turn up to get me? I could just run, to save myself, but that leaves you and Danny badly exposed, and believe me I want to solve this as much as anyone. So I've been making enquiries. I've been watching people. Amy included. And I'll tell you now, for an absolute cast-iron certainty, she's been having meetings that none of her bosses knows about. She's been using left luggage drops to store God knows what."

"Wow. I had no idea."

"It's the tip of the iceberg, as the saying goes. But I've been aware for a while that she had something huge to hide. And now I'm beginning to realise exactly what that is. She's playing an extremely dangerous game."

"But Amy isn't a killer."

"You have no idea what people would do when they're cornered."

I didn't know what to say any more. I was living in a surreal world of conspiracy and murder. Amy couldn't be a killer. Could she? But Clare was right. I had noticed a change in her over the last week. She was no longer the Amy I thought I knew.

Clare's next words were the last thing I expected her to say.

"Let's go and meet Danny and Mr Oakley," she said.

"What? You can't do that!"

"Why not?"

"Because Danny will be getting watched. You turn up and you're getting arrested, or worse."

"Nobody will know I'm there."

"You're not a bloody ghost Clare. You're not the invisible woman. If there are four people sitting at a table, and three of them are me, Danny and whoever this Simon is, you can be pretty sure that anyone who's looking will have a strong suspicion about who the fourth one is."

She smiled that annoying smile.

"Which is why I'm not going to be at the table."

"Oh God."

"I'm going to disappear into the background, just keeping an eye on things. Only you will know I'm there."

Chapter 33

DS Amy Cranston opened the left luggage locker, close to Kings Cross station, and removed a small bag, replacing it with a larger holdall. She opened the bag, checked its contents, then put it back on top. She closed the locker, pocketed the key, and then turned to leave. And came face to face with DC Lisa Miller.

"What the fuck are you doing here?" she said.

Startled, Lisa stepped back a pace. Amy didn't usually swear.

"Looking for you."

"Yeah, well I'm on a break, so if you don't mind leaving whatever it is until I get back to work, that'd be very much appreciated. And actually if you could stop stalking me altogether, that would be even better."

But Lisa wasn't moving.

"Going somewhere?" she asked.

"What?"

Lisa nodded at the locker.

"It's none of your business," said Amy.

"So what's in the locker?"

"Listen, I don't know if you've suddenly forgotten the English language, but I said it's none of your business."

"Whoa, there's no need to be so defensive. I'm only teasing you."

"Yeah? You need to focus on doing your job, DC Miller. Focus on catching Clare. And stop harassing me. Understood?"

Lisa nodded but still didn't move. She scrutinised her colleague, seeing a level of stress that she'd never witnessed before.

"Are you okay?" she said, finally.

"I was."

"No, sorry, Amy. I'm not having this. What's going on?"

"Do I need to say it a third time?"

They looked at each other. Amy wasn't going to back down.

"Okay," said Lisa at last. "Okay. I'll leave you in peace."

"Thank you."

But as Lisa walked away, she knew the time was coming when she wouldn't be able to turn a blind eye any more.

***

Amy left the station, making sure she wasn't being followed, and then checked her phone. One call now could end this. She was tired. Tired of running. Tired of hiding. Tired of breaking the rules. But she couldn't make the call. Not yet. There were still loose ends to resolve. She looked at the list. Olof Lindberg, Marzia Neri, Axel Meier, Lukáš Mäsiar, Eden Mills. Graham March himself. Six down, six to go. It was time to get back to work.

Chapter 34

CLARE dropped me off outside the Royal Scot hotel and said she'd be along in a moment. It was a different hire car. I don't know when she'd swapped it. Maybe the one she'd punched in the face last night had been the man in the rental place.

Danny was in the bar, chatting to a man who I guessed was in his mid-forties, with receding hair and an ill-fitting suit. Simon Oakley. I expected his handshake to be clammy but it was reassuringly firm and dry.

"Are you sure you weren't followed?" asked Danny.

"Positive. I got a taxi, and it took a few detours." It was kind of true. "How long are you booked in here for?"

"Just a couple of nights for now, but I'm playing it by ear."

"You can both stay at mine if you're looking for somewhere," said Simon. "It's not much, but it's reasonably clean."

"I appreciate the offer," said Danny. "And I appreciate you're doing your level best to come across as a reasonable person. But I do know you, you know. I'm happy to work with you on this but let's keep it professional, okay?"

"Danny, mate, I'm trying to put things right between us."

"One step at a time, then."

I ordered a Sauvignon Blanc because I hadn't had one in ages. Danny insisted on paying for it, which was decent. Perhaps he'd come to his senses and was trying to win me back. Or maybe he was just being nice. Either way, I was running out of money so it was handy. I kept the door in my eyeline for any sign of Clare.

"So," I said. "What's the plan?" I glanced at Danny, then Simon. Both seemed keen to let the other speak first. Simon was first to crack.

"There is something I need to tell you," he said, sounding nervous. "In the interests of being completely on the level."

Danny rolled his eyes. I think we both expected the worst.

"What?" he said.

"I told you I was working on a bigger story. About Mike. And that was true. But there was another reason why I didn't want you to run the Graham March story."

"It's coming out now. Which was?"

"Look, mate, this is embarrassing, all right? But I want to be honest with you. I used to have a problem. Gambling. I've dealt with it now but I got in a mess. I ran up debts. March sorted it for me."

"He lent you money?"

"Yeah. But not at the usual interest rate. As long as I made the repayments, there wasn't any interest. But he wanted to know what was going on at the Echo."

"Jesus. So you were protecting him?"

"No, he never asked me to do that. I think he wanted the insight on Mills more than anything. But if we'd run the story, it could have upset things, if you know what I mean. It was my self-interest. I'm sorry."

Danny's eyes narrowed. He didn't look happy.

"And did he get you to plant evidence against me?"

"No. God's honest truth."

"Were you up to date on repayments?"

"I was. But now he's dead, I can go back to being myself. Everyone has a secret. Don't judge by what you see unless you know the story. I had to tell you so there are no more skeletons."

"Don't judge. Don't assume. Question everything. That's Clare's mantra," said Danny.

"I know." Simon looked more vulnerable than I'd have ever expected, given what I knew of his reputation. Either he was being honest or he was an accomplished actor. "I am so sorry for the person I was. That's the motivation for doing what I can to make it up to you. And I want to clear your name so you can go back to work. You're a good journalist, Danny. And a good man. You don't deserve all that shit."

Danny took a sip of his pint.

"I don't know that I want to go back. I think I've lost that trust. I'm thinking of going freelance."

"Wow. Jesus. We'll miss you."

"You've survived without me the last three months."

"Yes, and look at the mess it's in. Seriously, though, if you do that I'll understand why. But I still want to clear your name. I'll give you a joint byline on this. And I could do with the help. This is all unpaid overtime for me."

I thought it was time to join in the conversation.

"You haven't got a story yet, though, have you? Everyone thinks it's Clare. She's adamant it isn't and she's being set up."

"I know," said Simon.

"So where does that leave you?"

"It leaves us either believing that she did it, or finding the person who's setting her up. Which seems the preference if the police aren't going to bother."

"But who's doing it?"

It was Danny's turn to take over.

"We're thinking it might be Curtis," he said.

"Who's he?"

"Detective Chief Superintendent. He's the main man running the search."

"Wow. You don't think it could be Amy Cranston?"

"*Amy?*" He sounded incredulous. Not surprising: put it like that, it sounded stupid. It had seemed a lot more plausible when Clare was explaining it. "Why do you think Amy?"

"I don't know. Just something somebody said. She doesn't seem herself. I wondered if she was connected."

Danny didn't seem impressed by the suggestion.

"I can't see it being Amy," he said, shaking his head. "Anyone but."

"I'll tell you what I'm going to do," said Simon. "First thing tomorrow I'm going to see March's wife."

"Rafaela?" said Danny. "Why?"

"To see if there were any links with Curtis. She might have heard them speaking. Maybe they met. Maybe he came round for dinner."

"Do you want me to come with you?"

Simon thought for a moment.

"Leave this one to me. I don't know if it would be insensitive given what happened and your history with her husband."

"I imagine she'd have been glad to see the back of him."

"Have you seen her?"

"No, I've just heard the name."

Simon exhaled.

"I'm telling you, I don't know what she saw in him. She's about twenty years younger and fit." He gave me an apologetic half-smile. "Sorry, that sounded sexist."

I shrugged. It did. But I was intrigued.

"But wasn't he constantly visiting prostitutes?" I said. "How long had they been together?"

"Not long, from what I can gather. Maybe she used to be one." He looked at me again. "Sorry."

"Don't mind me. There's nothing wrong with being a prostitute if you're doing it through choice."

I gazed around the bar. There may well have been a few not very far away. This was Kings Cross, after all.

"Do you know anything about this Lukáš Mäsiar?" I asked.

Simon looked blank. Danny explained about the Slovak arms dealer who'd mysteriously vanished.

"I don't think the police are making it public," he said. "Not until they've got a body, at least."

"I'll make some enquiries," said Simon.

I was getting increasingly worried about Clare's non-appearance.

"I'm just going to pop to the ladies'," I said.

There was someone standing at the sink when I got there, so I reapplied lipstick, waiting for her to leave. I thought I looked tired, and my hair was a mess. It's not always the easiest to keep under control. As soon as I was on my own, I took out my phone. Just as Clare emerged from a cubicle.

"You seem safe," she said.

"How did you even get in? I've been watching the door."

"I have ways."

"How are we getting home?"

"Keep your phone on you. I'll send a message."

"And are you okay?"

"I think so. How's it going?"

"They think it's Curtis. Simon's going to interview March's wife."

"Good." She stepped forward and gave me a hug.

"You're doing great," she said.

I didn't think I was doing anything.

I rejoined the others, leaving Clare behind. But almost immediately Simon had a message on his pager.

"I've got to call the office," he said, after reading it. "Sorry."

The call lasted less than a minute.

"Got to go. Keep in touch, okay? Anna, lovely to meet you." He shook my hand again. And then a moment later he was gone.

It seemed strange sitting at the bar with just Danny. It was something we'd done a hundred times before, but this was the first time since he'd completely betrayed me.

"Where are you staying?" he asked.

"Do you really want to know?"

"It's why I asked."

"With Clare."

"Are you sure that's safe?"

"No."

"How are you getting back there?"

"I'm waiting for a message."

"Do you want to come back to my room?"

I raised an eyebrow.

"I hope you're not thinking of any funny business," I said. Although to be fair, I wouldn't have been averse.

I was testing Danny's bed for comfort, in a sadly platonic way, while he set up his notebook computer on the desk and tried to find a phone socket for the modem. There was a knock at the door.

"Expecting anyone?" I asked. He shook his head. I had a suspicion I knew who it was, but my pulse quickened just in case I was wrong.

"Can I come in?" said Clare, when Danny opened the door.

She was wearing sunglasses, even though it was a dimly lit corridor. The hat was a nice touch.

Danny moved aside to let her pass.

"Simon will be gutted when he knows he missed you," he said.

"Will he?" I thought it was a strange thing to say. But then she seemed significantly more stressed than she had about fifteen minutes earlier in the ladies'.

"Are you all right?" I asked.

"Yeah. Is this a smoking room?" she asked, pulling out the chair from beneath the desk and then collapsing into it.

"No," said Danny.

"Sod it. I'll give you the money to cover the fine." She reached into her coat pocket and withdrew a packet of Silk Cut. But then presumably had a pang of conscience and didn't light one.

Danny moved to open a window anyway.

"You don't look all right," I said.

"I'm fine." She sat back and closed her eyes. Sometimes she scared me more than others. It was like living with a temperamental rottweiler. "Simon was Graham's best friend, Danny," she said.

"We discussed that. They had an arrangement."

"And you trust him?"

"I'm giving him the benefit of the doubt for the moment."

"Okay. Your decision."

Danny turned to me and pulled a "what's going on here?" face. I shrugged.

She opened her eyes and turned to me.

"We should get going. We've got an early start tomorrow."

"Yes, you said you had," I said.

She sighed.

"Anna, stop being annoying and do as you're told for once."

"But I don't want to go to Bratislava."

"Bratislava?" said Danny.

"Apparently Clare's going to find Lukáš. Wants me to go with her. I'm thinking that if there's a chance of meeting a murdering maniac of a gun dealer, I'd probably rather stay at home and watch Neighbours."

"I didn't know you watched Neighbours," he said.

"I don't. That's the point."

"It's important that you meet him," said Clare, butting in.

"Why?"

"Oh, just trust me for once, okay?"

There were so many things I could have said in response to that. I hadn't had a chance to choose the best before she turned to Danny.

"Danny," she said.

"Clare."

"We're going away for a day. I get the sense that the proverbial is about to hit the fan, because something has happened that was an accident, but keep the faith, okay? Just don't believe everything you hear about me."

"What accident?"

"Just, you know. An accident. Nothing to worry about. But I'll look after Anna and all will be okay. Can you please stay safe in the meantime?"

"I'll try."

"Lisa will want to know if you've seen me. Sorry, Anna. But she will. I'd prefer it if you said you hadn't."

"What if I say I have?"

"That really wouldn't be helpful."

"Okay." I could sense Danny was getting as frustrated as me. "So are you gong to tell me about the accident?"

She sighed again.

"I'd love to. But really, the important thing is to keep up the good work. Look into Curtis. Speak to Simon. I think it'd be worth talking to Rafaela too."

"We're already on that."

"Excellent work. I trained you well." She sounded tired. "Come on then, Miss Burgin. We've got bags to pack."

It would have been nice to stay with Danny, in the comfort of his hotel room, but I got the sense she wasn't going to take no for an answer.

Chapter 35

Wednesday March 20th, 1996

DC Lisa Miller was glad she'd skipped breakfast. It was one less thing to throw up. It was only 8am but she was standing in the basement of a building near Kings Cross station and already it was looking like a bad day.

DCI Rogan Court was talking to the forensics officer, close to the scene of the crime. The body was contorted, covered in blood, but still tied to the chair where he'd died. A tarot card lay on the floor amid the carnage.

"Time of death was Monday evening," he said when he joined her. "They'll know more when they get him back, but first impressions are late on Monday. Although ironically, it looks like heart failure rather than the beating."

It was eerily quiet in the basement. Outside she knew there'd be heavy traffic, but it wasn't permeating the walls. The room looked well equipped as a place of torture. A baseball bat lay on the floor. The only light came from a bare overhead bulb, which did little to illuminate the peeling black paint on the walls.

"What is this place? And where the fuck is Cranston?" Rogan continued. "Call her, can you? She should be here."

Lisa took out her mobile phone and called Amy.

"It's going to voicemail, boss. I do know a bit about the history of this place though, and I think I recognise him."

"Enlighten me."

"It looks like Jimmy Divine."

"Sounds like a made-up name. Should I know him?"

Lisa took a deep breath, and moved to the door. Anything to get away. Rogan followed.

"We questioned him last year over Graham March's loan-sharking scam. The suspicion was, Jimmy was the muscle. Don't pay on time and Jimmy would give you a reminder. Across the knees."

"Sounds a nasty bastard."

"Did you never come across him in Vice?"

"Should I have?"

"I only know what I heard last year, but apparently he had form for running private club nights. Function rooms full of punters and a handful of strippers who were expected to get interactive. He was the pimp."

Rogan let out a low whistle.

"Nice guy."

"It gets worse. Let's just say the girls weren't all willing participants. There were a lot of drugs. We think that's when he met March. But evidence magically disappeared and the prosecution fell apart. And then, a little while later, they're in business together."

"Coincidence."

"One of many."

They moved aside to let the photographer though.

"It's strange, though, isn't it? Yes, there's a connection with March, but I don't see him as part of some elite business network," Lisa continued.

"That's just what I was thinking. Unless he was there as a kind of enforcer."

She shook her head.

"I can't see it. Jimmy was lowlife."

Rogan went back into the room, and indicated for Lisa to follow. They walked around, giving the body a wide berth, taking in the depressing decor.

"You'd pity the poor bastards he brought down here," he said. "Still, it's one less scumbag on the streets."

One fewer, thought Lisa, but didn't correct him aloud. Instead, she walked towards the chair and pointed to the card left propped up, next to the body.

"It's different."

"In what way?"

"Take a look."

DCI Court looked down. Through the blood spatter he could make out the word "justice".

"So no longer the hanged man?"

"Presumably it symbolises retribution. An eye for an eye, a severe beating for a severe beating."

"So you're thinking revenge? Punishment?"

"Could be either."

"Same killer, though?"

"On the face of it."

They took a step back to let the photographer continue his work.

"But you're not so sure?" continued Rogan.

"There's a definite link to March."

"Was Jimmy Divine at the funeral?"

"I'd have to check to be certain, but I think so."

"Find out for definite. Where was Woodbrook on Monday?"

"If we knew that, we'd have arrested her."

"Sorry, stupid question." They walked back to the door. "I'll finish up here. You head back. Get hold of any CCTV you can of the street, and surrounding streets." He paused, frowning. "You don't look happy."

"It's just the card that's bothering me. If it's the same killer, fine, it's a different card but it's another on the list. But if it's not, it's either a huge coincidence, or some kind of a message."

"Somebody in competition?"

"Maybe. But we haven't released the information about the cards. Which means if it's not the killer, it's someone close to the investigation."

"Keep trying Cranston," he said.

"I will." But something told her it was going to be a futile task.

The wheels touched down in Bratislava before it was even time to wake up, and yet I'd already travelled nearly a thousand miles. One of the many benefits of chartering a private plane was that we didn't need to wait for our bags at a luggage carousel. But there again, the airport we'd arrived at seemed to be little more than a hut at the side of a field. And I was travelling light. Apparently it was going to be a day trip.

"Why, exactly, am I here?" I asked, as we stood in the freezing cold, beside the plane, presumably waiting for transport.

"I told you. I want you to meet Lukáš."

"Excellent, another corpse."

"Lukáš isn't dead."

"But why do you want me to meet him?"

"Because he's been a naughty boy."

"Clare, I don't go for bad boys. You know that. You've met Danny. I go for the type you could happily take home to your mum, albeit if you had a mum you wanted to go home to."

Clare grinned.

"What is it with your mum?" she asked.

"I don't want to talk about it."

"But we have an agreement. No secrets. Tell me everything about your mum."

"Clare, are you delusional?"

"No."

"You're telling me you don't have secrets from me."

"I told you everything in Venice."

"Since Venice. Very specifically since Venice."

She shrugged.

"A lot happens in life. I don't keep a diary. I may occasionally forget to tell you things, but that's not the same as keeping secrets. I'd like to meet your mum. Can you arrange it?"

"No I bloody can't." The less we talked about my mum the better. It was very much time to change the subject.

"So if we don't have secrets, where were you on Monday night?" I asked.

"Monday?"

"Don't pretend you can't remember. You went out and came back covered in blood."

"Hardly covered."

"Hardly a scratch on the arm, though, either. So where were you?"

"I told you. Just seeing an old acquaintance."

In the distance I could see car headlights approaching, even though it was daylight. I hoped it was a friendly taxi rather than some Slovak gangster coming to kill us.

"Who?" I asked.

"Let me tell you the way this works," said Clare.

"I already know. We don't have secrets. You just said so yourself. So I ask questions and you answer them."

"In the general sense. And I don't have secrets. You already know more about me than anyone else alive."

"That sounds ominous, knowing you."

"But sometimes it's better not to involve you in things for your own protection," she said, ignoring me.

"Right."

"So if, hypothetically, I had to go and meet someone who arguably wasn't pleased to see me, then you have to trust me that the reason I don't go into all of the gory details is not because I'm keeping a secret, but because it's for the greater good."

"The greater good?"

"Either because there's less chance of you getting into trouble if you don't know the details, or because I care about your opinion of me, and I'm worried that might change."

"But just to be specific, the details are gory?"

She was smiling again.

"It's a turn of phrase. Your mum, on the other hand. I struggle to imagine her as anything other than a lovely old lady."

It was an impressive conversational segue, but I wasn't falling for it.

"I'm still not going to introduce you."

"Why not?"

"Because I care about your opinion of me, and I'm worried that might change."

"Oh, you're clever. But I will get it out of you."

"You can try."

"I have ways."

"I'm sure you do."

"You don't want to test me."

"No, and equally I don't want to be standing at the side of a field in the middle of nowhere, freezing my tits off. So can you please take me to wherever we're going? And ideally not get me killed?"

The car pulled up alongside us. We climbed in the back. Clare spoke to the driver in a language that wasn't English. It may have been Slovak. It could have been completely made up for all I knew.

"Where are we going?" I asked.

"We won't be long," she said.

Within a few minutes we were pulling into a bumpy farm track, still in the middle of nowhere. The car stopped.

"Now what?" I said.

"We wait."

"For what?"

"To see what happens."

My mind was just beginning to wander into all kinds of unhelpful areas when a car appeared in the distance, slowing as it approached, and then turned towards us down the track.

"Wait here," said Clare, getting out of the car.

She closed the door. The other car stopped and a man got out of the driver's side and walked towards her, his breath clouding in the air. They didn't hug but I got the impression they knew each other. And then I remembered we were on the trail of an arms dealer who was possibly the person going round killing everyone, on the off-chance it wasn't Clare. Then I saw he was very definitely holding a gun, and not for the first time I knew I was way out of my depth.

Chapter 36

DANNY awoke to the sound of his mobile phone, interrupting a wonderful dream. The surroundings were unfamiliar and it took him a moment to gather his senses. He reached out to switch on a light, but it was excessively bright for first thing in the morning.

"Hello," he said, disorientated, his eyes too closed to see the number.

"Danny, it's Simon. There's been another murder. Another tarot card."

That made him sit up, wiping the sleep from his eyes, trying to focus his mind.

"Who? When?"

"I don't know the details. Just what I've told you. Can you call Lisa?"

"I'm on it. I'll call you back."

Danny stretched, trying to shake life into his body. He rubbed his face, had a sip of water, then pressed the preset for DC Lisa Miller.

"Is it true?" he asked, once they'd covered the basics.

"I can't really talk about it. But we will need to question you again."

"Me? Why?"

"Hold on."

He could hear footsteps, and rustling.

"Sorry about that," said Lisa, after a moment. "I just needed to get out of there. Are you okay to talk for a moment?"

"Of course."

"There are things that I need to tell you. Everything's escalating."

"Are you okay?" She didn't sound okay.

"I'm worried."

"You're scaring me."

"These are scary times, Danny. Where are you now?"

"I'm at a hotel. Kings Cross. Can I meet you?"

"That's perfect. Hold on." More footsteps. More rustling. "Which hotel?"

"The Royal Scot."

"Room number?"

"804."

"I'm not going to have long but I'll be there in a few minutes."

———

After an agonising wait, Clare got back into the car. She didn't look happy.

"That wasn't Lukáš then, I take it," I said.

"No, but I was rather hoping he'd take us to him. He says he doesn't know where he is. Hasn't heard from him for a fortnight."

"Since he went to London?"

"Exactly."

Clare said something to our driver, and we set off. The fields liked like any other fields at home, but the road signs were unintelligible. It didn't seem a good time to ask about the gun.

"That's buggered things, then," I said instead. "Would anyone else know?"

"Oh, he knows. He's just not saying."

Brilliant.

"Who was he?"

"Someone I thought I could trust."

"Is it possible to give him the benefit of the doubt? Maybe he just doesn't know."

She looked at me as though I was a child.

"It's all a game, Anna. Lukáš knows I'm coming for him. He's just being a dick about it."

"Unless he is actually dead."

"He isn't. Not yet, anyway."

I let that pass.

"So what now?"

"We're going for lunch."

"Lunch?" I hadn't expected that.

"Do you have a problem with lunch?"

"No. It just sounds remarkably civilised. And it's only technically still time for breakfast."

"I'll tell you what we're going to do. We're going to find a café, get a table, close to the window. We're going to make it easy for them."

I didn't like the sound of that.

"What are you talking about?"

"I'll tell you how this works. Lukáš now knows we're here. Which means he's going to want to do one of two things. Either he's going to disappear again, and we've had a wasted journey, or curiosity is going to get the better of him and he'll want to know why we're here. So he'll be watching us, seeing what we're up to."

"At the risk of stating the obvious, he probably thinks you're here to kill him. If you haven't already."

"That's always a danger." I searched for a flicker of humour, but she seemed worryingly serious. "But he knows that if I'd wanted to do that, I could have done it on Friday."

"Everyone thinks you did."

"And crucially, I didn't."

The fields gave way to buildings, as though we were entering the outskirts of a town.

"So what did you actually meet him about? Call me naïve, but why would a nice, apparently law-abiding person such as yourself want to have a covert meeting with a Slovak arms dealer?"

She looked at me, with a focus that scared me. I knew other people had died looking into the very same eyes.

"You know, it's a good job I like you," she said.

"You're not going to tell me, are you? I mean, why am I even here?"

"I'll tell you exactly once we reach the café."

We were dropped off close to Bratislava's pedestrianised city centre. It was quite quaint in an olde-worlde kind of a way. There were lots of shops with their shutters still down. None of the names looked familiar. There were lots of people, wrapped up against the cold, making their way, oblivious of my discomfort.

A small bistro appeared to be open. True to her word, Clare led me inside and then to a table by the window. I expected it would get busy later. The place was largely deserted.

Clare ordered me a bottle of wine while we looked at the lunch menu, and then took out her cigarettes, as though desperate to light one.

"Should we be drinking alcohol?" I asked.

"You like wine."

"I do, but equally it's still first thing in the morning and I think I'm going to need to keep my wits about me."

"And I think you're going to need a drink."

The waitress arrived with a bottle and asked Clare if she

wanted to sample it. She nodded and a small measure was poured. Clare swilled it around her glass and then breathed in the aroma and nodded. She didn't actually taste it. The waitress poured a measure into both of our glasses.

I took a taste. It was surprisingly good, but there again, I hadn't seen the price. Clare left her glass untouched. We ordered a couple of ciabattas, filled with something that resembled ham and cheese, but was no doubt the Slovak equivalent. It could have been anything.

"You're not drinking?" I asked when the waitress left.

"I'm going to tell you about Lukáš," she said, avoiding the question, but tapping a cigarette on the table. "I admit, I did go to see him on Friday. It was important that we met on my terms."

That was a start, but I was still far from happy.

"Call me a cynic," I said, "but would you describe sitting in the window of a restaurant in Bratislava as an extension of seeing him on your own terms? Or could it, perhaps, be argued that we are, in fact, sitting ducks?"

"The latter, if this had been before Friday. What did Amy tell you?"

"That apparently you were trying to broker some deal. She didn't give me specifics."

"Okay. Well, she wasn't wrong with that." She fired up her lighter, but then let the flame go out. "I have been negotiating with him. And on Friday it became rather urgent that I had to bring those negotiations to a conclusion."

"That sounds dramatic. Although obviously I've got no idea what you mean, because I still don't know what you were negotiating."

She was getting irritated, but I wasn't in the mood to pander.

"Well, listen and I'll tell you," she said. "Lukáš was one of the cabal. In many ways he was the leader of it. Certainly one of the most influential. And yes, somebody is going round killing all the members, but it certainly isn't me."

So she kept saying, but I still had my doubts.

"What were you discussing?"

She leaned across the table and lowered her voice.

"Anna, my darling," she said. "This is going to come as a bit of a shock. But there was only one thing on the agenda on Friday night. And that one thing was you."

Chapter 37

ANNY had not long emerged from the shower when there was a knock on the door. He grabbed the bathrobe and wrapped it around himself before opening it. Lisa extended her arms and gave him a hug. They kissed.

"I haven't got long but I just wanted to see you," she said.

"You look worried. Are you okay?"

"I've just come from a murder scene. It wasn't nice."

"Was that the one Simon was asking about?"

"I assume so."

He led her inside and they sat on the bed.

"Who was it?"

"Danny, is this you as a friend or you as a journalist? I shouldn't say anything. I told you - there's a massive conflict of interest here."

"As a friend. You know that."

"But you're talking to Simon at the Echo?"

"I won't tell him anything you don't want me to. But he knows about the body, even if he doesn't know the details. He was the one who rang me."

Lisa looked troubled. Danny hated to see her like this. He hated the thought that she was under so much pressure. But he knew that it was the adrenaline that drove her on.

"Oh, you know what?" she said after a moment. "To hell with it. It was Jimmy Divine."

"Wow. I've heard of him. March's muscle?"

"Yeah."

Danny let out a low whistle. Jimmy wasn't the kind of person you'd take on lightly.

"What happened?" he asked.

"Handcuffed to a chair and beaten up, but he actually died from a heart attack, according to forensics." She threw her head back, looking defeated. "Oh, Danny, there's some weird shit going on."

"What sort of stuff."

"For starters, Amy's gone AWOL."

"Amy? What do you mean?"

"She didn't turn up at the scene, she's not answering her phone. Nobody's seen or heard from her."

Lisa rubbed her face with her right hand. Danny reached out for her left.

"Should we be worried?" he asked.

"I don't know. I don't know anything any more. It's like... At the beginning, everyone was talking about this network, and going on about how Graham March wasn't the only one of us involved."

"One of us?"

"Police. But at the same time, all the attention is now on finding Clare. Nobody ever talks about the possibility of there being someone corrupt within the job any more. It's like, since the new DCS took over, all that's been forgotten. And yet this murder was different in some ways. Still close enough that if it wasn't the same killer, it was someone who knows a hell of a lot about the others. There was a tarot card, but it was a different one."

"You don't think the new DCS is the famous friend in high places?"

Lisa shook her head, looking worried.

"I don't know what to think any more. Because I did start thinking that, and I tried to talk to Amy about it, but she brushed it aside. Said I shouldn't give it any more thought. I should just focus on finding Clare. It was like she'd completely closed her mind and was shutting me out."

"You know what she's like. She likes to do things in a certain way, sticking to procedure and following orders."

"But that's exactly it. I don't think she's doing that any more. I followed her when she left yours yesterday because I wanted to try again, but she seemed in a hurry. So I followed her anyway because I was curious. And the next thing, she was putting some stuff in a left luggage locker at Kings Cross. Or taking it out. One or the other."

"Did she see you?"

"Yes. And she wasn't happy. And now she's disappeared. What if she's involved, Danny?"

Maybe it was time to think the unthinkable.

"You know, if you'd said this to me this time yesterday, I'd have said you had to be imagining it. But I spoke to Anna last night and she was talking about Amy as well. In front of Simon as well. Sorry."

"Shit." Lisa paused. "It's getting out of control. You spoke to Anna?"

"Yes. She came here."

"I don't suppose she mentioned where Clare was?"

"We agreed this was a friend-type conversation."

"Oh come on, Danny. We did, but did she? I'm sorry but this is still very much a live investigation. Which is why they want to drag you in for more questions, just so you know."

Danny let go of her hand.

"For the hundredth time, I have absolutely no idea where Clare is. Or Anna at this moment, for that matter. All I know is that Anna is spooked. Someone destroyed her studio. We've had armed police round the flat. Neither of us feels like we can go back there, and Clare, who has been a good friend to both of us, is seemingly number one on the Met's most wanted list."

Lisa still didn't try to explain. Anything would have been reassuring.

"What did she say about Amy?" she asked, instead.

"Not much. Just that Clare thinks she could be connected. Nothing specific, though."

"So she's been talking to Clare then? For God's sake, Danny. This is serious. If I find out you're lying to me or not telling me something you know, I'm going to be seriously pissed off."

Danny realised his error and backtracked.

"I'm assuming it was Clare. She said 'somebody'. I'm not hiding anything. I can't vouch for Anna. But whatever she does, she'll be doing it for the right reasons."

"The right reasons?" She turned towards him, then stood up. "Has the entire world gone mad? Danny, I can't reiterate this strongly enough. Anna is in severe danger."

"She would be if she was still at home, but Clare for all her faults has a habit of protecting her."

"For heaven's sake, please let's not fall out over this."

"I'm only telling you how it's always been."

"Really? Always? So there's nothing different this time, then?"

Danny sighed.

"Okay, it's different. There are lots of accusations. We don't know what's true, and you're not telling me what the hell is going on."

"There's a lot more than accusations, Danny. You know we've got DNA. And now we have a witness that places Clare at the scene just before Eden Mills was killed. Let her into the house. Didn't see her leave. I hate to say it Danny, but the fact is, Clare is on a killing spree. She's gone mad. Trigger happy. The powers that be think there's absolutely no doubt about it. And wherever she is, whatever she's got planned, if she's using Anna as some sort of shield then Anna is at mortal risk."

Danny stood up as well, and joined Lisa. He tried to hug her but she moved away.

"I'm going to have to go," she said. "I don't think I'm getting through to you. I've got so much to do, but it's good to see you. Just be very careful what you say to Simon, Danny. To anyone. And if Anna gets in touch, get her to come in and see me."

"Okay. But if Simon asks about the murder scene?"

"There'll be some sort of statement later." She turned to leave, but then softened. "If you're free this evening, Jessica would love to see you, I'm sure. And I would too. I'll cook you dinner."

"Will you even be home this evening?"

"I've got no idea, but I hope so. I'm not even supposed to be in at all today. Can we aim for seven?"

"Of course, but call me, okay? And yes, I'd love to."

They hugged and then kissed goodbye, but Danny didn't think her heart was in it. He started to get dressed, wondering if he would ever get to kiss her again.

"What do you mean, I was the only thing on the agenda?" I asked, feeling significantly uncomfortable at the prospect.

"It's why I needed you to come with me."

"Clare, I know I keep saying this, but you really are scaring me."

"You don't have to be scared."

"I'm permanently scared."

Outside, people were walking past. They looked different to people in England but I couldn't work out exactly why. Maybe it was their clothing. Maybe it was that more of them were smoking. Everyone seemed to be on a mission. Nobody was hanging around, obviously watching us. But still I wondered if any of them were spying for a gun-dealing psycho nutcase. Clare reached out for my hand and squeezed it. I looked down at her ring, imagining the stories it could tell.

"Lukáš wasn't - isn't - a pleasant man," she said. "You remember during the Balkan war, how lots of weapons were shipped through Vienna?"

It rang a vague bell. I nodded in the absence of anything better to do.

"Well, he was very much part of that. Bratislava may be in Slovakia, but it's right on the Austrian border and Vienna's just up the road. But as well as that, he's fiercely loyal to his own."

"What does that mean?"

"What that means is that when Graham died, he took it personally. He wanted to take revenge on those he thought were responsible. But despite his job, and what you might expect, he's not a killer. He's a hard-as-nails businessman, but he's never knowingly been violent."

"Knowingly? So who did he think was responsible for Graham?"

Her expression was worrying me.

"Three people. And bizarrely, none of them pulled the trigger."

"Who then?"

"Me, obviously. But then also, by association, Danny, and you."

"Oh, for fuck's sake." I just wanted to go home. "This is outstanding. So you're telling me some possibly deranged Slovak arms dealer has a vendetta against me? And you've brought me here - to what? Get brutally murdered?"

"No. I've brought you here because when he meets you, he'll begin to understand what I told him last Friday."

"Oh God, you're talking in riddles."

Clare topped up my glass but still didn't touch her own.

"He's been looking at ways to destroy us all," she continued. "Not to kill us. But to get me banged up, to destroy Danny's career, and to put you so far out of business that you never work again. I've been meeting him. Trying to make him see sense. Telling him that I'm fair game, but that none of what happened has anything to do with you. But he wasn't responding well to those negotiations. And when I heard about your studio on Thursday... Well, I knew exactly who was behind it, and I knew things were getting way out of hand. So it was time to act."

I was beginning to get a headache. I drank more wine to numb it.

"So you killed him? For me?"

"Oh Anna, how many bloody times? No, I have not killed anybody. Get it into your head, will you? He admitted to me what he'd done, and I told him in no uncertain terms, that it was completely unacceptable. And you know what? He was scared of me too. As far as he was concerned, it was me who was going round killing members of his group over the last few days, and I did nothing to try to dispel that impression. So I gave him an ultimatum. Put everything back. Leave you and Danny out of it. Never bother you again. And if he did that, then just possibly I'd leave him until last on the list, giving him time to make himself scarce and difficult for me to find him."

"Excuse my language but fucking hell."

I reached for her cigarettes but she slapped my hand away,

"You're excused. And no, it wasn't easy, but eventually he did come round to my way of thinking. I gave him forty-eight hours to return everything or face repercussions. I even told him to leave you a bottle of Sauvignon by way of an apology. Have you been to the studio since Thursday?"

"No. I haven't had a car, if you remember."

"Good point."

"So are you saying everything will be back?" I felt a moment of real excitement and potential hope.

"No," she said, dashing it. "I drove past on Monday and it was still empty."

"Brilliant." The only other customer left the bistro. "Well, it's good to know you haven't lost your touch." I paused for a moment to let that sink in.

"I'm sorry." She didn't look happy, but I didn't know if it was with me or with herself.

I took a moment to process everything she'd said to me.

"You said he'd face repercussions. What sort of repercussions?" I asked at last.

"Let's just say, I know people who could make things very difficult for him. I have - somewhat unfairly, I think - developed a bit of a reputation over the last few years."

"So you said what? Lay off me or he'd have a visit in the night from someone with a baseball bat? Or an Uzi?"

"Not exactly. I gave him an ultimatum. Put everything back and leave a contribution towards the refurbishment, and we'd say no more. He could attempt to take it out on me if he could ever find me. But in the meantime, he had to promise to leave you alone. And he had forty-eight hours in which to do it."

"And again, what did you threaten?"

"It's not bad. Not really. Lukáš said he thought I was killing his network, which might have been a bluff if he was covering for himself, but for once it was actually quite useful. And if it wasn't me personally, then associates of mine, under my command. It's complete nonsense, of course..."

"Of course."

"... but it didn't seem a bad impression to leave him under. The only snag, of course, is that it isn't me. And if it was actually him who was doing it, as some sort of clean-up or retribution against his former friends, then he would have known I was bluffing him."

"Clare, nothing you're telling me is giving me a warm feeling about sitting in a restaurant window in Bratislava."

"But if it's not him," she continued, ignoring me, "then the recent loss of Eden Mills will have helped to get the message across."

"But if it is?"

"We may have an issue."

I'd heard enough.

"For fuck's sake. And yet we're still here?"

"We are. I wouldn't worry about it."

"What do you mean? Wouldn't worry about it? Just to reiterate, and correct me if I missed anything, some gun-dealing psychopath has got it in for me? The only possible way to stop that is for him to heed your warning, which if I'm not mistaken he has thus far ignored. And this, quite possibly, is because he's the one on a killing spree. So we've decided to visit him in his own backyard, to what? Make it easier for him to bury the bodies?"

"You're missing something."

"It had better be something big, because right at this moment I'm about to hail a taxi and leave on the first available flight, even if it means hitching a lift on a cargo plane."

"It's quite big. I'm pretty sure he's not the one going round doing the killing."

"I thought you just said he might be?"

"No, I told you. He doesn't do violence. Not that kind, anyway."

The cargo plane option was looking ever more appealing.

"Are you armed?" I asked.

"Do I look armed? Of course I'm not armed. Where would I get a gun from?"

"Er, hello. You're on the trail of a Slovak arms dealer. Presumably you've mixed in those circles."

"You have such a bad impression of me."

"Based on evidence, in fairness to myself."

"The cheek of it. No, I'm not armed. They don't know that, though."

That didn't exactly reassure me.

"But if we find Lukáš, he almost certainly will be?"

"Without doubt."

"There's the clincher, then. See you. Taxi time."

She reached out a hand to stop me.

"I guarantee he won't kill us."

"You're giving a guarantee? Like a money-back type of deal? You promise I'll get reincarnated if you've stuffed this up?"

"I won't stuff this up."

I sat back.

"Because what? He does what you tell him? I think we've just proved that he doesn't." I had another, even bigger gulp of the wine, and she topped me up again. "I'm putting a lot of faith in you here."

"Have I ever let you down before?"

"I can think of times where it hasn't gone altogether smoothly."

"Well, take my word, this will be fine. We just wait here for a bit and somebody will meet us."

I checked the street. There were even more people milling around, but still none looked like a spy. I was just giving up hope of anyone coming for us - or perhaps starting to succumb to feelings of utter relief - when a woman entered the restaurant. Clare nudged me under the table. But I'd already clocked her as she gave us the once-over before exchanging a few short words with the waitress. Then, to my surprise, possible dismay and almost certain joy, she turned and left as quickly as she'd arrived.

I looked at Clare but her attention was fixed elsewhere. The waitress was approaching.

"Your bill has been settled," she said, which took me by surprise. The food had yet to arrive and I still had most of the wine to devour.

Clare said something in a language I didn't understand, but which was possibly the Slovak equivalent of "thank you", or else "are you throwing us out?". The woman's expression intrigued me. She could almost have been fighting back tears.

"You need to come with me," she said. Clare nodded. I quickly finished my glass and looked forlornly at the rest of the bottle. Clare was already standing and I didn't want to get left behind.

The waitress didn't say another word as she led us through the deserted kitchen. It was a good job I wasn't hungry, as nobody was cooking. I momentarily considered grabbing one of the knives that were arranged side by side on the work surface, but I couldn't imagine ever stabbing anyone, and suspected it would make the situation substantially worse.

A doorway led to a ramshackle office-cum-storage room full of cardboard boxes and chaos, together with an overpoweringly musty aroma. The waitress indicated to a sofa, which was only partly covered in detritus, then turned and left us, closing the door behind her and sniffing as she did so.

"This is nice," I said. And then added "what now?" when Clare didn't immediately respond.

"We wait," she said.

"What did you make of her?" I nodded in the direction of the door.

"Very curious."

"She looked upset."

"But only after that woman came in."

"I don't suppose you heard what was said?"

"Slovak isn't one of my strong suits. I'm just pleased we haven't fallen asleep yet."

"What? Are you tired?"

"No. Some of the places here are notorious for spiking the drinks. Rohypnol. GHB. You wake up in the street, your money has gone, your cards have been used to empty your accounts."

"Now you tell me."

"I thought it best not to worry you."

"Anything else you've elected not to mention?"

"No, I'm not big on secrets."

"Either you're taking the piss or you're deluded."

In the event, we didn't have to wait for long. A back door opened and a man entered. I didn't like his expression, but I liked his bodybuilder physique even less. He could have crushed me between two fingers. I didn't even dare think about what he could be carrying in the inside pocket of his jacket.

Chapter 38

ONCE he was dressed, Danny called Simon.

"I spoke to Lisa," he said. "She couldn't say much but confirmed it was March's enforcer, Jimmy Divine."

"Jesus. Jimmy!" Simon let out a breath. "Did you ever meet him?"

"No."

"Consider yourself lucky. He was an absolute sadist. Loved nothing more than beating the fuck out of vulnerable people. Men, women, didn't matter. Be a day late and Graham would be on your case. Any more and it was an appointment with Jimmy's famous chair. Not many walked out of there. Or walked ever again, given the state of their kneecaps."

"But you still protected him?"

"Not Jimmy. I had no option with Graham, but Jimmy was scum. I'm not sorry he's had a taste of his own."

"Even so, though..."

"Look, Danny. It's a dirty, mixed-up world, okay? I was playing the long game. I was going to get him eventually. Hold on."

Danny could hear traffic noise in the background, with lots of indistinct voices. He was glad of the calm of his hotel room, and yet simultaneously felt isolated and powerless. After a few moments, the noise diminished and Simon came back.

"Sorry about that. I went somewhere better," he said.

"Where are you?"

"I just left March's wife, so I'm heading back."

"How was Rafaela? Any links?"

"Nothing, which is a bit of a bastard. Never heard of Curtis till the eulogy, apparently. I gather she didn't have much to do with Graham all round. She could definitely have done better."

Anyone would have been better than Graham.

"So what's your instinct?" asked Danny.

"My instinct is that we're still a bit up shit creek. I'll keep working on it, though."

"Okay. Let me know if you hear anything."

"Likewise, mate. And keep working on tracking down Clare."

"Bye."

Danny lay back on the bed, staring at the ceiling, trying to work out what he was missing. What was it Lisa had said? *"This murder was different in some ways. Still close enough that if it wasn't the same killer, it was someone who knows a hell of a lot about the others."*

Could it be someone else? Someone taking the opportunity to take revenge on an enemy while in prime position to blame it on someone else? Or was the different card deliberate? Giving a different message to someone?

Suddenly he had a disturbing thought. Who would want Jimmy dead? Someone who had suffered in his torture room. Someone Graham had lent money to, and who knew lots of details of the other murder scenes? He could only think of one name. And he'd just spoken to him.

Was Simon really capable of that? How well did he really know him? Yes, Simon had been all charm recently, but the four years previously? He'd always been a devious, conniving bastard.

But then, if that was possible, what did anything mean any more? Then Danny had darker thoughts still. Murderers like to return to the scene of their crimes. It's a classic trait. They want to pry into the investigation, checking how close the police are getting, feeling pride in their own cleverness at staying one step ahead.

Was Simon cosying up because he wanted to pin the murder of Jimmy onto Clare? Danny remembered Clare's words. *"Simon was Graham's best friend."*

That would explain why he was so keen to meet Clare. Not to hear her side of the story, but to copy what he thought were her methods, so she would take the blame. But Clare would see through that, and then what? Would Simon kill again? And once Danny had served his purpose, what then?

He was suddenly aware that things could be going very wrong indeed.

***

"You've come to see Lukáš?" he said, in heavily accented English.

I thought it best to keep quiet and let Clare do the negotiations, although I reserved the right to change my mind on that at any point. Equally, I thought it best not to mention that last bit out loud.

"Who are you?" she asked.

"I'm Stefan. A family friend. You should come with me now," he said. I suspected we weren't going to get much more out of him. The words sounded rehearsed.

I could see Clare processing this development. It seemed too easy. He could be genuine and this could be a significant advance. But equally it could be a trap. If we got in a car with him, we could easily end up buried in the woods. I waited for Clare to tell him we were good, and thanks but no thanks.

"Thank you," she said, indicating for me to stand and then

holding the door for me as we followed him outside. An ageing, dark blue Škoda that was badly in need of a wash was waiting, with its engine running. The lack of hubcaps gave the impression of a questionable service record, but I decided a breakdown would be the least of my worries.

Another man was behind the steering wheel. As Clare and I got in the back, I gave her a look that hopefully conveyed both a sense of extreme nervousness and absolute trust that she knew what she was doing. She seemed to understand it.

"Anna, sometimes you learn to rely on the fundamental decency of most human beings," she said. "Not everyone is going to attack you."

"If it's all right with, you I'll err on the side of caution," I said.

It was only a short journey, but we still saw a glimpse of the Bratislava that was clearly off the standard tourist trail. There were narrow, cobbled backstreets, walls covered in graffiti, but very few pedestrians. The car pulled up outside a dilapidated looking building, with ageing, sun-bleached bricks exposed through patches of missing render. Stefan got out and opened our door for us. I followed Clare, who in turn followed Stefan through an ancient wooden gate. There was a brass plaque on the wall, but I didn't know what it said.

It soon became obvious. We were shown through to a darkened room, decorated with flowers and candles. And there in the middle, in an open casket, was the body of a man I took to be Lukáš. Clare made a cross sign across her heart, then bowed slightly, reaching out to touch his hand. Then she stood aside for me to do the same. The hand was stone cold. He was very definitely dead. Oh fuck.

"It is good of you to come to pay your respects," said Stefan. "The family say they do not know you but they are very honoured that you have made the journey. That you have come all this way just to say farewell."

I nudged Clare with my foot but she gave me a look that said stay silent.

"Do you know what happened?"

"He was taken ill while overseas. We're still trying to find out exactly the circumstances. His family are very upset. We will all miss him."

"Yes, his passing has come as a great shock to us, too," she said, looking at me. I admit, I almost laughed.

But something about the way Stefan was looking at Clare suggested he was not going to let us off lightly.

"You were good friends, yes?" he asked.

"I can't imagine being anywhere else," said Clare.

"But you knew him well, yes?" Full marks for persistence. But before Clare could answer, he pulled us to one side and lowered his voice.

"His widow wants me to ask a... difficult question. Two beautiful women come to see him from England. She asked if you were, how shall I say... More than just friends?"

My bad feeling about the whole escapade was rapidly plumbing new depths.

"You must reassure her," said Clare, taking care to speak slowly and clearly, pronouncing every word with care. "We met through business. Through mutual acquaintances. I just found it hard to believe that such a strong man could... you know..."

"I understand," he said, then took a step back.

"How long are you in Bratislava?"

"Just for the day."

"So short. You must join us for dinner. Drink some Borovička. Let us show you our beautiful city."

"That's a very kind offer, but sadly we have a very tight schedule. And I already know Bratislava. My knowledge, of course, is not as in depth as yours, but I am familiar with its beauty."

"That is a shame. We would like to spend more time with you."

"And we likewise, but we have to fly to Berlin this afternoon. I am so sorry. This was just a brief stop to pay our respects to our great friend."

"I understand."

He stayed looking at us, alternating his focus from Clare to me and back again.

"Can I give you transport to the airport?" he said.

"Just back to the city, if that is okay," said Clare. "We have one small thing to do but will order a taxi from there."

"As you wish."

We spent the next ten minutes standing in increasingly uncomfortable silence, before eventually Clare linked her arm through mine and led me towards the door. Stefan followed. I was glad of the fresh air but temporarily blinded by the brightness of the sun after the dimly lit room.

Stefan opened the car door. This time I really did think we were going to be murdered, but true to his word, he dropped us back at the rear entrance of the bistro. Once we had said our goodbyes, it was just the two of us standing in the street.

"You're bloody good at faking it," I said. But Clare wasn't really listening.

"I have no idea who they thought we were," she said, "but we need to get out of here before they work it out."

Chapter 39

DS Amy Cranston parked her car in the middle of a derelict industrial estate on the eastern edge of London. She connected a call to DCS Paul Curtis.

"Your absence was noted this morning," he said, in lieu of pleasantries.

" I didn't have any option. It's getting serious. Lisa is beginning to ask questions. She keeps following me."

"You know her better than me. Do you think she knows?"

"About us?"

"Of course about us."

"I don't know. I don't know what she knows."

"That would not be helpful."

"I am aware of that."

How had it come to this? Amy had been well aware of the stakes at the outset, but now they were getting higher. Suffocatingly so.

"Do you think I would have agreed to this if I'd known the scale of it?" she said. "It's way out of control."

"We knew the risks, Amy."

"Did we?"

The DCS coughed, and cleared his throat.

"I'm speaking to you, not as a colleague. Not even as a friend. But as a partner, okay?" he said. "There's no good to come from looking inwards, blaming ourselves. But it will be finished soon."

"When they discover the other six bodies?"

"We should try to make sure that doesn't happen."

Amy looked out at the grey sky and the depressing landscape. It seemed appropriate to her ever-worsening state of mind.

"I think it's time for a new approach," Curtis continued.

"Really? At this stage?"

"Yes, my dear. I think it's time to start thinking about our end game. How we get out of this alive."

"I've thought of little else." She paused, while deciding to take a risk. "Lisa saw me at the drop."

There was an extended silence.

"Are you still there?" she asked, eventually.

"What did you tell her?"

"What could I tell her? Nothing. Just to stop stalking me and concentrate on finding Clare."

"I think it's time to forget Clare."

"Really?"

"Not officially, of course. It is convenient that she's so elusive. But we need to escalate this now. End it all, for good. It's time."

Danny was on the verge of phoning Lisa, telling her his theory and suggesting she should immediately arrest Simon Oakley, when his phone rang. It was the man himself.

"There have been some developments, Danny," he said. "The police seem to be falling apart. Amy's gone missing."

"I know. I heard about that."

"I need to see you. I really need you to find Clare."

Danny almost laughed at the ridiculousness of it.

"Listen, I'll tell you what I'll do. I'll get her round mine and book everyone in for half-hour slots, shall I? I'm sure she'll be up for that."

"Hey, there's no need to take it like that, mate."

"And can you please stop calling me mate?"

"Whoa, what's happened to you?"

Danny could feel his stress levels reaching breaking point.

"I've got to go," he said. "Call me if there's anything you need to tell me."

He ended the call then thought twice about calling Lisa. What if he was wrong? He wouldn't do anything without speaking to Clare, but where the hell was she now?

I don't think I'd ever seen Clare look quite as agitated. The usual calm professionalism had gone and she looked genuinely flustered. We headed to the nearest taxi rank. She spoke to the driver in something that wasn't English again. Presumably giving him the address of our airfield.

As we set off, Clare pinched the top of her nose, then put out a hand to stop me when I tried to start speaking.

"Sorry," she whispered after a moment. "Just keep an eye out, okay. Make sure we're not being followed."

I didn't know quite how I was supposed to do that. We were in a line of heavy traffic. Of course we were being followed, by probably thirty or forty cars. How on earth was I supposed to work out if any of them were doing it with malicious intent?

The driver's CB radio crackled into life. It sounded like a control room asking his whereabouts. I have no idea what he said but it sounded vaguely similar to the words Clare had used. The radio voice seemed to give an affirmative, and then the transmission ended. The driver turned up his radio, playing some mass-market, middle-of-the-road euro-pop.

Clare kept looking from side to side, then spoke to the driver again, raising her voice against the music. She must have asked him to change direction, because suddenly he turned hard right, followed the road for about quarter of a mile, then executed a U-turn, before waiting a moment and rejoining the road we'd just left.

"Do you see anyone else turning?" she asked me.

I didn't. I took that as a good sign.

"No."

"Keep looking."

Gone were any attempts to reassure me. This was about survival. I desperately wanted to speak to her, but I didn't want to break her concentration. This was what she did. She was good at this. But my attempts to convince myself weren't working. She looked scared. I'd never really seen her look scared before.

The driver continued, through several sets of traffic lights. Some were red, some were green. Some changed as we approached them. Others as we passed through. Finally Clare seemed to relax.

But then the driver did another hard right, and this time she hadn't given him an instruction. And I saw a look of panic in her eyes. A moment later he stopped the car outside a deserted farm building.

Stefan was standing there, waiting for us. I didn't like the look of him. Nor the gun he was holding in his massive fist, pointing directly at us.

He walked to our door. The gun seemed to get even bigger.

"Get out, both of you," he said, in his accented English. "Did you think I did not recognise you?"

Chapter 40

"HOW are you doing with the CCTV?" asked DCI Rogan Court.

Lisa turned her screen to face him.

"Shit," he said. Lisa nodded. They were looking at a grainy image from the street near Kings Cross where Jimmy Divine's body had been found. Lisa pressed play. Clare was clearly visible, walking towards the camera.

"Can we see where she's come from? Where she's going?"

Lisa rewound the tape.

"It's difficult. There isn't a camera that covers the entry to the basement. But this is just around the corner." She pressed play again, and then pointed to a section of the screen with the rubber end of a pencil. "She appears here. That's the corner. See the way she's walking when she comes into the shot? There's a definite change of direction. So yes, I think we can almost guarantee she's coming from the direction of the scene."

"And the time stamp fits?"

"It's perfect."

"Can you see her approaching if you go back earlier?"

"Not on this camera. It's a busy street, but I've gone back over the previous hour and there's no sign of her. But there are loads of roads round there. She could have come from any one of them."

Rogan patted Lisa on the shoulder.

"Good work," he said, but then exhaled. "Of course, the defence would say all it really proves is that she was still in London on Monday. So where the fuck is she hiding?"

"I'll keep looking, boss."

"Good girl."

Lisa bristled at being called a girl, but didn't let it show. For now. The DCI moved off, but she called after him.

"Still no sign of Amy?"

"Not yet," he said, turning back.

"You don't think Clare's got to her?"

"You mean like a hostage?"

"I..." She stopped. She didn't know who she could trust any more. Maybe nobody but herself. "I'm sure she'll turn up. She'll have her reasons."

Rogan turned and walked away, leaving Lisa to continue with the CCTV. But her mind was elsewhere. What was Amy up to? Was she the corrupt one? Or was it DCS Paul Curtis? And yet all of this had started just as Rogan Court made the transfer from Vice. Coincidence? Hadn't Graham March been involved in trafficking? Maybe it was all of them, all in it together.

She contemplated the image of Clare, staring out of the screen, thinking of the two most obvious questions. Where are you? What do you know?

"Sorry, Anna," said Clare, squeezing my hand.

I didn't know whether to be terrified or furious, so settled on a combination of the two. So this was it, then. Time to claim on the guarantee.

Stefan didn't wait. He pulled open the door and dragged me out. I stumbled and got a shove for the privilege. Clare followed, looking deeply concerned. He pulled her roughly by the arm. I rather hoped she was going to do some ninja combat move to disarm him, but he was huge, and it would have been a futile use of energy.

"Clare Woodbrook," he said. "And Anna Burgin."

He kept pointing the gun at us. We were standing on dried mud at the side of the road, away from anywhere apart from the derelict barn. There were cars on the main road, but they were all oblivious to our imminent execution. The chances of somebody turning down the track were beyond minimal.

"I admire your bravery," he continued. "But more amazed by your stupidity."

"We didn't know," said Clare. "We thought he was still alive. We came to negotiate. We had no idea he'd died."

Stefan laughed.

"And yet you are the woman who killed him!"

"No."

Without warning, he swept his arm up and smashed her across the face with his gun, breaking her skin. She reached up to her face. I saw blood seeping through her fingers.

"Move to my car," he said. It was parked a short distance away, but the engine was running. There was someone behind the steering wheel. I couldn't see if it was the same driver as before, but it was definitely the same car.

"Where are you taking us?" I asked.

He raised a fist, and I flinched, but the threat was enough and he didn't connect.

"The family want to meet you," he said. "What is the English expression? An eye for an eye?"

"Seriously," said Clare. "He was taken ill. I only helped him back to his room."

"You poisoned him." It was a statement, not a question.

"No. I promise you."

"The car. Try to run and I will shoot."

I looked at Clare, but she didn't return the glance. She was fixated on Stefan.

"Do you really think we'd have come all this way if I had something to hide?" she said.

"You came to gloat."

"No!"

He hit her again, this time a sickening punch to the stomach which left her bent double, gasping for air, blood running down her face. She looked smaller than normal. And far less in control. I reached out and helped her up, watching Stefan as his face turned ever more angry and insistent

"Are you okay?" I said, my voice weak with terror. But she shook her head. Tears in her eyes. Still fighting for air.

"I'm pregnant," she whispered.

Whatever I'd been expecting, I hadn't been expecting that. Speechless, I wiped her anguished, bloodied face, and then watched as she wrapped an arm instinctively and protectively around her stomach. It wasn't the time for the who, when, how, or even the what the fuck?

Stefan was five paces behind us. At least he couldn't hit anyone from that distance. Except possibly with a bullet. We walked slowly, and awkwardly, towards the car, tripping over the uneven surface. Stefan shouted us to get a move on. Threatened to shoot.

I stopped and turned back towards him, to tell him to piss off, but he was standing tall, legs apart, both hands holding his gun, pointing it directly at Clare. She stood motionless beside me. As though she was on the verge of giving up the fight.

"I shall count to three," he said.

But Clare still stood motionless.

"One."

Again, there was no attempt at movement.

"Two."

Clare hobbled forward. I had no option but to follow. We reached the car.

"Open the door and get in," said Stefan.

I reached out to the handle. Took one last breath of fresh air. One last look at the scenery. Thought one last time about running, but knew it was pointless. I'd die with a broken heart. I hoped Danny would miss me.

I helped Clare into the car then got in alongside. There were tears in her eyes. I didn't know if it was pain or genuine sadness, or a combination of the two. Stefan closed the door. The driver reached forward and pressed a button, and the central locking clicked into place. This was it then. We were captive. There was no turning back. Stefan walked round to the passenger door and opened it, said something to the driver, and bent down to climb in, his gun still fixed firmly on us.

Chapter 41

AND then he stopped. And his face changed. First surprise. Then anguish. Then pain. I hadn't registered the sound of the shot, but the echoes and the smell of the smoke filled the car. Stefan fell, dropping the gun, revealing our taxi driver standing behind him, holding a rifle.

A second volley of shots did for the driver. I heard those all right. The ringing in my ears somehow mingled with the spatters of blood and brain that appeared on the window. The taxi driver opened our door.

"Come," he said, walking back to his car.

We sat in silence as he pulled a U-turn and accelerated back up the track before rejoining the main road. There were so many questions that needed to be asked, but my first thought was for Clare, who looked to be in agony.

"The nearest hospital, please." I shouted to the driver, hoping he would understand me.

"No," gasped Clare.

"Seriously, you need to be looked at."

But she shook her head.

"Just give me a minute to get my breath," she said. "I've had worse than that." Then she called something to the driver, who raised a thumb, and floored the accelerator.

"What the fuck just happened?" I asked when she appeared ready for interrogation. "And what do you mean you're pregnant?"

"Which first?" she asked, in a slightly breathless and significantly pained voice.

"Let's take them in turn."

"All right." She paused, adjusted herself, and winced. She didn't look a good colour. "You didn't think I picked a random taxi, did you?"

"What?"

"I knew Stefan would realise, sooner or later. And I knew there was a risk he'd try an ambush."

"Jesus. So you planned all that?"

"No, believe me." She moved again, turning towards me, then reaching out for my hand. "But we had to know. If he called the taxi company, we were to divert. I didn't know he'd be so..." She winced. "Enthusiastic."

"I thought that was it. I thought we were getting killed."

"I told you. I guaranteed you wouldn't. I don't tell lies, Anna."

I exhaled, forcefully.

"Next time can you actually forewarn me?"

"Hopefully there won't be a next time."

"Quite."

The driver slowed slightly to navigate an intersection, and then sped up again. I started to recognise the scenery. The airfield wasn't far away.

"But he said Lukáš had been poisoned."

"Yes, I noticed that," said Clare.

"You've joked about poisoning me."

"For God's sake. I haven't poisoned anyone. It was a joke. Admittedly, bad timing."

"So who did?"

She frowned.

"That's what I've been wondering." She gazed out of the window, eyes fixed on a distant spot, as though trying to make sense of everything. Good luck with that.

"Okay. And what do you mean you're pregnant?" I said.

"I'm pregnant," she said, turning back to face me. "What more is there?"

"Er, hello. Like, who's the father? How long? Why are you still smoking fags?"

"I've had one and a half since Friday. If that makes me a bad mother..." Her voice trailed off.

I thought about it. She'd had cigarettes, but kept playing with them, rather than smoking them. She hadn't touched her wine. If it hadn't been such a ridiculously unlikely concept, I'd have maybe seen the signs.

"How long?"

"Not very. I found out that morning in Venice when I awoke with a storming hangover. Thanks to you."

"It was very much self-inflicted."

"Whatever."

"And the father?"

"More difficult."

"What do you mean more difficult?"

"You don't know him."

"Obviously I don't know him, unless it's either Danny or Graham March."

"Oh, please."

"Well, who then?"

"A one-night stand. I was feeling frisky."

"Jesus. You don't even know, do you?"

She looked at me with real pain in her eyes.

"I've narrowed it down to one or two."

"*What?*"

"What do you want me to say?"

"But you never even have sex."

"Evidently I do."

"Jesus." Why was I the only one who never had sex? "And you didn't use protection?"

"I thought I had."

"Well, it didn't work."

She closed her eyes. I hated myself for sounding angry. What sort of a friend was I?

"I'm sorry, Anna," she said.

"What are you sorry for?" I said, reaching out for her hand, my voice softening.

"For not telling you."

"Oh, Clare." I wanted to give her a hug but she looked in too much pain. "Don't worry about that. I'm not sure I'd have believed you if you had. I can't imagine you as a mother."

"No." She winced again, but sat up straighter this time. "It's going to cause complications."

"I think that's probably understating it."

"But now do you believe me? Why I'm not going round killing people? I've had other priorities. It's not the world in which to raise a child."

And for the first time in a long time, I did believe her. But if the killer wasn't Clare, then who?

The driver pulled up at a gate, then said something unfathomable, to which Clare responded. We got out of the car, then somebody opened the gate for us. Our plane was standing ready, but Clare excused herself, to clean up in the bathroom. I was left standing on my own, trying to make sense of it all. Clare as a mum? Changing nappies and going to playgroups? Assuming she wasn't actually behind bars at the time. Fuck me. Sideways and relentlessly.

DS Amy Cranston answered the call.

"It's time to take Lisa out of the equation," said Curtis.

"Yes," she said. "I understand."

"Good."

For a moment Amy pictured her colleague, with her red hair, innocent smile and enthusiastic devotion to duty.

"Be gentle with her," she said.

"I will."

She pressed the red button. Almost immediately the phone started ringing again. She took a breath before connecting. It would all be over soon.

This time there were no niceties. She listened to the instruction. It wasn't hard to remember.

"Yes," she said, eventually. "I'll see you there."

Clare returned from the bathroom. Most of the blood had gone, but she didn't look comfortable. I was desperate for her to see a doctor. My experience of pregnancy was minimal, garnered purely from being born, and I wasn't sure my memories of that were reliable.

"So, what now?" I asked.

"We go back to London and lie low."

"But why London? Why not one of your other bases?"

"How do you mean?" She looked at me with a clear-eyed innocence that was obviously fake.

"Clare, I sometimes wonder if you are actually on drugs. Have you just done drugs in the toilet?"

"What?"

"Seriously? Have you just been snorting something? Don't

worry. I won't judge you if you have. It must be tempting if you've got lots of money. Getting off your head occasionally."

"It is, but not at the moment, obviously. Anyway, you bang on about my smoking, but do you ever think what you're doing to your liver?"

Where had that come from?

"First things first, I don't 'bang on' about your smoking," I said. "You're perfectly entitled to have a fag if you want one, although possibly not every five minutes while you're pregnant. But you're the one who said you were giving up, so I may have occasionally asked for a progress update. And second, my liver is absolutely fine, thank you very much."

"Are you sure?"

"Any alcohol I have is severely diluted by nice cups of tea."

"That must be a hell of a lot of cups of tea."

The cheek of the woman.

"Can we change the subject?" I asked.

"Gladly. But for your information, no, I don't do drugs. If 'do' is the correct verb."

"Okay. But in that case, going back to the original question, why do you want to go back to London?"

She paused for a moment, and screwed up her eyes. She really did worry me. She looked in a hell of a state. Eventually she spoke.

"Because I'm British. It's home," she said.

That seemed faintly ridiculous as well.

"But it isn't, though, is it? You're number one on the wanted list back in London. Go back to Sunderland, yes. I'd understand that. Stand on the beach like Danny told me you like to do. Shout at the waves. Visit your old flat, assuming you've still got it. Or Cologne or any of the other places you told me about. Places you have places, if that's not some sort of tautological bastard of a sentence. Anywhere, to lie low. You're out of the country. You're safe. Why not just instruct your pilot to take you wherever you want. You like Germany. You can speak German. You've got friends there. So stay there until it's all resolved, one way or another."

She shrugged, as though confused.

"But I want to go back to London."

"Why?"

"Because this isn't going to blow over until we put a stop to it. And I owe it to you above everything."

"Why to me?"

"Because Lukáš was the bastard that destroyed your studio. And he's not going to be able to put it all back now, is he?"

I hadn't even thought about that.

As the plane taxied away, I tried to read Clare's expression but it was impossible to fathom. I closed my eyes, pretending to sleep, but really just needing time to process my thoughts. What was I going to do? Was there actually any point in anything any more? Did I even want to rebuild my studio? Should I just move away and start again, doing something completely different, somewhere far away? And, of course, of more pressing concern, what was I going to do now my primary duty of care was towards Clare and her unborn child?

LISA left Holborn after another tense day. So much of the job was everything she'd ever dreamed of. But nobody told you about the really dark times. The feeling of isolation, as though working in a bubble, detached from whatever plans and schemes all those around you were concocting. No wonder so many police officers' relationships failed. So many colleagues retired early, through stress-related illness. And yet there were good people as well. There must be. It was a job you took because you wanted to make the world a better and safer place. So why did it seem like there was nobody left she could trust?

She called Danny from the car.

"Hey, Danny," she said when he answered. "You still okay for dinner?"

"Of course, if you're free," he said.

"I won't have time to cook but I've got wine. I'll arrange a takeaway."

"Don't worry - we can phone for something when I get there. Think about what you fancy. You deserve a night off. Jessica will be pleased to see you."

"Ah." She stopped.

"What?" asked Danny.

"She won't. She's staying at my mum's."

"That's a shame." He paused. "Although it does mean it's just the two of us."

"Haha, don't get your hopes up. I'm exhausted."

"Bad day?"

"The worst, but I'm heading home now."

"Are you okay?"

"I'll survive. But can you promise me we won't talk about work? Anything else you like. Or frankly, I could just do with a great big hug if your ribs are up to it."

"I'm sure they are."

They ended the call, arranging for Danny to arrive at eight. Lisa navigated her way through the evening traffic. The rain reflected headlamps and brake lights, making her eyes tired and her head ache. There should just be enough time for a shower, though. Maybe the healing power of water would work wonders. And of course it would be good to spend time with Danny. An opportunity to forget about everything, and switch off and recharge before the mayhem started again tomorrow.

Yawning, she parked and closed her eyes for a moment, breathing deeply. She was off duty now. Tidy the flat. Get changed. And maybe, if he wanted to stay the night, she'd find some way of feeling less exhausted after all.

As Lisa crossed the road, heading towards her home, a car pulled into a space a few places behind. The driver didn't get out, but stayed still, watching, waiting for the right moment to make a move.

By the time we arrived back in Belgravia, I was exhausted. We'd travelled to another country and back and yet it was still only early evening. It felt like the middle of the night. I helped Clare up the stairs.

"I'm getting too old for this," I said.

"You're twenty-six," said Clare, leaning against me.

"Precisely my point."

We reached her front door but she stopped, hesitating, suddenly looking very worried.

"Are you going to open it?" I asked.

But she raised her hand to stop me.

"Somebody has been here," she said.

"What?"

"Somebody's been inside the flat."

"How do you know?"

"I just do."

"Nobody knows you live here."

But evidently somebody did.

Chapter 43

LISA sighed. She'd prioritised the shower, and changing into a subtly sexy dress, but she'd only just finished her make-up when the doorbell sounded. He was ten minutes early. So much for arranging the cushions, and loading the dishwasher, and lighting the candles. Nothing ever went quite to plan, but nonetheless the butterflies in her stomach told her she was excited to see him.

The doorbell sounded again.

"Coming," she shouted. And with one last check in the mirror, she made her way to the door, and undid the latch.

But it wasn't Danny.

"Oh, hello, sir," she said, momentarily confused.

DCS Paul Curtis looked at her with hard, unforgiving eyes.

"You need to come with me," he said.

Lisa opened her mouth to protest - and then she noticed the gun.

Clare put her finger to her lips. I got the message and stayed silent. She slowly put her key in the lock, then turned it delicately, as if she were opening a safe in a bank vault. I flinched as the lock snapped back, the unnaturally loud sound echoing through the hallway.

Clare edged the door open. I stood behind her, terrified. Part ready to run. Part ready to fight. We couldn't call the police. There was no back-up. And she was far from in the best of health.

The flat was dark apart from the light from the hallway. We moved slowly forward. Clare signalled for me to close the front door. Everything went black. My sense of hearing was heightened. But aside from a quiet electrical hum, I couldn't detect a sound. Maybe it wasn't an electrical hum. Maybe it was still the ringing in my ears.

Clare reached for my hand then we stood still, listening. Eventually she guided me slowly forward. She opened the door to each of the bedrooms in turn, flicking on the light, exploiting the element of surprise - but all three bedrooms and the en suites were empty and looked undisturbed.

With all of the lights back out, I felt disorientated. Clare guided me to the staircase. We crept up, taking each stair slowly, pausing after three or four to listen out for any movement above.

At last we reached the top. The door to the living room was closed. She reached out for the handle and turned it slowly, and then pushed gently at the door. Again there was darkness. And then there was an almighty bang.

Danny cursed the Underground. Maybe Anna had a point. By the time the delay was cleared and he arrived at Kilburn station, he was already five minutes late, and Lisa's flat was at least another ten-minute walk away.

He crossed the road, turning up his collar against the evening drizzle, and quickened his pace. But as he stopped at the next crossing, waiting for the lights to change, he could sense someone approaching.

He turned. It was Simon. But there was no greeting, no handshake. No "mate".

"Come with me, Danny," he said. "No fuss. No arguments. Just do as I tell you."

Clare flicked on the light. There was a mess all over the kitchen floor where the plant had fallen. Behind it, a curtain swung in the breeze from the open window. There was nobody else in the flat.

"Did you leave a window open?" I asked.

"No," she said, moving towards the mess, and then reaching up to close the window.

"Do you ever open the windows?"

"Of course. It's nice to get fresh air."

"But you're sure you left them shut."

"Yes."

"Why would someone leave a window open? We're too high up to climb out of it."

"To spook me out. It's mind games."

"But who even knows you live here?"

Before she could answer, there was a knock at the door. She looked at me. We weren't expecting anybody.

Clare flicked on the light in the hallway and I followed her back downstairs. She peered through the spy hole, and then turned the latch. An elderly lady was standing there, looking worried.

"I'm so sorry," she said, in a refined Scottish accent. "I heard the noise and I knew what had happened."

Clare visibly relaxed. She turned to me.

"Anna, meet my neighbour Elsie. Elsie, this is Anna," she said. "Elsie looks after the place for me while I'm away."

"Yes, but I must apologise," said Elsie. "I opened the window to let in some air and forgot all about it. Was it the plant?"

"It was, but don't worry. I can find a new pot," said Clare.

"But you must let me come up and clean up the mess."

"Oh thank you, but honestly, there's no need. We've just got back. It won't take me a moment."

The old lady still looked worried.

"If you're sure," she said.

"I am," said Clare with a smile. "Good night, Elsie, and please don't worry."

The old lady turned to walk back to her own flat across the landing.

But as she moved away from the door, a familiar face took her place.

"Hello," said Amy. "Are you going to invite me in?"

Chapter 44

CLARE stood aside, allowing Amy to pass.

"This way?" she asked, pointing to the staircase. Clare nodded. I expected the armed response. I expected handcuffs. I expected flashing blue lights. I didn't expect Clare to follow Amy up to the kitchen and offer her a glass of wine.

Amy sat at the table while Clare took a bottle from the fridge, and showed it to me, with a questioning look. I nodded. It was the very least I was going to need.

"How was Bratislava?" asked Amy.

"It didn't go quite as planned," said Clare, passing her a very full glass.

"I was going to say. You look like you've been in the wars." She had a point. Clare's clothes were still dusty from the farm track, and there were dried bloodstains on her collar. The broken skin and fast-developing bruise were a bit of a giveaway too. "What happened?"

"Nothing much."

"Ha!" I said, taking a big sip. They both looked at me.

"We got stopped on the way back to the plane," Clare continued, reluctantly, then shrugged.

"And what happened in your kitchen?"

"Oh, that? Just an accident with a plant pot. I was about to clean it up when you arrived."

It was all most bizarre. It was like a normal conversation between two people, regardless of the fact that Amy had been haranguing me for the last four days, telling me all the bad things that Clare had done, and stressing how important it was to find her. How she was a psychopath on a killing spree and needed to be stopped.

"Are you two back friends again?" I asked, looking at each of them in turn. "Can one of you tell me what's going on?"

But before they had the chance to do that, my phone burst into life. It was Danny.

"You should get that," said Amy.

"Put him on speaker," said Clare. I pressed the green button a second time and put the phone on the table.

"Danny," I said. "Where are you? How are you?" I could hear traffic noise in the background.

"I'm with Simon. They've got Lisa."

That stopped me. Clare and Amy both leaned towards the phone.

"Who's got Lisa? What do you mean?" I asked.

"Curtis," he said. I looked at Amy. "Simon made a connection and went to verify it with her off the record, but when he pulled up, she was being put in the back of a car."

"Have you tried calling her?"

"Yes, but there's no answer."

"Shit." I turned to Amy. "Danny, I'm with Amy now. She'll know what to do. You're on speaker."

"You're with Amy?"

"Hi, Danny," said Amy, taking over. "Where are you?"

"I..." He hesitated. "I don't know. Somewhere in Kilburn."

"That's good. Can you do me a favour? Stay there but keep your phone on. I'll give DCS Curtis a call."

"Amy, I'm worried." He wasn't the only one.

"I understand. But give me a minute, okay? I'll call you back." She ended the call and pushed the phone across to me. I took it, baffled. Why wasn't Clare running? And where were the armed police? And more importantly, despite everything, where was Lisa?

Lisa sat at the table, staring at the door that had just closed behind DCS Paul Curtis. "Don't move" was the last thing he'd said to her, before leaving her on her own. The room was dark, cold, and musty. The chairs and table must have dated from the 1970s, if not before. A low-wattage lamp hung shadeless from the ceiling, casting a depressing glow over the ageing wallpaper that hung limply, only partially still glued to the walls. She could hear movement from the next room, a scraping sound, as though furniture was being dragged over a cheap linoleum floor.

She knew she was in danger. But equally she knew there was no escape. She would do exactly as he said and hope to get out of this alive. From the next room she heard the sound of a phone ringing, and then a low, muffled voice. She strained to listen, but the words were indistinct. From within came an inner strength. She could deal with this. She had to. For the sake of Jessica, if nobody else.

Amy reached into her pocket for her phone and pressed a preset. As it rang, she put it on speaker mode and placed it on the dining room table.

"Returning the favour," she said.

Before long a male voice answered.

"Curtis," he said.

"Sir, it's Amy."

"Amy. I'm glad you called. Where are you?" There was a waver in his voice, as though he was on edge.

"I'm with Clare and Anna," she said. I looked at Clare. But again her expression was emotionless, as though she was purely concentrating on the words.

"That's good. Are they safe?"

"For now."

"Keep them that way."

I should have been reassured by that, but I wasn't.

"You have Lisa?" Amy continued.

"I do. She'll be safe if you do everything I say."

I didn't hear the rest of the call. Amy picked up the handset and took it off speaker before continuing. It sounded like she was getting instructions. She kept alternating between "yes" and "okay". Clare sighed and shook her head. We shared a similar frustration, but I expected she had slightly more clue about what was going on.

Eventually the call ended. Amy took a deep breath, then stood up.

"I've got to go," she said. Clare rose to show her to the door. I followed.

"Is Lisa okay?" I asked.

"I hope so," said Amy. As we reached the door, she turned back towards us.

"Anna, good to see you. Clare, you know what to do." And with that, she disappeared down the staircase and out into the London night.

Chapter 45

"CAN you please tell me what the actual fuck is happening?" I said, as Clare closed the door.

"Come with me," she said, leading the way back upstairs. I wasn't having any of it.

"But that was Amy. Amy has been searching for you." She continued walking, but I remained close behind. "She's been followed around by armed police trying to capture you. And then you told me she was the one doing the killing, which would have been almost believable if I didn't actually know her. But she didn't try to arrest you and apparently she also knows exactly where you live."

"That is a bit awkward, to be fair," said Clare. "I really didn't want to have to move."

"Oooh, you're going to make me scream. How long has she known where you lived?"

"Since this afternoon."

That didn't make any sense.

"What do you mean, this afternoon? How do you know that? We weren't even here. I specifically do not remember her mentioning that, so you cannot possibly know."

"So why did you ask?"

I was getting exasperated.

"Because I didn't think you were going to say 'this afternoon', did I?"

"I'm not going to lie to you and say it was yesterday."

We reached the kitchen. Clare sat back at her chair. I downed the rest of my wine in one and then eyed Amy's untouched glass longingly. Clare pushed it in my direction.

"So what's going on? Who's got Lisa?"

"Curtis."

"DCS Curtis?"

"Yes."

"Why?"

"Her life is in serious danger."

I'd kind of gathered that. I didn't quite know where to start.

"Why didn't Amy arrest you?" That would do. "And one more time: how does she know where you live?"

Clare's eyes narrowed as though puzzled by my insistence.

"She didn't arrest me because I haven't done anything. And she knows where I live because I told her."

This was making even less sense. I banged my fist on the table in frustration, and immediately regretted it because it hurt.

"That was impressive," said Clare.

"Will you just shut up and answer the frigging question?"

"I can't answer a question if I'm shutting up, can I? They're mutually exclusive acts."

"Jesus, I'm warning you." I think she could tell by my expression that I was getting seriously pissed off. "I don't want to labour the point, but you just said she's known where you live since this afternoon, and equally you were the one who told her. But I was with you all afternoon in sodding Slovakia, so evidently that didn't happen."

"I phoned her."

"But you didn't! I was with you all afternoon."

"I rang from the toilet."

That stopped me.

"From the toilet?"

"Yes. Just before we got on the plane."

I tried to cast my mind back.

"You went to clean yourself up," I said

"I did. But I also called Amy."

"God help me."

"You don't believe in God."

"And again, I'm warning you." The most irritating thing of all was that she appeared to be enjoying herself. "Why did you ring Amy? What did you say to her? 'I know I've been a bit elusive but why don't you pop round for a glass of wine and watch while I try to piss Anna off by being obtuse'? Because I'm telling you, I've had a seriously long and stressful day and you do not want to see me when I'm angry."

That made her laugh. Which had the opposite effect on me.

"Okay," she said. "I'll tell you what happened. I rang her. I said something along the lines of, 'I'm sorry for a being a bit elusive, but if you promise to turn up on your own and not arrest me, I'll tell you where I am, and then we can resolve all this with the minimum fuss'."

"And she agreed?"

"Yes. I think she'd been working along the same lines."

"And how do you propose to resolve it?"

"That was the other thing I mentioned. There's only one way to resolve this. To make sure you're safe. Lisa's safe. Danny's safe. And everybody else is safe."

"Which is?"

"I'm going to have to turn myself in. But I had conditions. Out of respect to Joe Leyland, I want it to be to him. We go back years."

I hadn't been expecting that either. I looked at her, not quite sure that I'd heard correctly, then decided that I had. She shrugged and reached for her cigarettes. I reached across and grabbed the packet from her.

"But you haven't done anything," I said, my voice softening.

"That's not strictly true."

She looked tired, and pained, her expression almost pleading.

"Clare?"

"You're the one who keeps pointing out that I've done bad things."

"And you're the one who keeps telling me you haven't."

"I suppose I have a different perspective on the difference between good and bad."

"You're doing my head in."

She looked down at the table.

"Can I have my cigarettes back, please?"

"No. And anyway, I thought you said Amy was the one going round killing everyone."

"No. I just said not to discount it. What did Sherlock Holmes say? 'When you have eliminated the impossible, whatever remains, however improbable, must be the truth.'"

"Which is why I thought we were supposed to be looking at Amy."

"It was never Amy."

Not for the first time, I felt the bottom fall out of my world. I sat in a stunned silence. Trying to understand the woman opposite me. Trying to understand what on earth went on inside her head.

"Why, Clare?" I said at last, my voice full of defeat. "Why did you do it?"

Danny stood next to Simon Oakley outside a terraced house in Kilburn, north London. The same one Simon had seen DCS Paul Curtis enter with Lisa. The curtains were closed, with no light visible round the edges. The traffic noise drowned any sound coming from within.

"What did Amy say?" asked Simon, as Danny returned the phone to his pocket.

"Just reiterated what she said the first time. Stay where we are. Don't worry. Lisa's safe."

"And you believe her?"

Danny didn't know what to believe any more.

"You said you saw a gun."

"I definitely did."

"So why is Curtis taking Lisa away at gunpoint? How does that equate with her being safe?"

"I don't know, mate. I wish I did."

"I don't know what to do."

Danny tried to think. He didn't notice the worsening rain. The plunging temperature. All he cared about was Lisa.

"I'm going in," he said at last, with a granite determination.

"Don't be stupid. He's got a gun."

"I've been shot before."

"Precisely my point. Third time unlucky."

"But if Curtis has got Lisa..."

"Danny, if he's going round killing everyone, he's not going to blink an eye with the pair of you."

But Danny wasn't listening.

"Are you coming with me?" he asked.

"Look - no, please. Wait for Amy. Think of your ribs, for God's sake. You've just come out of hospital."

"And I don't mind going back in. I thought we decided Amy was as corrupt as any of them. What if she's making it up? What if she's working with Curtis as some sort of elaborate friends-in-high places double act? She's the new March. He's still the ringleader, eh? What then? We wait here, pissing about while Lisa's inside getting murdered? I'm going in. *Mate.*"

And with that he examined the wall of the tiny front garden

until he found a loose rock that was large enough to do the job. Then, with Simon following close behind, he crept to the front door, smashed a pane of glass, and in one swift movement reached through, opened the latch, and burst into the hallway. His momentum carried him through to the dining room at the end, where Lisa sat terrified and DCS Paul Curtis stood alongside her, his finger poised on the trigger of his gun.

Chapter 46

"WHAT do you mean, why did I do it?" asked Clare. "Kill all those people," I said. "And repeatedly lie to me. I am so pissed off with you. I trusted you."

"What *are* you talking about?"

"You."

"God, you don't listen, do you? How many times. It isn't me."

"But you just said it wasn't Amy and you're going to turn yourself in."

"Yes, to put a stop to this."

"So who is it?"

"March's friend in high places."

"Curtis?"

"I can't give myself up to Curtis," she said, answering the wrong question. "If I'm going to do this, it has to be someone I can trust."

She was already making a call.

"Joe Leyland?" I said.

She nodded. The call was answered. I moved to stand beside her so I could listen in.

"Joe, hi, it's me," she said. "How's your wife?"

"Clare. I hope you've done what I told you to."

"Speak to Amy? No, not yet. But I do want to come in. Make a full confession. I'm tired of running but I want it to be you. I think I owe it to you."

"Interesting."

"But we need to act fast or I may change my mind. When are you next in London? And how is she, by the way?"

"She's in a bad way. But I'm actually here now. I was picking up some things."

"Perfect. Tonight, then."

"Are you lying to me?"

"I'm serious, Joe. You know what? I was beaten up today. You'll be shocked when you see me. I've had enough. Of this. Of everything. I just want it to end."

There was a pause at the far end.

"Okay," he said at last. "Where are you? I can come to see you. There's no need to make this painful."

"I appreciate that, but I'd rather meet you somewhere."

"Such as?"

"Hold on."

Clare pressed the mute button on her phone.

"Can we do this at yours?" she asked me.

It seemed like a faintly ridiculous suggestion, but it had been a day for ridiculous things, and I was too tired to even begin to process the request.

"If you want," I said.

"Thank you."

She resumed the call.

"Do you know Anna Burgin's house in Camden? Rochester Square?"

"What number?"

She told him.

"I'll meet you there, in an hour," she continued. "You won't need back-up but bring it if you wish."

"I'll see you then." He ended the call.

Clare turned to look at me, reaching out for my hands, and cupping them in hers. Her eyes were beginning to water.

"I need to do this alone," she said.

"I'm coming with you," I replied, defiantly.

"You're not."

"You're doing it in my bloody house."

"All the more reason not to come. I need you to stay here. You're safe here."

"I'm coming."

"Anna, please. Listen to me. This has to be just the two of us, okay? Me and Joe. Seriously."

And when I looked at her bruised face, her pleading eyes that had seen so many bad things, and the beautiful hands that had fired bullets but had also come to my rescue repeatedly over the last few years, she did what she was always capable of doing, and completely melted my heart.

"You'll need my keys," I said.

"Danny, what the fuck are you doing?" asked Lisa.

He stopped in the doorway, trying to assess the scene. Curtis was pointing the gun, but not at Lisa. It was aimed squarely at the doorway where he was standing, with Simon. Slowly it was lowered.

"I've come to get you out of here," he said, sounding braver than he felt. "Step away, Curtis, if that's who you are."

Lisa looked confused.

"But, Danny," she said, pointing a thumb at her boss. "He's the one who's protecting me."

That didn't make any sense. Danny paused, trying to take everything in. Curtis stepped to the side. Lisa stood up and ran towards Danny, arms outstretched. She was laughing.

"You've seriously come to rescue me?" she said. "That's so sweet."

Danny shook his head, trying to clear his thoughts.

"But you were abducted at gunpoint?" He turned to Curtis, watching for any reaction.

She hugged him tighter, causing his ribs to ache.

"No! God." She sighed, then turned to her boss. "You tell him."

"Danny, pleased to meet you," said the Detective Chief Superintendent, stepping forward, and offering a handshake. "I've been hearing lots about you."

Danny hesitated before accepting. Maybe this was all part of the trap.

"We had a credible report that Lisa was in serious danger," the DCS continued. "I've brought her here until back-up arrives and they can take her somewhere more secure."

"What sort of report?" he said, still struggling to believe it.

"It's kind of a death threat," said Lisa. "Primarily because I've been getting close to you."

"To me?"

"Yeah."

"Why me?"

"To punish you. That's the theory."

"For what?"

"Your part in Graham's death."

Danny stepped back.

"Are you being serious?" he said. She nodded.

"Where's Anna?" asked the policeman.

Danny didn't know what to say.

"Is she still with Clare?" Curtis continued. "It's okay now. You don't need to hide them any more."

"Why?" asked Danny, slowly feeling reality sinking in.

"Because if people who are close to you are being targeted, Anna's at very serious risk."

295

Chapter 47

NO more than a minute after Clare left, my phone rang. It was Danny.

"Anna, thank God, where are you?" he asked, sounding breathless.

"I'm still at Clare's." I yawned, snuggling into the corner of the sofa. The day was catching up with me, but I had to try to fight it.

"Is she there with you?"

"No, she's gone. Any news on Lisa?"

"Lisa's safe. Hold on."

There was a rustling on the line, and then a new voice came on.

"Anna, this is DCS Paul Curtis," he said. "I need to know where you are. We need to come and pick you up."

That didn't sound right.

"I can't tell you where I am," I said. I couldn't betray Clare's trust. Especially not to the leading suspect.

Danny came back on the line.

"It's okay," he said, trying to reassure me. "You can tell Curtis."

"It's not okay, Danny. He's the last person we should be trusting."

"You know what? Ten minutes ago I thought the same thing. But Lisa is here for her own protection. And you need someone too."

"I can't just give out Clare's address." My protest sounded increasingly feeble. Amy already knew it, but telling her had been Clare's decision, and I wasn't going to make others on her behalf.

"Okay," Danny continued. "Let me come and meet you somewhere."

My head flopped back against the sofa. The thought of going anywhere just made me feel more tired. Clare had told me to stay. I was hoping she'd come back. I had no idea any more.

"I'm fine," I said. "I'm safe here."

"Where's Clare?"

"She's gone out. To ours, ironically."

"What? Why?"

"To turn herself in, apparently. Still says she hasn't done anything, but enough is enough."

"Wow," said Danny.

"She told me to wait here," I continued, to fill the void while he took that in.

"Do you always do as you're told?"

"No, but she was deadly serious."

"She didn't say I couldn't go."

"Danny, she wants to do this on her own."

"It's got beyond that," he said. "I'm going to go there. I'll call you."

And before I had a chance to protest, he killed the line.

Charming, I thought. But then, more than that, I knew exactly what I had to do. Stuff what Clare had said. She was trying to be brave. She hadn't been acting rationally. And if Danny was going, then I wanted to be there too.

Clare looked around the flat, trying to make sense of everything, trying not to think the unthinkable, but knowing that sometimes the unthinkable was the only plausible option. It was still festooned with streamers and balloons from Danny's homecoming. Some of the balloons had partially deflated, adding a sad, neglected edge to what should have been a happy place. But so much had changed over the last few days. She'd never be able to shake the ghosts of her past, but she was determined, now, to do the right thing.

And yet she was tired. Her face was still sore from where the gun had connected. Her stomach still ached from the punch. She'd survived this far by being one step ahead. Keeping alert. Out-thinking everyone. But her energies were failing. It was too late to keep running.

Noises came from the front door. She'd left it ajar so she wouldn't have to open it, and face the prospect of being arrested on the street. She wanted her moment, her chance to tell her side of the story. To put things right with the one person in the police she'd always been able to trust.

DSI Joe Leyland walked into the room.

"Long time no see," he said, and then noticed the state of her. "What happened to you?"

"It's been a long day," she said. "Come in, have a seat. I'd shake your hand but standing up is painful." She smiled.

The policeman did as directed, taking the armchair opposite Clare, who was sitting crossed-legged on the sofa.

"Your face?" he said, his own face etched with concern.

"I did warn you. But don't worry about that. It'll heal. Thank you for coming."

"We've been looking for you."

"I know."

"You've given us quite the runaround."

"I know."

"But you've decided it's time?"

"I have."

"That's good."

There was silence in the room apart from the ticking of a clock and the faint hum of traffic from the nearby main road. Clare was glad she'd turned the lights down low.

"I know this is the end," she said. "But I can't do this any more. I can't go on pretending. You didn't bring back-up?"

"I've got someone waiting in the car. But I took you at your word. Despite everything, I do still maintain a degree of trust."

"That's good. Don't worry, I don't think you'll need her."

The "her" seemed to land. Clare looked into his eyes as she said it, saw a flicker of confusion, but almost immediately it passed.

"Why?" he asked.

"Why what?"

"Why are you turning yourself in? Why not keep running?"

"Because I want this to stop. Enough people have died. Once I'm out of the way, it can't continue."

"That's very noble of you."

She laughed, the stress of the day giving way to a sense of relief that it was nearly all over.

"Have they found Chris Stokes yet?" she asked.

"No, not yet."

"But they will."

Joe nodded.

"I mean, it's not me," said Clare. "I think we both know that. But someone is following me round killing people, and using me as the scapegoat. Once I'm out of the way, they can't continue or else the jury will see that it wasn't me after all."

"That's a valid point."

"So unless I disappear between here and the police station,

that'll be the end of it." Again she watched him. Looking for any moment of doubt.

"Of course, we still only have your word that it isn't you," said Joe.

"It's all you need."

"But do you have any idea who it is?" He shifted in his seat, loosening his jacket. "Actually, it's warm in here. Do you mind if I take this off?"

"Be my guest."

He removed the jacket, then folded it carefully over his lap, as she knew he would.

"I've given that a lot of thought," said Clare. "Because you know what? It didn't make any sense. Every crime needs a motive."

"Like greed, for example?"

She laughed.

"Touché. And yes, that was my downfall. But I was never a bad person. Not really."

"There are those who would disagree. If they were still around and able to do so."

"But they aren't." She paused, still watching him. He seemed calm, and in no rush, happy to give her time to explain. "But as I say, I started looking for a motive."

"And?"

"There didn't seem to be one. Or at least none that made sense." She recrossed her legs, and ran her hand through her hair.

"Go on."

"Let's look at the victims. All members of Graham's secret network. Who would want to kill them? Why, and why now?"

"We've been working on the theory that it was your German friends."

"I know." She laughed again. "But if that was the case, why try to pin it all on me? They'd want me to get on with the job. Be discreet. Not manufacture evidence to try to get me arrested. It doesn't make sense. It never made sense."

DSI Joe Leyland rubbed his chin and smiled.

"Unless of course you were just getting careless. You can't argue with DNA."

"No, I know. And my DNA was found at the crime scenes. I can't deny that. But I know, and you know, that that means nothing. What was it in Seattle? A hair? And Venice? A cigarette? Do you really think I'd kill someone and leave a cigarette behind that could incriminate me?"

"Maybe, if you were losing your touch."

"I'm not losing my touch." She looked at him again as she said it, watching for any reaction before continuing. "All it means is that someone was following me around, picking up evidence, then killing people and leaving the evidence behind where they knew it would be found."

"It's an interesting theory."

"It is. Because if someone was following me, then it meant they had the opportunity to kill me. But I was more use to them alive. They needed me to act as the fall guy. They needed to keep me alive. Until maybe one day when the last of the victims had been found, and then who knows? They could arrange to have me arrested, or perhaps they'd make sure it never went that far."

"And again, an interesting theory."

"And again, it is. Because it means I was never running from the police." A shooting pain through her stomach caused her to pause. Finally it passed. "I was running from whoever was following me. There's corruption deep within the heart of the Met, Joe. We both know that. We've worked together to try to uncover it. But the person in charge would ensure that I wasn't found until the moment was right. They knew I'd try to avoid arrest because of things in my past, but the last thing they wanted was to actually find me."

"And you think this is Curtis?"

"Do you?"

He shrugged.

"I'd be interested in your view."

Clare nodded.

"I'm sure you would." She ran both her hands through her hair then rubbed her eyes with the heels of her hands. "I thought it was. Then I decided it couldn't be."

"So who?"

"That only left the new guy. DCI Rogan Court."

"He did seem to turn up at just the right moment," said Joe.

"He did."

"How did you work it out?"

Clare thought for a moment. There were so many things she could tell him.

"The evidence was there," she said at last. "We know March had a weakness for massage parlours. If he had a friend on the inside, there was always a chance it would be someone from Vice."

"Quite."

"And then everything changed as soon as Rogan arrived in Holborn. I don't like coincidences."

Joe reached into his pocket for a pair of handcuffs.

"They won't be necessary," said Clare. "I'm doing this through choice."

"Even so..."

She shook her head.

"No, Joe. I'm doing this on my own terms. If I'm taking the fall, I want to do it with dignity."

"Okay." He rested the handcuffs on the arm of the chair.

"You see," she continued, "whoever was doing this wanted me out of the way. They wanted me to think it was Curtis, because he was the new guy too."

"He's been there years."

"He has. But he's only been in charge of finding me since your wife had the crash."

She watched for a reaction, but his attention was focused on her words.

"But then they made a fatal mistake," she said.

The words hung in the air. Clare detected a change in the mood. It was small, but instantly perceptible.

Joe fixed his eyes on her.

"Which was?" he said.

"Lukáš."

He frowned.

"Why Lukáš?"

"Because up until then, someone had been following me. This time they were one step ahead."

"Meaning?"

"Meaning Lukáš was poisoned. But he was taken ill while I was with him, and that means the poison was administered first. And that means it wasn't someone who was following me. It was someone who knew in advance where I'd be going. That could mean only one thing - and that was when I realised who the person was."

Chapter 48

I'M not sure if I've ever mentioned it, but I hate the Underground. The thought of getting the Tube from Knightsbridge back to Camden filled me with horror. I called Danny.

"I'm going to get a cab," I said. "Where should I meet you?"

"Bear with me." He disappeared for a moment. Eventually he returned. "Curtis says Amy is coming to collect you."

"Amy?"

"Apparently she knows where you are."

That was a point. But before I could speak further, there was a buzz from the door.

"That'll be her," he said, hearing the noise.

I went to the door, as quickly as my aching legs could muster, and looked through the spy hole.

"Yes, it's Amy," I said.

"Good. Go with her."

"How's your wife?" asked Clare, changing the subject.

DSI Joe Leyland looked surprised.

"You've already asked me that. She's in a bad way."

Clare nodded.

"I'm sorry to hear that. Do you know what happened?"

"It's still being investigated. It looks like mechanical failure."

Clare lifted a cushion from the sofa and hugged it to her stomach.

"It's tragic. And so close to retirement," she said. "I do feel for you."

"Can we get back to your theory?"

She laughed again.

"I'd rather talk about your wife. I never met her."

"No, well, you move in very different circles."

"Yes, I do." It was coming to the moment. "The thing about her, though, is that I don't understand what she was doing driving a car in the Lake District."

"You already know that. We've just bought a house there."

"Yeah, exactly. But why was she driving a car? I mean, it's a miracle really, given that she died three years ago."

And then it was out in the open. The temperature seemed to drop. From beneath his jacket, Joe produced a gun, and pointed it directly at her.

"Oh, you think you're so clever, don't you," he said. Clare shrugged.

"I have my moments."

His eyes narrowed, hardening.

"How long have you known?"

"Since Amy confirmed it for me. She's been gathering evidence on you. Keeping it off-site. She didn't want to believe it, of course. Had to keep it a secret. You don't know who you can trust these days." Clare gestured to the window. "Did you leave the door on the latch? Why don't you call Rafaela and ask her to come in? I think she'd appreciate my confession."

I followed Amy down the stairs and out to her car.

"Are we heading straight to Camden?" I asked.

"I'm keeping you safe," she said.

"But I'm supposed to be meeting Danny."

"You are. But this time we're going to keep a safe distance."

Clare watched while Joe Leyland made a call, never letting the gun waver for a moment. A couple of minutes later, Rafaela March stepped tentatively into the room, wearing a knee-length black coat over a well-tailored, dark grey trouser suit.

"Joe," she said, in her soft Spanish accent. "Is everything okay?" Her eyes alighted on Clare with undisguised venom.

"Ah, the merry widow," said Clare. "You're looking very chic, as ever. Excuse the low lighting. Take a seat."

"Stand behind me," said Joe. She followed the instruction and stood silently, observing.

"I know you can't kill me," Clare continued. "At least not here. Believe me, it takes a lot of effort to get the bloodstains out of the flooring. I know. But I imagine you're going to take me somewhere and make me disappear."

"You're very perceptive."

"And again, I have my moments. I just wanted to see the two of you together before I go. You make a lovely couple."

Rafaela stepped forward and rested her hand on Joe's shoulder.

"Of course I should have spotted it earlier. I saw you both at the funeral. I saw the way you looked at each other. I even captured it on camera. It just took me a while to work out why."

Joe smiled.

"Is this another of your theories?"

"It is. Shall I tell you? From the beginning?"

"Briefly, if you can manage it. We've got a busy evening."

Clare chuckled.

"Indeed we have. Okay, so here we go. Stop me if I've got any of this wrong. You and your pals were up to all sorts, but you needed a dirty cop to pin it on if it all went wrong, so you settled on Graham. You knew what he was up to. You'd seen the evidence. You pretended to be the one fighting the corruption and enlisted me, but really it was just to keep an eye on me, trying to control me. Better that my evidence came to you so you could bury it rather than risk giving it to anyone else. Warm so far?"

"Moderately."

"But Graham was a maverick and he was out of control, so you arranged to have him killed on the rooftop. Issued the order 'shoot to kill', although that's since disappeared into the ether. But then you had a problem. You wanted to retire, but without anyone to pin things on, you were dangerously exposed if the truth should finally come out, so it was time to disband the network. Correct?"

"It's interesting."

"But is it correct? At least be honest with me."

"Essentially."

Clare was warming to her subject. Despite the pain and fatigue, it was good to clear the air.

"Okay. Thank you. But you couldn't rely on everyone keeping quiet, so you had to silence them permanently. And the lovely Mrs March was only too happy to help you. It was her husband who'd died, after all, even though the marriage was largely a farce. But she's also greedy and you're rich, and you think it's love, but she's just a gold-digger, temporarily short on funds. Sorry to break it you." Clare turned to Rafaela. "No offence."

"You twisted bitch," she spat.

Clare shrugged, unfazed.

"So you got her to follow me. Sometimes even pretend to be

me. You took two weeks of annual leave and planned it all. Persuaded me to investigate the network, and each time I discovered a new one, one or the other of you would pop along straight after and kill them. And of course, because you knew me and we'd spent time together, you'd been able to collect souvenirs like hairs and cigarettes that you could leave behind. How am I doing so far?"

"You're very good." His grip on the gun intensified.

"In fact I made it easy for you," Clare continued. "Because I told you I was going to see them. But it wasn't just the network, was it? You" - she turned to Rafaela again - "also blamed others for making you a widow. Me, for one. Then Danny and Anna. So you thought you'd have a bit of fun with the two of them too. You got Eden Mills himself to plant the evidence against Danny that got him suspended. You were going after Lisa to break his heart. Lukáš raided Anna's studio, out of spite, having cancelled her insurance. Then you tried to kidnap her, on the pretence of taking her to me, but really so you could either kill her or just use her as a way of getting to me. Still warm?"

"It's warm enough."

"But of course you needed to orchestrate things. So you invented the car crash so you could disappear for a bit. Then you could keep an eye on us. You even followed us to Welwyn. Shooting to miss, of course, but doing enough to scare us."

She paused for a moment of reflection.

"It was almost a perfect plan. If you hadn't got carried away and effectively killed Lukáš before I even got there."

She looked from one to the other.

"That's pretty much it, really. I take it you don't want me to say all this in court?"

"I don't think it need ever come to that," said Joe.

"I thought as much. But before you take me somewhere to dispose of my body, can you at least do me the courtesy of telling me if I'm right? Because it seems to me like the least you can do, if the only person I could trust was secretly plotting to kill me."

Joe stood up, but still aimed the gun directly at Clare.

"Pretty much," he said. "You always were a good investigator. You were wasted on a newspaper."

Clare smiled.

"It's funny you should say that. Because I mentioned court and you didn't flinch. And yet DCI Rogan Court would be very interested to hear all of this. As would Simon Oakley from the Echo. It would make quite a story."

"Well, we'll just have to make sure they don't, won't we?"

"Ah," said Clare. "It's a bit late for that." Her focus shifted. "Because both of them are standing behind you."

His expression changed, from smug satisfaction, to disbelief, to horror as he turned and saw she was telling the truth. In a moment of panic, he turned the gun on the new arrivals, but Clare was one step ahead. She fired twice from beneath the cushion, both bullets hitting him in the leg. It wouldn't be fatal. That would be too good for him. He collapsed, his gun falling away. Rafaela went to grab it, but Rogan tackled her to the ground.

Clare stood up.

"Sorry, Joe," she said. "Do you mind if I leave you to it? Anna's going to be furious about the state of her floor again, and I really don't want to hang around for that."

Chapter 49

W E arrived in Rochester Square just in time to see someone being taken to an ambulance, handcuffed to a stretcher. Amy told me it was DSI Joe Leyland. Paramedics were giving him oxygen. A moment later, a glamorously-dressed woman with long dark hair was led away in handcuffs, with DCI Rogan Court gripping her upper arm. He did the pressing-down-the-head thing and bundled her into the back of a police car.

"That's Rafaela March," said Amy, before she left me standing on the pavement and went to speak to her colleague.

Danny came to join me, watching the events unfold. He put his arm around me, gathering me close. I looked up at him, and then beyond to where Lisa was standing, looking at the pair of us.

"I can't believe we actually got through this without you getting shot," I said. "It makes a pleasant change."

"It does." He smiled. He had a beautiful smile. I wanted to kiss him. I wanted to wind back the clock to Saturday morning, when I'd still been brave enough to dare to dream.

Lisa started walking towards me, her red hair looking ever

more striking in the orange glow of the street lamps. I sighed. I knew when I was beaten.

"Come here," I said. I opened my arms and gave her a hug. "I hope you'll be very happy together. He's a good man. Look after him for me."

There were tears in her eyes.

"Thank you," she said. "I will." The hug intensified. And I genuinely wished her well.

Amy came to see me once Danny and Lisa had disappeared into the night. Something had been puzzling me.

"Where exactly is Clare?" I asked.

She had a bemused expression.

"I don't know. She seems to have disappeared."

"But she's not very well. I need to look after her."

Amy nodded.

"She told me about the baby."

"Did she tell you about being punched in the stomach?"

Before she had a chance to answer I felt a buzz from my pocket. I pulled out the phone. There was a new SMS message.

Sorry I had to dash off. I've gone to the hospital to get checked out. See? I do listen to you. Don't worry, I'm sure everything will be okay. I'll come to see you. There's something I need to tell you.

I thought about replying, but Amy said the flat was clear to enter. Apparently I had to prepare myself for a mess. She wasn't wrong. There was a dark stain in the middle of the front room floor. A police photographer was taking pictures. DCI Rogan Court came over to join me.

"Sorry about the floor," he said. "We'll get it cleaned up for you."

"Thank you."

"Amy tells me you've had a busy day. Can I make you a cup of tea?"

I shook my head. Nobody knows how to make a cup of tea how I like it, apart from me. And Danny, and he was no longer here.

"Thanks but no." It was long past midnight. "I'm going to head to bed, if that's okay. I'm knackered."

He reached out to shake my hand.

"We'll finish up now and leave you to it," he said, as he held my hand in his vice-like policeman's grip. True to his word, he proceeded to usher everyone out. And then I was left on my own. Standing in my flat. Not knowing even where to start in putting my life back together. But tomorrow was another day.

Chapter 50

One week later: Thursday March 28th, 1996

I STIRRED two mugs of Yorkshire tea, then removed the bags, added the milk, and carried them to the kitchen table.

"Thank you," said Clare.

It was the first time I'd seen her since Joe Leyland's arrest. I put my arm around her shoulder, pulling her close. She'd spent a few days in hospital, although I have no idea what name she'd given them.

"I'm sorry about the baby," I said.

She nodded and looked at me, her eyes failing to mask the emotion.

"Do you mind if we don't talk about it?" she asked.

"Of course not."

"I'm still getting my head round it all."

"I understand." I let go of her shoulder. "Come on, let's go through to the front room."

True to their word, the police had cleaned things up as best they could. All evidence of the party had been cleared away, too.

Instead, the floor was covered in cardboard boxes. I'd started to pack my life away.

"You are actually moving, then?" she asked.

"I haven't got an option. I can't pay the rent. It's the end of an era."

"You know I've offered to help."

"I do, and it's lovely, but I have to face up to things. Decide what I want to do with my life."

"I know that feeling."

We lapsed into an easy silence. Then I remembered the text message.

"You said there was something you wanted to tell me."

"Did I?"

"You know you did."

"I was hoping you'd forgotten."

In truth, I almost had. I waited for her to tell me.

"I did a bad thing," she said at last.

"Oh God, do I want to hear this?"

She took a cigarette from a packet and looked at me for permission. I nodded. She lit it than sat back and closed her eyes.

"I accidentally killed someone," she said, blowing smoke at the ceiling.

I hadn't been expecting that.

"Who?"

"Jimmy Divine."

I'd forgotten all about him too.

"Go on," I said, moving slightly further away.

"It was the night you stayed with me."

"The night you went out and came back and went straight in the shower? The night I found clothes with blood on them? And you said you'd punched someone in the face?"

She nodded.

"I didn't mean to."

"Christ."

She looked incredibly guilty.

"I didn't. Really. That would have been too good for him. I just showed him what it feels like to be strapped to a chair and beaten to a pulp. Because, you know what? That's his speciality and I thought it was about time he felt it from the other perspective."

"But you killed him?"

"I honestly didn't intend to. I just wanted to teach him a lesson. Did I enjoy it? No. Am I proud of myself? No. And do I care that you're upset about it? Yes. Because vigilante action is never a good thing. But I thought that if it stopped him doing that to one more person, then it was worth every moment of the self-disgust I felt in the process."

She was refusing to look at me.

"But you did actually kill him?"

"No, I think you'll find he died of heart failure. But given everything he'd pumped through his veins over the years, that could have happened at any time."

"And the tarot card?"

"That was just childish. I was trying to get a message to whoever was going round doing the other murders. To freak them out a bit. I regret it now. I regret all of it."

At last she turned her head towards me. Then reached into her pocket for a tissue to dab her eyes.

I looked at her, trying to make her out. She was still a dangerous woman. I should never forget that.

"I'm sorry, Anna," she said. "I feel like I've let you down."

"That's hardly an exclusive club," I said.

"No." She paused. "How's Danny?"

"God knows. I've hardly seen him."

"That is so sad."

"It's life. You know what? I try to be the best possible version of myself, but I just wasn't good enough. But every day feels like torture. I thought it would get easier. It doesn't. Every minute of every day, I'm thinking about him, just desperate for a call or a message. Just to say hello. I suppose I'm not a priority any more."

She sighed.

"We make a fine pair."

I smiled.

"What are you going to do now?" I asked. "I take it you're no longer on the wanted list?"

"Oh, I wouldn't go that far. I don't know. Lie low. Evaluate things. What about you? Where are you moving to?"

My eyes roved around the place. I loved my flat. We'd had so many happy times here, but everything comes to an end one day.

"I've got no idea. I've got no job. No money. I suppose I ought to put a CV together and try to find someone who'd employ me. But what could I do? Really?"

"You're a brilliant photographer."

"But I'm not, though, am I? I mean, I know what I'm doing. But I can't even do it any more."

"I've told you I'll help you."

"I know."

"But you won't accept it?"

"No."

"Because?"

"Because it's not your problem."

"Oh, but it is. If you'd never met me you wouldn't be in this mess."

I moved towards her and reached out my arm. She shifted slightly, and I gave her a hug.

"Thank you for not killing me," I whispered. She extinguished the cigarette, then turned towards me and smiled. Then she returned the whisper.

"Should we just run away together?"

I thought about it for a moment, as though she was being serious.

"Where to?" I asked.

"Anywhere you want."

The thought of leaving everything behind was as tempting as it was fanciful. New beginnings. A new life. Telling everybody and everything to sod off.

"Being with you is dangerous," I said.

But she was smiling at me. And at that moment my heart began to sink. I knew she had a plan.

The end.

SPECIAL THANKS...

Court Me Kill Me was, as ever, a lot of fun to write - despite a house move a month before the deadline. That made things a bit hectic for a while...

Special thanks for encouragement and support go to Mary Cafferkey, Rebecca Asselin, Cathy Kisbey-Green, Carol Lewis, Tim Atkinson and - of course - my two Slovak friends: Blazena Kovalikova and Daniela Elzaki. It is a pleasure to know you all. Thank you also to Sara Ielden for the police advice and Simona Knox for the upgrade and having Anna's best interests at heart.

Many thanks, of course, to everyone who has left a review of one of the books on Amazon, Kobo, Nook, Apple, Goodreads or elsewhere. Your feedback and encouragement is a huge help and motivation.

And, as ever, huge thanks to my editor, Carrie O'Grady, for vision, clarity, commas, and making me smile.

FEEL FREE TO SAY HELLO... :-)

If you enjoyed the book, have any queries, or just want to say hello, I'd love to hear from you via www.davidbradwell.com. While you're there, you can download a **FREE copy of the series prequel** - In The Frame:

You can also follow me on Twitter: @dbshq - or see what Anna is up to: @AnnaBurginNW1

If you enjoyed Court Me Kill Me, you should read **Cold Press** - the first full-length book in the Anna Burgin series.

London. 1993. Investigative journalist Clare Woodbrook goes missing on the brink of unveiling her biggest-ever story. Is it kidnap? Murder?

Worse still, the police investigation into her disappearance is being headed up by a corrupt DCI - himself the subject of one of Clare's current investigations.

Clare's researcher Danny Churchill sets out to find her, and enlists the help of his flatmate - feisty fashion photographer Anna Burgin. But they soon realise that nobody can be trusted. And as the search becomes ever more desperate, suddenly their own lives are very much on the line.

Packed with intrigue, twists, conspiracies, and dark humour, Cold Press is a hugely entertaining British thriller, with a sting in the tail.

Order Cold Press NOW in print or ebook format at Amazon, Kobo, Barnes & Noble, Apple and more.

After Cold Press, the story continues in **Out Of the Red** - book 2 in the Anna Burgin series.

The gripping, twist-filled sequel to Cold Press.

Investigative journalist Danny Churchill is hot on the trail of Graham March - the disgraced former police DCI. The investigation takes him to Germany where he soon starts to uncover dark secrets and new depths of depravity.

Back in London, and aided by his flatmate - fashion photographer Anna Burgin - Danny's investigation intensifies, but as he gets closer to the truth, the body count starts to rise.

Help is offered from the most unlikely of sources, but if Danny accepts, is he doing a deal with the devil herself?

Order Out Of The Red NOW in print or ebook format at Amazon, Kobo, Barnes & Noble, Apple and more.

Book 3 - **In The Frame,** the series prequel novella, is available as a FREE ebook at www.davidbradwell.com.

In The Frame takes us back to Anna and Danny's student years and explains how they became friends in the first place.

Photography student Anna Burgin didn't expect to be arrested, but she's the only suspect for a series of crimes, and the Police have found damning evidence in her room.

But Anna has no recollection of doing anything wrong. Was it a moment of madness? Or is somebody setting out to destroy her?

And is the stranger in the bar really trying to help, or just part of an evil conspiracy?

The sequel to Out Of The Red is book 4: **Fade To Silence.**

You know you've got problems when being hunted by a Serbian hitman is the least of your worries...

Balkan gangsters, corporate spies and a fugitive killer are all on the loose in London, but when a body shows up, all of the evidence points to the victim's wife.

Journalist Danny Churchill wants to find the truth. But when reports emerge of a huge shipment of weapons heading to the UK, it soon becomes the most dangerous and action-packed investigation so far.

Packed with twists, intrigue and dark humour, Fade To Silence is book 4 in the bestselling Anna Burgin series.

Order Fade To Silence NOW in print or ebook format at Amazon, Kobo, Barnes & Noble, Apple and more.

Book 6 is Anna in 2019.

There's Tinder. There's trouble. There's mystery. There are lies and heartbreak. It's a dark psychological thriller of jealousy and deception, and oh my goodness, the twist.

Coming 2019. Stand by.